Other Regan McHenry Real Estate Mysteries

Backyard Bones
(coming in spring 2009)

The Death Contingency

A Regan McHenry Real Estate Mystery

Nancy Lynn Jarvis

Good Read Mysteries
A Subsidiary of Good Read Publishers

This is a work of fiction. Names, characters, places, and incidents are either products of the author's imagination or are used fictitiously. Any resemblance to actual events, locales, or persons, living or dead, is entirely coincidental.

Good Read Mysteries

Good Read Mysteries © is a registered trademark of Good Read Publishers
301 Azalea Lane, Santa Cruz, California, 95060

Copyright © 2008 by Nancy Kille

Library of Congress Control Number: 2008934564

ISBN: 978-0-9821135-0-9

Printed in the United States of America

www.GoodReadMysteries.com

Books are available at special quantity discounts through the website.

Acknowledgements

To my eldest son, Brennan, who slogged through the very first draft, reading for consistency. To AJ, my youngest, who told me my surfing references needed work. To Shirin and George and their family, who devoted some of their Christmas time to reading and editing. To Mom, who kept reading, but not at bedtime, because she was worried about what was going to happen to Regan. To Morgan, who helped with copy-editing advice. And thank you especially to Craig, my Tom, who asked hard questions — the right hard questions — for all his reading, editing, dealing with endless computer issues, and everything else he did.

The Death Contingency

Nancy Lynn Jarvis

Of course the fictitious disclaimer is true. Murderers, motives, and characters are made up. But, if you have worked in the real estate industry for any length of time and think you recognize clients or associates, or if some of the things that happen to Tom and me feel like déjà vu to you...well, what can I say? It's quite a business, isn't it?

Regan McHenry

Signs every few yards along the cliff edges warned that they were dangerous and unstable. But he'd had a few beers and needed to relieve himself. If the cliffs were unstable, why hadn't the signs fallen into the ocean, he sniggered with intoxicated logic?

An impish grin crept across his face; he was seventeen, invincible master of the world. He moved to the very edge of the cliff and stood, feet spread, hand tauntingly on a warning sign, head thrown back crowing at the sky as he sent his stream arching into the ocean below.

He was stunned by the suddenness of the fall.

He didn't cry out for help as he plummeted. There was no time.

He plunged deep into the ocean. Frigid water slammed his body, contracted his muscles, and forced the air from his lungs.

He strained for the surface, battling his emptied lungs that were desperate for oxygen, struggling against the urgent need to take a killing breath.

He surfaced with a gasp, gulping air until his lungs hurt

less than his skin.

He wasn't afraid. Just shaken and angry. Sobered. This was the Pacific. The ocean was warm where he came from near San Diego. How could it be so cold here? He was partying just north of Santa Cruz, home base to so many world-class surfers; how could they surf in this water?

He shivered violently. His entire body felt like it was being slashed by tiny, sharp razors. Except for the long pants and the tightly zipped sweatshirt that covered him, he half-expected he would see his blood oozing from a thousand cuts.

The plunge left him disoriented. By the time he turned to face the cliffs, he was surprised how far he had drifted out to sea.

Not a problem. He was a strong swimmer. He kicked and paddled hard in the direction of the cliffs. But despite his efforts, after a few minutes they seemed farther away, not closer. The music from the party was growing fainter. Not good.

The cliff face was sheer where he dropped into the ocean. He was going to need help getting back to the top. By now, some of his friends should be climbing down with flashlights, calling his name, ready to lend a hand when he got near land. Why didn't he see lights moving down the cliff face?

He rubbed his ears — they must be affected by the cold — he could hardly hear the sounds of the party anymore. And he was getting tired fast. He took as deep a breath as he could manage and called to his friends. No response...

His arms and legs didn't feel like they belonged to him

any longer. They were heavy and stiff — his joints almost old-man arthritic in the cold sea. It took real determination to kick his legs and reach out his arms to paddle.

Maybe taking off his shoes would make swimming easier, less tiring. He stopped his ineffective strokes to reach down and take them off. But his fingers were numb and lacked strength; he couldn't be certain when he grasped the Velcro tabs on his shoes. A task that should have taken a few seconds stretched into exhausting minutes.

Finally one of his shoes popped to the surface behind his head. He didn't notice it…

At least the water wasn't as cold anymore. He felt prickles — pinpoints of pain rather than the overwhelming agony of razor-cut cold.

As he struggled with his shoes, the sounds of the party faded more and more, growing softer and farther away until he couldn't hear them at all. The beacon of light given off by the party bonfire on the cliffs had become very faint, more a memory of warmth than luminosity.

Perhaps he should have been concerned, but he wasn't. He was comfortable in the water now. The moon came out from behind a passing cloud and shone brightly. Cool silver light reflected off little lapping waves all around him. The sounds they made were soothing…restful. And he was so tired…

He had no fear of sinking; the salt water buoyed him up. Maybe he'd turn on his back, close his eyes, and just rest for a few minutes, enjoying the warm Pacific and the lapping of the waves before he got back to the hard task of swimming to shore.

Another man was resting momentarily in the ocean, too, well beneath the young partygoer. He hadn't expected rescue when he went into the sea. He never struggled to return to the surface after his drop into the Pacific. His breathing had been regular and deep. His lungs had filled with water as naturally as they had with the air that would have buoyed his body and kept him afloat in the dense, salty sea. Instead, the weight of the water in his lungs had quickly sent him to the ocean bottom.

A school of surfperch swam around him near the marine floor. They were small fish in a vast ocean, but the unified movement of their silvery bodies caused a slight ripple in the dark underwater world. Caught in the flow, the man gave up resting and swam, his arms and legs lacking coordination and purpose, on his random undersea journey.

Kaivan arrived precisely at 10:00 for his Thursday morning appointment, encouraged into the escrow company lobby by a strong burst of wind against his back. He ran his hand lightly over his head to return any stray hairs to their proper place and gave the knot on his tie a quick wiggle to make sure it was perfectly positioned.

Realtors are trained to dress up at least one level from their clients. In the laid-back beach community of Santa Cruz, Kaivan could have met that standard with khakis, a shirt open at the collar, and because of the February chill, a casual zippered jacket. But he was always conscious of what he wore and how he looked. He knew he was an attractive man, and by dressing well, he could count on being favorably noticed by women. He liked that.

Besides, it was a signoff, and realtors always upped it a notch for a signoff. It was an important occasion for their clients, and for them, too — they were close to a job completed and to a paycheck.

Even so, it didn't seem fitting to wear one of his designer-label suits today. Instead he chose charcoal flannel slacks, a well cut custom-made navy cashmere blazer, an Egyptian cotton shirt, and a navy and dusky blue silk tie. Expensive classic clothing: his trademark.

Kaivan left the lobby and walked through the employee work area. He walked slowly, showing off, strutting his stuff for the benefit of the women working there. He noted their glances and approving smiles. He made it a point to catch each woman's eye in turn and offer a returned smile. Perfect, he thought.

He stuck his head into Arlene's cubicle. "I'm here," he said jauntily. "Where have you put my client?"

"He's not here yet," the escrow officer replied.

"Sorry about that. He's usually right on time." Kaivan grinned sheepishly and raised his eyebrows in apology.

"There's a lot of traffic on Highway 1 this morning. They closed another exit for the widening project and the road was backed up when I came in. Everyone's running a little late."

"That's probably what's happened to him. He doesn't have a mobile, but let me try him at home one more time." Kaivan pushed the appropriate speed dial on his cell phone, held it to his ear, waited a few seconds, and announced, "No answer. He must be on his way, inching through the backup as we speak. I'll wait for him in the lobby."

Kaivan checked the time on his watch again. The watch wasn't top-of-the-line, but it was a genuine Rolex, purchased and registered at Dell Williams Jewelers, a reputable store on Pacific Avenue that had been in business for generations. 10:14. His seller was almost fifteen

6

minutes late.

When the sale closed, his client, who was also his favorite uncle, would net well over half a million dollars in profit, even after all the taxes and commissions were deducted from the proceeds. But first there were papers to sign, and his uncle still hadn't arrived.

Arlene came out of her cubicle at 10:23, her arms full of documents, and went to the lobby. She glimpsed Kaivan checking his watch.

Cyrus Ansari, Kaivan's uncle, was now very late. Mr. Ansari's tardiness, understandable if he was caught in unexpected traffic, was going to mean she'd be running late for the rest of the morning. She might even have to forgo some of her lunch break to catch up. His fault or not, Arlene was less than pleased with Mr. Ansari.

Regan arrived just as Arlene reached the lobby. A nippy gust of wind caught her before she made it all the way through the entry door. She came in with a shiver.

Her clients weren't due to arrive until 10:30, but she had come a little early to review their escrow summary pages, just to make sure Arlene got everything right. Regan was thorough. She paid attention. Even though Arlene was very good at her job, Regan always double-checked all the details.

Her clients were young, enthused, very pregnant, and like most first-time buyers, nervous. Signoffs were an exciting but also an anxious time for buyers, so she often liked to break her clients' tension with a little lighthearted jesting. One of her favorite devices was telling buyers that the small print on the documents they were initialing said they agreed to give the lender their first-born if a mortgage payment was more than two days late.

Parents of teenagers normally enjoyed that gag and feigned enthusiasm. Most hastily asked, "Where do I sign?" But she planned to skip that line today, considering her buyer's condition.

Regan spotted Kaivan and noted what he was wearing. Like other women had done that morning, she smiled at him, although her smile was more than just one of approval. He was a friend, that was part of it, but the main reason for her smile was some self-directed amusement at how predictably she reacted to Kaivan's expensive custom-tailored clothing.

She wore clothes well. She had willowy long legs and was tall enough to be a model, but his impeccable wardrobe always made her feel disappointingly turned out, like a poor relation.

Nothing she wore, probably nothing she owned, was in his league. Case in point — today's outfit: knee-high brown suede boots, worn against the chill rather than as a fashion statement, a simple brown wool skirt and jacket, and a three-year-old turquoise-colored angora turtleneck sweater. All very ordinary and off the rack.

The only thing striking or custom about her outfit was her earrings. They were large silver and turquoise pieces made from an old two-part belt buckle she found during a vacation prowl in a little Durango bookstore. She brought the buckle back to Bead It, a bead and jewelry findings store on Pacific Avenue across the street from Dell Williams Jewelers, where she had one of the tattooed and pierced employees divide it and make it into earrings according to her specifications.

Like so many things she prized, the earrings had a story and a memory behind them. They never failed to gain her compliments, but they weren't expensive, and unless she wanted to call herself a designer, they didn't have a fashionable derivation either.

Regan smiled a greeting and joined her associates. "Hi, Arlene. Morning, Kaivan. Are you here for your uncle's signoff?" she asked, slipping ever so slightly into real estate jargon.

"Yeah, I am, but he's running late," Kaivan said, checking his watch another time.

"Traffic's really backed up this morning. I bet he's stuck," she said sympathetically.

"That's what Arlene thinks, too," he replied.

Regan turned her attention to the escrow officer. "How are the Beltran's docs doing?"

They had worked together many times. Arlene expected Regan's inquiry and was prepared. She took the top sheets off the stack she was holding and handed them to her.

"We're all set for your clients. Here's their balance sheet and summary for you to review."

"Thank you, madam." Regan nodded her head in a small bow as she took the proffered pages. "It seems you're on top of everything, as usual.

"Kaivan, how are we doing keys for your uncle's house? I can come by your office the morning we go on record and collect them for my clients, if you want."

"That would be great, Regan. Thanks."

"I set up my clients' walkthrough with your uncle for today, right after we finish…"

"Today?" Kaivan interrupted. His smile remained fixed and friendly, but his voice exuded tightness. "You're going by my uncle's house today?"

"Uhh," Regan grimaced. "Sorry, Kaivan. I should have set it up through you, but I asked your uncle about it directly on Monday, or maybe it was Tuesday, whenever it was that he called me…"

"He called you?" Kaivan interrupted again, he seemed attentively curious rather than irritated. "What did he say to you? Why did he call you?" he pressed.

Kaivan's pointed inquiry made him seem territorial. Where did that come from, Regan wondered? Some realtors guarded their clients in the same way that certain societies sequestered their maidens, afraid to let them have outside contact, but she'd never known Kaivan to behave like that. That wasn't his style.

"Your uncle called because he wanted to know if we were going to close by the eighth," she explained. "He mentioned something about having plans. He didn't elaborate, but you probably know what he meant."

"About his plans…uhm…"

This time a rush of cold February air interrupted, announcing the escrow company door was being opened again. All three looked toward it, Arlene and Kaivan, hopefully.

"My clients are here already," Regan said, as she spotted the Beltrans. She smiled, waved at them, and motioned for them to join her.

"Stephanie, Ed, I'd like you to meet your very talented escrow officer, Arlene Smith."

"We've talked on the phone. It's good to have a face to go with your voice," Stephanie said.

Ed reached for Arlene's hand to shake it, realized she was holding too many papers for that to be practical, and quickly transformed the aborted grasp into a little fan wave of his hand.

"And this is Kaivan Nasseri. He's the agent for Mr. Ansari, the seller of your about-to-be new home."

Kaivan extended his hand to Stephanie. "My client should be here any minute. We're almost ready for the big event, and it looks like you might be, too?"

"Just about a month to go," Stephanie beamed.

"Then double congratulations are in order," he said as he shook hands with Ed.

"Arlene, should we wait for you in one of the conference rooms?" Regan asked, pointing from one room to the next in eeny-meeny-miney-moe fashion.

"Yes, in the big one. Some of your docs are already in there," Arlene said.

"Sounds good." Regan motioned her clients toward their signoff room. "Your mortgage broker called. He said he'd be joining us."

Arlene had set up a small signoff room with its little round table for Kaivan and his client. Mr. Ansari had few papers to sign, and she'd expected they would be in and out well before Regan and her clients arrived. That was another thing Mr. Ansari's lateness was going to affect.

"Shall I wait a little longer for your client, Kaivan, or

get started with the buyers now? My assistant, Larissa, went to the Recorder's office this morning, but she should be back any minute now. I can leave a note for her to help you. Larissa's very capable, almost as good as me," Arlene giggled. "You've met her, haven't you?"

"Yes, I have." Kaivan tilted his head in the direction of the conference rooms. "Sure, you go ahead with them. I'll buy my uncle a cup of coffee when he gets here. We can entertain ourselves for a while if we need to, but those people shouldn't have to wait around because my uncle's stuck in traffic."

"You understand I'm not trying to abandon you?" Arlene apologized. "It's just that the Beltrans are first-timers. You know what that means," she rolled her eyes toward the ceiling. "I don't feel comfortable turning them over to my assistant."

"Really, it's no problem. I won't tell my uncle what he's missing," Kaivan flirted. "Go on ahead with them."

"Thanks, Kaivan," Arlene flashed him a quick smile, put her papers down, scribbled a note for her assistant, collected her papers again, and headed for the large conference room.

Stephanie watched attentively as Arlene added the documents she was holding to the other papers already in the room and then took out her notary book, a little inkpad, and a box of tissues from a drawer under the table.

"Do you expect us to cry?" Stephanie asked. She sucked in one cheek in a nervous little twist of her face.

"Cry? Oh, certainly not. The tissues are for wiping off

the ink after I collect your thumbprints," Arlene quickly explained, stifling an amused grin.

Regan suppressed a smile, too. The Beltrans were even more edgy than most first-time buyers. She needed to lighten things up a little. "You should own your first house by this time next week; that's pretty exciting, isn't it?" she began.

Both Stephanie and Ed gave tense little nods of agreement.

"Let me warn you right now, escrow companies always like to overestimate your final closing costs. They want to give themselves a small cash cushion in case the escrow runs long and the closing amounts need to go higher. Right, Arlene?"

"That's what we do," she replied.

"Arlene thinks it's much easier for her to cut you a refund check than it is for her to get more money from you after escrow has closed," Regan told them, winking at her confederate.

"For some reason, she seems to think you'd rather buy that amazing sofa you'll find — you know the one I mean, the sofa that's perfect for the living room and on sale, too — than send her what's left of your life savings, just so she can balance her books."

"Oh, we don't need a new sofa," Ed said with a small lopsided grin on his face. "But should I tell Regan about the great rug we just bought?" he asked his wife.

"I think he just did," Regan stage-whispered to Stephanie and Arlene. There was easy laughter all around. That's better, Regan thought.

"Anyway, these numbers are a little high. If everything goes according to schedule, you'll get a nice refund check from Arlene. It won't be big enough to treat the friends who helped you move to an elegant dinner at Shadowbrook Restaurant, but it should be enough to take them for some great Chinese at O'Mei," she smiled.

"That's fine with me," Stephanie said. "O'Mei is a favorite of ours. I know Shadowbrook has the big reputation," she used a falsely deep voice and a newscasterish style to describe the restaurant: "romantic atmosphere in charming Capitola by the Sea, blah, blah, blah. But I don't like the glass-sided funicular you take to get there; it scares me. And with all this in front of me," she patted her pregnant belly, "I don't think I could do the stairs very well. There must be three hundred of them," she laughed.

"Oh, before we forget," Ed interjected, "can we skip going by the house after we finish here? A problem came up at work and I have to take care of it today, so I don't have the rest of the day off, like I thought I would. I don't know that we need to see the house again, anyway. We know what it's like; we're really happy with it."

Stephanie nodded her agreement.

"We can reschedule," Regan said, "but we should make sure Mr. Ansari made the repairs we negotiated and that everything is as you expect it to be."

"Really, we'll just skip that part," Ed said firmly. "The repairs weren't that significant, and we trust Mr. Ansari. I'm sure the house is fine."

Arlene sat down next to Regan, opposite the Beltrans,

turned the papers toward them so they could follow along, and started to explain the first set of documents. She read the pages upside-down, an unusual skill, but one she had absolutely mastered.

The mortgage broker they were expecting rushed in about twenty minutes later. Except for the fact that he was fully dressed, he did a credible impression of Tom Cruise's famous *Risky Business* sliding entrance.

"Oh, people," he flustered, waiving his fingers, with their perfectly manicured fingernails, in front of his face like a menopausal woman in the midst of a hot flash. "Sorry, people, I'm late," he stated the obvious, as he looked from side to side to make sure he acknowledged everyone in the conference room. "I had an earlier signoff."

He clearly hadn't learned to read upside-down, so he sat at the end of the table and twisted his head to read as Arlene returned to her explanations.

"I'm sorry to interrupt again, darling," he leaned forward and splayed the manicured fingers of one hand on the table to stop Arlene. "Can we start with the loan package? I'm cutting things pretty close today. I've got another signoff in Watsonville at eleven-thirty. I don't know what I was thinking — being here to explain your loan, and then getting from Santa Cruz all the way to the other end of the county in an hour. Duh!" He hit his forehead with the palm of his hand. "But if I hurry after we finish here, and traffic isn't too bad, I might just make it."

Regan took a discrete peek at her watch. 10:47. Not likely.

Arlene accommodated him, and he disappeared as

hastily as he had arrived, twenty minutes later.

Regan envied him his escape and wished she had a good excuse to leave. She had an active mind that dreaded tedium, and the reality was, once she had checked Arlene's calculations, her presence at the signoff wasn't really necessary. It was expected, however. She had to stay.

Regan looked for ways to keep from getting bored.

11:25, she guessed, placing a bet with herself on the precise minute when the signoff would end.

No, probably longer, she thought. They're both engineers — well technically, Stephanie is a systems analyst, but they both think analytically and behave like engineers when it comes to decision-making. They'll read every word. Better make that guess 11:40.

She didn't even need to look like an active participant because all of the Beltrans' attention was focused on Arlene's explanations. Her thoughts began to drift as the signoff continued.

Regan idly looked out the conference room window toward the parking lot. That was Kaivan, wasn't it? He waved to someone she couldn't see and got into his black BMW. He and his uncle must be finished with their part of the signoff.

She tried to stay focused by mentally reviewing the details of the transaction, checking off each of the disclosures she'd duly discussed with the buyers, and recalling each of the property inspections she'd arranged. All there, all reviewed, all accepted, all done.

And all too easy. A disquieting thought flitted through her mind: nothing had gone wrong during this deal.

Even if most realtors would consider that a good thing, she didn't. It made her uncomfortable. She'd only closed one sale in her career where nothing went wrong. That experience left her apprehensive and unsettled, anxiously waiting for a post-sale calamity, waiting for the proverbial other shoe to drop.

After that experience, she always welcomed the sense of unambiguous closure that resolving some small problem provided. A trivial last minute renegotiation of some piece of the contract was always the easiest, but she could, in fact she had, handled more unusual matters.

A tiny smile crossed Regan's face as she recalled a raccoon-initiated chicken-coop tragedy that happened during one transaction. She had hurriedly phoned every egg production company in Santa Cruz County, searching for replacement poultry whose feather patterns mimicked the late night murder victims' plumage. She bought two replacement hens and drove them to her buyer's new house the day before escrow closed. Driving with the crated chickens on the seat next to her, clucking and studying her with their beady little dinosaur eyes, had been oddly disturbing, but the effort had been worth it. She had saved the buyer's young daughter, who had named each of the now deceased chickens and was looking forward to caring for them as pets-who-produced-eggs, from having to learn the harsh reality of predator and prey at the tender age of eight.

Regan's mind returned to the Beltran's escrow. Nothing had gone wrong during this sale, nothing at all.

Her boredom slowly morphed into gnawing uneasiness.

17

She tried to persuade the sensation away. *You've sold hundreds of houses. Aren't you due for a second flawless escrow? Of course you are.*

She didn't persuade herself. The feeling remained.

What could possibly go wrong before this smooth sale closes?

Nothing came to mind — still, her anxiety grew. She fidgeted in her seat. Finally Regan gave herself a silent command. *Stop it. You're not a worrier by nature. Stop seeing trouble where none exists.*

But as silly as it seemed to her, she couldn't shake her growing sense of foreboding.

3

On Monday morning, Regan, who was compulsive about punctuality, was running late. It wasn't helping that she seemed to get behind every indecisive driver on the road and hit every stop light she came to just as it turned red.

She was meeting some buyer clients, the Poliches, at a newly listed house. She'd previewed the house and met the sellers before calling her clients about it, and was sure they'd like it — maybe even make an offer.

It was just what they wanted: a gracefully detailed home in a nice location, with four bedrooms, and what realtors call a gourmet kitchen open to a family room.

It was in their price range and had a couple of superb bonuses in their kitchen and location requirements. The kitchen had just been tastefully redone with top-of-the-line appliances and finishes, and even more bells and whistles than her avid cooks specified. And it was one of the twenty or so unique homes that ringed Westlake Pond.

It was also a single-level, a critical requirement for her clients, since Jena Poliche had been diagnosed with multiple sclerosis just before Christmas, and might be faced with using a wheel chair in the future. The house had been built in the early 60's, the end of the era for large scale single-level houses. After that, land prices in Santa Cruz started to increase and parcel sizes started to shrink. Builders stopped constructing single-level homes — they went up, instead of out, to gain square footage.

Houses around the pond didn't have the current buyer hot buttons. There were no ten to twelve-foot-high ceilings, arched windows, or three-plus car garages. But they did have real hardwood floors, the kind made of solid thick oak that could be refinished and restained light or dark as tastes changed; wonderfully rich, textured walls that had been plastered by master craftsmen who were capable of creating a feel no longer seen in this era of hurried sprayed-on finishes; and generously sized lots with mature trees.

When they were built, they were the choicest properties on the west side of Santa Cruz because of those features and because of their view of the pond. They still had a certain cache for those same reasons. The Poliches were definitely going to be impressed.

As Regan pulled up to the house, just a bit too fast for neighborhood driving, a uniformed officer emerged from behind a hedge at the side of the property. For a second she thought he had been hiding with a speed gun, caught her, and was about to give her a ticket. She hit the brakes hard enough that it should have been clear to him that she was aware of her excessive speed and felt she deserved one.

But he waved her on. "Phew!" she whistled. "Dodged that bullet," she said out loud in a slightly guilty voice.

Two more police cars rolled up. Their sirens were silent, but they parked at hurried angles. By the time she found a place to park and walked back to the house, the officer who motioned for her to keep going had unrolled yellow crime scene tape across the front of the property. The tape stopped her at the sidewalk.

Her clients pulled up just then, slowed their car in the roadway, and lowered the passenger side window.

"What's going on, Regan?" Jena Poliche asked. Her husband Bob, who was driving, dipped his head a bit so he could get a better look out the passenger side window and hear what was being said.

"I just got here. I don't know yet."

"Keep moving, please," the officer said to the Poliches as he waved them forward. "You can't stop here."

"What's happened, officer?" Jena asked him.

"It's none of your concern. Just keep moving, please," he said, more forcefully this time. "You're blocking an official vehicle here on police business."

Regan's still-curious clients inched their car forward enough to give the newly-arrived white van space to stop in front of the house. The van pulled forward as the officer undid the tape, turned sharply into the street, and then backed into the driveway. A couple of men wearing uniforms, although not regulation police uniforms, climbed out, opened the back doors of the van, and pulled out a stretcher with drop wheels. The officer retied the yellow tape as the men rolled their stretcher into the house.

"Lady, how many times do I have to tell you to get out of here?" he shooed Regan away.

21

"I'm a real estate agent," she said. "I'm supposed to show this house this morning. I have a ten o'clock appointment with the woman who lives here."

"Well, you're too late. She's not going to be keeping any more appointments," he replied. "Now move along."

Regan took a better look at the vehicle. *Santa Cruz County Coroner* was written on the side in plain black block letters.

🏠🏠🏠🏠🏠🏠🏠🏠🏠🏠🏠

Most Santa Cruz real estate companies held office meetings on Tuesday morning. Regan and Tom, Regan's husband and partner, had never figured out why Tuesday was the day. Nevertheless, when they started their own company, Kiley & Associates Real Estate, they stuck with the convention. The meeting at their Swift Street office wasn't due to start for a few more minutes, so Regan had time to finish reading the *Santa Cruz Sentinel* article about the Westlake Pond Murder, as it was being called, that she had happened upon the day before.

Regan lowered the newspaper to her lap. "My clients weren't as upset as I was," she said to Tom. "But then, they hadn't met the murdered woman just the day before like I had. She introduced me to her children. They're little kids, Tom," Regan frowned. "I'd guess about four and maybe six. She told me she and her husband were getting a divorce, but that it was a friendly one. They were keeping it that way for the sake of their children. He hadn't even moved out yet. She said they planned to just go their separate ways when the house was sold. They were going to keep it all very positive and amicable."

Regan tilted her head to one side and sighed as she recalled the dead woman's demeanor. "She put on a good show, but she seemed awfully sad to me. I thought she had been crying; her eyes had that look about them. I wished her well and told her I'd been through a divorce when my children were young, so I had a good idea what she was going through. I promised her things would get better. I sure was wrong about that, wasn't I?" Regan finished her rhetorical question with lips pressed hard together. "I had such a cheerless feeling when I left."

Tom asked, "Are you OK, sweetheart?"

"Uh-huh. Sure," she shrugged. "It's just that the newspaper account says her husband is alleged to have stabbed her at least twenty times. It says the children were in the next room and probably heard her screaming." Regan shuddered. "What's something like that going to do to them?

"The article says her husband's a law professor; he teaches at a prominent school in the Bay Area. I talked to him briefly, too. He was just coming in as I was leaving. He seemed so…so ordinary. I think of murderers as creepy, deranged monsters who leap out of the dark, not people with normal lives, people you might know and talk to every day."

"You're sure you're OK?" he asked again, very gently this time.

"I'm fine. This is closer to a murder than I ever thought I'd be, or ever want to be again, that's all." She refolded the newspaper and put it down.

"I need a distraction," Regan's tone was wistful, "and not the kind that comes with work. I need something really fun to think about. After the office meeting, could we talk about something completely different, something like deciding how to celebrate our anniversary?" she asked, managing a weak smile.

"Good plan. You got it." Tom's returned smile was broad and wholehearted.

The four other agents who did business out of their brokerage drifted into her office one by one, ready for the weekly meeting.

When the last had arrived, Tom asked, "Everybody got their coffee? Good." He half-sat, half-leaned on the corner of Regan's desk as he began directing the get-together in his role as broker. "This should be a quick meeting. Let's start with the new county ordinance about swimming pools."

Tom's prediction proved right; the meeting was a short one. February was a quiet time on the real estate calendar. Their colleagues had no new listings to announce, so the office didn't need to set out in a car caravan to view properties. Tom had done most of the talking as he conducted the meeting, the normal pattern since he was the broker; but Regan, who usually had something to add, hadn't said a word. She was unquestionably still in the same dark place she had been before the meeting began.

Tom wasn't about to leave her there. As soon as the meeting ended and their associates returned to their separate business dealings, he plopped into one of the seats opposite her desk, tilted back at what seemed like a dangerous angle, and put his feet up on the edge of her desk. His heels rested on the slightly worn spot his shoes had created there because of this frequently repeated pose.

Regan smiled. "One of these days, you're going over," she said as he tilted back even farther to drain the last of his coffee.

"Never going to happen," he promised with great certainty. "Now, about this anniversary you're so eager to plan — it's ten years, isn't it? I can't quite remember."

Regan tossed a paperclip at him. "Yes, it's ten years. I looked up tenth anniversary gifts. You're supposed to get me diamond jewelry," she teased.

Tom's tone was flirtatious, "Diamonds, huh? You wouldn't want me to give you something legendary instead?"

"You do mean legendary like our engagement, don't you?" she asked coquettishly, playing off his double entendre. "Or do you have something else in mind?"

"Do I have to pick one or the other? I'd hate to have to choose, because either way, I've got some impressive suggestions," Tom offered in waggish reply, continuing their playful exchange.

Regan and Tom met in a conventional way, at a party thrown by a mutual friend. They decided to marry in a conventional way, too. Tom proposed during a romantic moonlit walk on New Brighton Beach in Aptos. But according to the Santa Cruz real estate community, their engagement had a more unique beginning, a somewhat mythological beginning.

Regan was a realtor when she and Tom met. When they decided to get married, she felt comfortable selling her house and his house. Buying *their* house was a completely different matter. She was as nervous as any other homebuyer, and asked her broker to present their offer.

Her broker went to the seller's house to make the presentation to the sellers and their agent. He'd barely begun on the offer details when the elderly seller-husband noticed that Regan and Tom's last names didn't match.

"I see that her name is McHenry and his name is Kiley. She's not one of those uppity feminist types who won't change her name, is she?" the husband scowled.

"No, no. It's nothing like that," the broker said, trying to avoid telling the obviously anti-feminist owner that Regan was *indeed* one of those types. "They aren't married," he explained.

"They aren't married?" This time the question came from the wife, whose sharp gasp, followed by pursed lips, told the broker all about her unmistakable shock and displeasure at the possibility that her house could become home to a wickedly cohabiting couple.

The broker was concerned his latest retort was about to cost his agent her house. "Well, um, not yet. But they are planning to get married," he fumbled. His eyes darted around wildly while he tried to come up with something to say that would put Regan and Tom back in the seller's favor. "In fact…" he stammered, "I think they want to get married here…I mean as soon as they buy the house." He decided to embroider his story with an appealing yarn.

"Those stairs…wow…what a great place they'd be for a bride to make her entrance from. Don't you think so?" he asked, trying to recover by refocusing them on a positive image.

It worked on the wife. Her rigid reserve dissolved immediately. "Oh yes," she cooed. "Both of our daughters and one of our granddaughters were married here, and that's exactly how they made their grand entrance. They were such beautiful brides."

"You know, dear," the husband tapped his wife's hand rapidly, "I do think I heard them say something about what a lovely setting this would be for a wedding when they were looking at our house."

"More weddings here; how perfectly wonderful," the wife chirped with joyful fervor.

The house had been on the market for a while, even had received some offers, but every time a sale appeared close, the owners found a reason to avoid selling — possibly because they weren't yet truly ready to give up the home where they had been young and raised a family. Their agent had spent thousands of dollars in advertising and invested a great deal of time with them, but they were threatening to take the listing away from her. She read their reaction to the other broker's tale and saw this offer as one that might finally work, get to a sale, and earn her some long overdue income.

"Oh, it's so romantic, isn't it?" the seller's agent gushed. "I think I heard them say that, too, John," she confirmed the husband's imagined remembrance, "In fact, I think he proposed here, right by the window in the living room, where there's such a nice view out over the rooftops of Santa Cruz. He probably thought that lovely panorama made a perfect backdrop for a proposal." Her eyes were positively misty as she said it.

Regan's boss suppressed his mirth and surprise at how well the seller's agent remembered a scene he had just made up. Her tactic was clearly working, and he wasn't about to threaten her triumph by challenging her embellishments.

Tom and Regan got the house, but that's when their engagement got tossed into the real estate gossip mill, and the myth around it started.

Names and places quickly disappeared, as they do in all urban legends. The rumor could have been started by Regan's broker or the seller's agent — the former because he found it amusing — the latter, having talked herself into believing it by then, because she thought it truly was romantic. Neither ever admitted to being the rumor's source.

However it began, word spread that an agent's boyfriend proposed to her while she was showing him property. It didn't stop there. As delicious a bit of gossip as that already was, the details got juicier as the story looped through the local real estate population.

On the second iteration, the buyer wasn't a boyfriend — he was a client the agent had met at an open house a couple of months before and had been working with ever since. And by the third time the story came around, the agent had answered an up-call for an advertised property. When she met the potential buyer at the house, they fell in love at first

28

sight, and before the showing was over, he had dropped to one knee and proposed. Regan's smile grew as she recalled the details of their *legendary* engagement.

Her mood brightened; being around Tom usually had that effect on her. She was about to tell him so, when her ringing phone interrupted. She glanced at the name on caller I.D. and sighed. "I probably need to get this."

"To be continued tonight, then." In a final attempt to cheer his wife, he left his chair with a theatrical bound, and as he headed for her office door, said, "But right now it's Tuesday morning, time for work. I've got calls to make, people to see, websites to update." Tom raised his hand to his temple and shook it like a vaudevillian performer shaking a straw hat. "Showtime! And you've got calls to answer," he added, pointing to her ringing phone.

"This is Regan," she greeted the escrow officer with a little leftover chuckle, still smiling from Tom's animated exit. "How are you this morning, Arlene, and how's the Beltran's escrow doing? I bet you're calling to tell me we're on schedule for a Thursday close, aren't you?"

"I'm good, but I'm a little unsure about the close date. You might lose your money if you placed that bet."

"What's up?" Regan asked.

"Well, the lender can fund the Beltran's loan whenever they're ready, so that part is all set; but…" Arlene wavered, "you did know Mr. Ansari still hasn't come in for his signoff, didn't you?"

Regan wasn't pleased with that news. "No, I didn't. I thought he was doing that last week, the same day my clients signed all their docs. What happened?"

"I don't know. My assistant said she and Kaivan waited for him; they kept expecting him to turn up at any moment. Larissa said Kaivan waited for an hour, but his uncle never showed up."

"How did I get left out of the loop on this?" Regan asked.

"I don't know the answer to that one, either. I'm surprised Kaivan didn't let you know," she said. "Anyway, now Kaivan says he's misplaced him."

"Misplaced him?" Regan raised her eyebrows, "What does *that* mean?"

"I'm not sure. All I know is, that's the exact phrase he used," Arlene replied.

"Do me a favor? Don't call for funds, yet. In fact, don't let the loan fund until I tell you to. I don't want my clients paying interest for a house they can't close on. I better talk to Kaivan. Thanks for the update, Arlene."

Regan took a deep breath and exhaled slowly as she returned her phone to its cradle. The anxious mind-set that started at the Beltran's signoff returned. But now, her anxiety wasn't something vague and free-floating, it had a focus. Her gathering sense of trouble was centered squarely on Cyrus Ansari.

It was after 8:00 that night and several messages left before Kaivan returned Regan's calls.

"I'm sorry. I don't know what to tell you," he apologized. "I've gone by his house every day since he missed the appointment. His car is there, but he isn't."

Regan frowned. "Have you checked with your family? Have any of them seen him?"

"Of course I've checked with my family and all of my uncle's friends as well. It took some time because we're a sizable group," he chuckled, "but that's where I started. No one has seen him, and no one seems to know where he is."

"OK," Regan drew out the word, making it seem longer than two syllables. "You've gone through your family connections. We need his signature on a grant deed. What else are you doing to find him?" she asked, attempting to keep the edge out of her voice.

There was no point in annoying Kaivan, but her clients had given notice and might not have anywhere to live in a few days if escrow didn't close soon, and he didn't seem to be taking his uncle's disappearance that seriously. He hadn't even called to give her a courtesy heads-up that there could be a delay with her client's purchase.

That was irritating. If her clients found out from someone other than her that there was a problem, she looked bad. It made her seem like she wasn't paying attention for them.

"Well, I'm working on it," he paused, "but mostly I'm waiting for him to turn up. He's probably just gone out of town for business or to play." Regan could almost see him shrug over the phone. "He loves to gamble and likes to get on a senior citizen bus, flirt with all the widows, and go to Vegas every once in a while. Maybe he's done that."

"Wouldn't he have told you if he was going to leave town for a while, especially if he was going to miss his signoff appointment?"

"Umm...not necessarily," Kaivan replied. "He's kind of a free spirit when it comes to his travels. Although, now that you mention it, I am kind of surprised he didn't let me know to reschedule for him. He must be on quite a winning streak if he can't take some time out to call me," he laughed.

Now that I mention it? Come on, Kaivan. How could you not have thought of that, Regan questioned silently.

"I know he wants the house sold. He'd really been after me to get him an offer before you and your clients came along. This isn't the first time he's sold real estate, so he should remember he has to sign docs before the sale takes effect. I guess I could have done a better job reminding him of that."

Oh, yes. Again not out loud.

"I'm sure he's not going to blow the deal. He'll be back. Don't worry, Regan. I'll work on it. I'll make sure this sale closes."

"I'm going to have to call my clients and tell them your uncle has inexplicably disappeared without signing the transfer documents. Then I get to say, 'by the way, even though the seller's agent doesn't know where his client is or when he'll be back, you don't need to worry because he says he's working on it'. That's a call I don't look forward to making, Kaivan."

This time, Regan didn't try to keep the edge out of her voice. "Let's think of something proactive for you to be doing. Has he ever set up power of attorney or given anyone authority to sign legal documents for him?"

Kaivan tried to deflect her ire with an encouraging reply. "Maybe. That's something I *am* working on," he said. "Relax Regan, your clients will be OK, I promise. I'll let you know as soon as I hear from him. How's that sound?"

"Not great, but I guess that's all I'm going to get for tonight." Regan acknowledged temporary defeat. "Call me right away when you hear from him, even if it's two in the morning."

"Really? OK, two in the morning it is. I promise." He laughed again and said goodbye.

Regan tried to shake the image of a slightly overweight senior citizen flitting about on free-spirit wings, and concentrate on her knowledge that Kaivan's promises weren't given as lightly as they were by so many other realtors, who used "I promise" with no more gravity than "talk to you soon" or "thank you so much" as a phone sign off.

Kaivan was better than most at making the phrase meaningful since he so often worked with his family and in their emigrant community, which seemed, at least from her outsider perspective, almost like an extended family. Certainly he had more control over his familial patrons than other realtors had over their unrelated clients. But Kaivan wasn't a magician; he couldn't promise to materialize a missing person, even if that person was his uncle.

Regan and Kaivan had worked together at a local Century 21 office some years before and had been friendly, so she knew a lot about him and his family. They were originally from Iran. The first of his uncles had emigrated while the Shah of Iran still ruled, over thirty years ago. The rest came later.

They were Christians in a predominantly Muslim country, but had no problems living there and practicing their faith when Iran's government was secular. That began to change shortly after the Shah was deposed and Ayatollah Khomeini's influence and power increased.

When Iran officially became an Islamic Republic in 1979, it became increasingly difficult for his family to remain in their home country. Daily confrontations with the more militant factions running Iran were the new routine.

One by one, his uncles had packed up their immediate families and joined the growing Nasseri clan in Santa Cruz. They did well in America and found Santa Cruz, with its liberal sensitivity and large population of University of

California students, especially open to newcomers.

Encouraged by their relatives' success, and increasingly feeling less comfortable in Iran, Kaivan's parents brought him and his two sisters to Santa Cruz when he was eleven.

Like other family members who immigrated after the American hostage crisis — that four hundred and forty-four day drama that enfeebled Jimmy Carter's presidency and helped Ronald Reagan gain the White House — they told their new neighbors they were Iraqis. They didn't acknowledge their true heritage until the First Gulf War started in 1991.

Many émigrés chose to preserve their old way of life and culture in large part. The Nasseri family did so in the extreme. They were embarrassed by the conduct of their homeland toward the citizens of their adopted country, and because of that, kept to their expatriate Iranian community almost exclusively.

That wasn't the case with Kaivan. He approached life in America very differently from the rest of his clan. He still remained close to his family, but he also enthusiastically embraced his new life in Santa Cruz, even briefly joining a garage band and learning to skateboard and surf, like so many other Santa Cruz teenagers. He remained fluent in his native Farsi; although the fact that he had mastered English and eliminated any trace of an accent by the time he was in high school was a great source of pride for him.

In all the years she had known him, Regan only remembered one time when he referred to Iran as home, and that was rather indirectly.

He came to their house for a barbeque shortly after she

35

and Tom moved out of Santa Cruz proper to a house in the country setting of Bonny Doon. They had been excited about their new home and wanted to show it off; so when some agents at Century 21 said it would be fun to have an office barbeque, they volunteered their house with its private acreage, swimming pool, and outdoor kitchen.

Kaivan was impressed with the house, and came back a couple of days later with a cherry tree as a house warming present. He said this type of cherry grew at his family home in Iran, and his mother thought special houses should be blessed with cherry trees. That small phrase was his only acknowledgement of his Iranian homeland. By then, Kaivan had truly become an unhyphenated American.

He talked fondly and often about his uncle Cyrus. Cyrus Ansari, the absent client, was Kaivan's uncle on his mother's side. His uncle was close to fifty when he came to Santa Cruz almost twenty years ago as the last member of Kaivan's family to immigrate. He was something of an oddity, being the family's only bachelor.

Kaivan's mother was his baby sister, but she felt a maternal need to make sure he ate well, so he was invited to dinner with the Nasseri family every evening. He quickly became the boy's favorite of his five Santa Cruz uncles and was elevated to a unique status, filling a function more like a godfather than an uncle.

Mr. Ansari relished his role, and lavished special attention on young Kaivan. As his uncle succeeded in business, gifts followed. By the time Kaivan got his real estate license, Mr. Ansari was comfortable enough financially to present him with what he called a 'proper realtor BMW'.

He encouraged family members and his friends to use Kaivan's services, and his sponsorship and referrals got the new real estate agent's career off to a strong start. Kaivan owed him a lot — but their relationship was based on genuine affection, not obligation.

Over time, Nasseri children grew up, married, and started their own families. Still, they remained a close-knit group, adding, rather than subtracting members. Nothing much happened to one of them that everyone else didn't know about immediately. That's why it concerned Regan that none of Kaivan's family seemed to know where Cyrus Ansari was. It was unusual. Unusual was disturbing. Unusual wasn't what she wanted in the midst of her sense of brewing trouble.

What she wanted right now was routine: predictable, reassuring, even boring routine.

Regan looked at the clock in her office. 8:30. She was exceedingly perturbed. Too late to call Stephanie and Ed tonight, she decided. Anyway, what good would it do to have them worry all night? She could just as easily call them in the morning. Maybe Mr. Ansari would turn up by then. She'd get a great-news communiqué from Kaivan and never have to make the call at all.

Right.

She turned out the light in her office. Their house was a single level, built hacienda-style around a courtyard, with a wall of glass on the outside to take advantage of distant bay and ocean views, and more glass on the interior side so the courtyard garden could be enjoyed from most rooms. She looked through the courtyard-side windows, searching for a lighted room and Tom. The house was dark except for the living room.

Regan knew the house so well, there was no need to turn on lights. She walked through the dark and found him reclining on the sofa, reading. His shoes were off and his stockinged feet were aimed at the warmth of a huge fire he'd started in the fireplace.

"That was a late finish for work," Tom said without looking up from his book. "Problem? Problem solved?"

"The most annoying kind of problem, one that I'm not sure is real, and one that I can't do anything about, if it is." Regan sat down cross-legged on the floor, leaning against the sofa with her back to him.

"Mr. Ansari, the seller of the Beltran's house, has disappeared."

"Disappeared?" Tom queried, finally looking up over the top of his book.

"Well, maybe. That's the problem. No one knows where he is, but that may not mean anything. He may just have gone away for a while. Kaivan Nasseri — you remember him?"

"Of course."

"Kaivan is the listing agent involved. He says he'll let me know as soon as he finds his client," she sighed, "but for now, it's limbo time."

"And I can guess how you feel about that," Tom declared.

"I think a backrub would help put it all out of my mind," she said, wiggling her shoulders until he put his book down and obliged her.

"Umm," Regan murmured. She could feel the tension leaving her neck. "In keeping with the romantic fire and the backrub, and with not expecting any interruptions tonight, could we get back to our anniversary? I think we should definitely dub our anniversary H-M-II, honeymoon two," she explained her new acronym, "and go to Italy or Ireland like we've been meaning to."

"Do I hear a preference?"

"Ireland. We could spread it around that we glimpsed a leprechaun and see where the story goes. Given our history, I bet with time, realtors will say we found a whole village of little people and discovered the pot of gold at the end of the rainbow," she laughed.

"I bet they will," Tom hooted.

"The only problem with Ireland is the food won't be as good as if we go to Italy."

"Ah, but the Guinness will be," he countered.

"Since I don't like beer, there's a real chance you'll be forced to drink my share, too." She ran her tongue over her lips as she gleefully presented Tom's potential dilemma. "We wouldn't want to offend any pub owners, would we? Do you think you could handle drinking my beer as well as your own?" Regan's tone was filled with pretended concern.

"Ireland is sounding better all the time."

"There's another thing to recommend it: if we go to Ireland, couldn't we call it a business trip? We could say we were researching the origins of Irish storytelling, you know, to help us recognize when other realtors are telling us tall tales." She started to giggle. "That should count as part of our risk management credits for license renewal, shouldn't it?"

"I've always enjoyed the way you think," Tom chuckled. "I'm just not sure the Department of Real Estate would let us have that one. Anyway, I'm pretty good at 'not quite the truth detection' already, and I think you're better at it than I am. "

"It's because of me Irish heritage, don't 'cha know. I recognize Blarney when it comes me way," she said with an exaggerated and not very good brogue.

"Being Irish again are ye now, Mrs. McHenry? And with Saint Patrick's Day still so far away?" he rejoined with a perfect Irish inflection.

"Listen to you. You don't have a drop of green blood in your veins, my documented American since before the Revolutionary War, but with that lilt, your love of Guinness, and a fine Celtic name like Thomas Michael Kiley, if we go to Ireland, our legend will probably put a very tall leprechaun in your ancestral line."

"That settles it, then. Ireland it is."

It was late when they went to bed. They'd had a pleasantly diverting evening, just what Regan needed, and she'd almost managed to put Mr. Ansari's disappearance out of her mind.

When she'd been new in the business, little glitches would send her into fitful sleep, if not outright nighttime pacing. Something like a missing seller would definitely have kept her awake all night. She would have fretted endlessly, trying to figure out what to do, or once she realized she couldn't fix the problem, how to break it to her clients, in a non-alarming way, that things weren't going well.

Now after many years as a realtor, she was not only experienced, but also seasoned, tough, and detached.

Since the fix-it ball was in Kaivan's court, she would

42

put everything out of her mind for tonight, get a good night's sleep, and think about what to do tomorrow at a convenient time, which would definitely be during daylight hours.

At least that's what she told herself.

It was easy enough to talk the talk; walking the walk was much harder. It was the detached part she had trouble with.

As soon as the lights were out and there wasn't anything to distract her, the missing Mr. Ansari pushed back into her thoughts.

Where was he? What would happen if he didn't turn up soon? She knew a realtor whose client vanished during an escrow — the man just stopped returning phone calls and was never seen again. Could the same thing happen here?

Those were the questions on her mind as she fell asleep. Her restless psyche spent the night attempting to answer them and produced a series of bizarre dreams as a result.

Regan saw Kaivan's uncle kidnapped and thrown on a Las Vegas bound bus by a farcical group of large frogs with heavily mascaraed eyelashes. Some had white hair coiffed with 1930's chic finger waves. The rest wore Queen Elizabeth II style hats.

Mr. Ansari tried to flirt with their leader, who bore an uncanny resemblance to Dame Edna, the Australian comedian who impersonates a female celebrity, but she wasn't receptive. She ordered him tied to an oversized lily pad and set adrift on the Upper Owyhee River. "But I love widows," he asserted forlornly. Regan startled awake as he was sucked under water at The Widow Maker, a level four rapid.

Next, she dreamt that a now homeless Stephanie was giving birth to quadruplets in the children's section of the Clothes Cottage, a Capitola clothing consignment shop. "Please," Stephanie begged between contractions, "I don't want my babies to have to live here." Awake again.

She even had the archetypal realtor nightmare about locating a forgotten septic tank by falling into it. She knew two people that had happened to: one a brand new agent, clipboard for taking notes in hand, showing property for the first time; the other, just to prove experience offered no protection, an old hand at country property. And that wasn't even counting the broker Regan knew who lost her whole Mercedes to a long-abandoned and rotted wooden tank in an upscale neighborhood in the Rio del Mar section of Aptos.

But in her dream, it was Mr. Ansari who disappeared into a massive undiscovered septic tank at the touristy Old West settlement in Felton — home of antique steam locomotives — known as Roaring Camp.

"I'll never be found if you don't help me," he cried. "Please don't let me disappear. I have plans for the eighth."

As he struggled to keep from descending into the muck, he somehow set off toots and whistles on all the Shays, Heislers, and other geared locomotives in the railway yard. Languid whistles morphed into urgent telephone rings, jangling her awake a third time.

She'd never been a morning person, especially during the winter, preferring to be eased into the day slowly, teased awake by increasing daylight. But now, her heart pounded as she searched for the illuminated numbers on the clock next to her bed. 6:30.

Her near-panic reaction to a pre-dawn ringing phone was a new phenomenon. It started when Maxine, her east coast sister-in-law, called before dawn on September 11th, 2001, and told them to turn on their television. The second World Trade tower had been deliberately pierced by a jetliner. All speculation about a horrible accident was over; the country was under attack.

Then, two years ago a sympathetic caregiver had called from Pacific Coast Manor Nursing Home at six-fifteen, in the still dark morning, to let her know her father had died minutes before. After a year and a half in a slow downward spiral, they both knew his life was almost over. She had been with him until late the night before, when the staff told her to go home and get some rest. Regan said a special goodbye to him, just in case, but intended to be back before eight the next morning. She still regretted not being with him when he passed away.

Occasionally, a contractor she was using to make repairs would call before seven. 6:30. *Try to be positive.* She was expecting bids for work on a house she was about to put on the market. Maybe it was an enthusiastic contractor calling with a very competitive bid.

6:30. *Try to be very positive.* Maybe it was Kaivan. As unlikely as it was that he would be calling at this hour, never mind his promise, there was always the possibility the call could be from him.

If it was, it was probably good news — his uncle had turned up and was going to the escrow company as soon as

45

it opened — and she could call Arlene to get everything back on track to close this week. What a great way to start the day that would be.

Optimism won out again, as it usually did with Regan. She bounced out of bed, not stopping for a robe or slippers, and hurried to their office to answer the phone. She didn't turn on lights, relying instead on the red charging light in her phone's cradle to find it.

"Hello," her voice was still husky with sleep.

No attacks, no deaths, no contractors, and no Kaivan. It was Stephanie.

"I hope I'm not calling too early," the young woman began with a level of effervescence and energy that overwhelmed Regan's sensibility this early in the morning. "The baby seemed to be practicing soccer kicks again and woke me up before five. I've been trying to wait for a reasonable hour to call. Ed just found out he can have tomorrow and Thursday off. Do you think there's any chance we could buy our new house today? We could let the owner live there until when he was scheduled to move out, but maybe he could take all of his stuff out of the baby's room, and we could start painting it a nice sunny yellow," she bubbled.

Regan had explained how the last few days before the close of escrow worked to the Beltrans, but the reality of all the details that still had to be attended to before the house changed owners had been overridden by Stephanie's hopeful enthusiasm.

Regan had to tell her what was going on. It didn't come out well. She wasn't awake enough to choose her words carefully, not that there was a good way to tell Stephanie about the trouble Mr. Ansari's absence was causing. She had to tell her client to forget about closing early. For the moment at least, there was a hitch in the escrow which, if not resolved, might mean it couldn't close at all.

"Try not to be too concerned, Stephanie. We're working on a way to get this taken care of. I'm sure we'll find a solution," Regan said with a practiced confidence that she didn't necessarily feel.

6

The disappointing conversation she had with Stephanie left Regan wide-awake and cold. No use going back to bed, she'd never get back to sleep.

Instead she grabbed her robe and warm slippers and went to the kitchen. She put fresh food and milk out for the cat who, like Tom, thought it was too early to be awake. Regan set up the coffee pot so when Tom got up, he could just flip the switch to start it brewing. Then she fixed breakfast for herself.

Still in her pajamas and robe, she took her second cup of tea back to their office. She checked her email and reviewed the latest changes to the real estate listings in Santa Cruz County. Once it was past eight o'clock, she made phone calls to some of the professionals she needed to talk to as listings and escrows progressed. Her definition of a respectable hour to call clients was much later than Stephanie's was for calling her. She waited until it was almost nine to call a couple of prospective clients. She reviewed paperwork. She fidgeted.

She never had been very good at doing nothing. To her

way of thinking, even spinning wheels was preferable to passively waiting for something to happen.

Tom, who was even less of a morning person than she was, came into their office a few minutes after nine, coffee cup in hand, and put his free hand on her shoulder. She tilted her head slightly as he leaned over and kissed her cheek by way of a good morning greeting. He sat down at his desk and braced for a news flash, but Regan didn't turn from her computer, something she would have done immediately if there had been any news about Kaivan's uncle.

After a few minutes of silence, he asked, "You'll need to have a look for yourself, won't you?"

"I've been thinking about it, but I have a lot of work to do today…"

He interrupted, "Which you're not going to do very well until you…"

"Make sure Mr. Ansari isn't playing a little hardball or negotiating in absentia?" she finished Tom's thought. Regan exhaled deeply and then laughed, "It scares me sometimes, how well you know me."

"And it scares me how you can finish my sentences. We're even. Go," he said, with a flourish of his hand.

Tom was right about her having no peace until she checked for herself. Besides, didn't she just tell Stephanie "we" were working on finding Mr. Ansari? Didn't that mean she should be doing something, too, and not just waiting for Kaivan to produce his uncle?

She got dressed, put what was needed for a later meeting into her briefcase, and left early so there would be time to swing by Mr. Ansari's house first.

Regan had done other deals with Kaivan and found, although he was a wily negotiator who might bend the truth about little things, like how conscientious his clients had been in maintaining their property, once he agreed to something, the games ceased. He was one of those people you could have counted on with just a handshake — not that she ever conducted business that way. Years in real estate had given her too healthy a respect for signed contracts.

But, she didn't know if Mr. Ansari was as trustworthy as his nephew when he made an agreement. Rather than Kaivan controlling his uncle and the escrow, it might be the other way around. Mr. Ansari might be using Kaivan unwillingly or unwittingly to fake a disappearance.

Even though she'd heard a lot about Cyrus Ansari, she'd only met him once, when she presented the offer for his house. When they were introduced, he took her extended hand in both of his. "Call me Cyrus, lovely lady," he insisted. "I want all beautiful women to call me Cyrus." He was charming and flirtatious in the same way Kaivan could be, and a practiced flatterer. He probably taught Kaivan his moves, Regan mused. The student had mastered the technique — the teacher was a little over the top for her taste.

She remembered that he asked very little about the offer. Most of his questions were about her clients. He wanted to know everything about them, about what they were like. He asked if they were nice people, and she recalled his pleased reaction when she told him Stephanie and Ed were expecting a child soon.

At the time, she decided he was what he seemed: a genuinely warm, highly expressive man with just a touch more theatricality in his manner than she appreciated.

But today, Regan, who was usually very good at getting a sense of people quickly, didn't trust her initial impression of him. Masterfully deceitful people were sometimes hard to recognize, especially during one brief meeting. Cyrus Ansari might be a slick flim-flammer or worse. Maybe he had asked questions about her clients, searching for innocence he could dominate.

In her current mood, that assessment of Mr. Ansari seemed more and more likely. Maybe he wasn't missing at all, just hiding out, refusing to sign the deed, and planning to do a last minute power play, hoping to force her or her clients to pay for something that was his responsibility to pay for right now. Midnight manipulators certainly weren't unheard of in this business.

Past manipulations and power plays filled Regan's mind as she drove. She thought about Rickie Longland, the one-time president of the local Association of Realtors, pillar of the local real estate community that she was, who had called with some surprising news at nine o'clock the night before a sale they were doing was to close.

Rickie said the seller, who also happened to be her father and a retired real estate broker, was refusing to compensate the buyer's agent according to the commission she had advertised and her father had contractually agreed to pay.

An apologetic Rickie said she had no idea this was coming, but her father told her that unless Regan agreed in writing to eliminate all but a trivial remainder of her commission, he would stop the sale.

She called her client immediately and asked if he was willing to forgo closing the following day. A day's delay would give her some time — she could find out what her rights were.

Her client told her his movers were scheduled to begin work at eight the next morning and pleaded with her not to hold up the closing over a thing like commission, which he rightly felt she shouldn't make his problem.

So Regan signed the document Rickie faxed to her and let escrow close. She naïvely thought she might be able to get compensation later. She confirmed that Rickie's father was still paying his daughter her part of the commission. Surely Rickie would be honorable and make up the retracted amount out of her own pay. That's what she would have done. At the very least, Rickie would certainly share her commission.

But Rickie never did either of those things. Evidently, the highly regarded Santa Cruz realtor learned about ethics at her father's knee.

Regan's client was very grateful she hadn't inconvenienced him, and he sent some referral business her way, but she still got a bad taste in her mouth every time she ran into Rickie Longland.

She worried something like that might be setting up here as she pulled up to Cyrus Ansari's Royale Street house.

There was a dark blue Lexus parked in the driveway, Mr. Ansari's, she assumed, and another car parked in front of the house. Regan pulled to the curb in front of the next house and walked back.

1215 Royale Street certainly had what real estate agents call "curb appeal". It was a 1930s Spanish-style bungalow. Though small, just two bedrooms and one bath, it oozed charm.

It had a clay tile roof, arched windows, and a heavy, rounded wooden front door with an old-fashioned brass mail slot. The cream painted stucco was in keeping with the traditional Californio color scheme. The risers going up the steps to the front porch were faced with Mexican tiles in an array of bright colors and various designs, giving the house a cheerful fiesta presence even in the otherwise cheerless middle of winter.

The lawn was carefully mowed and edged, and the foundation plants were neatly trimmed. Not much was in bloom this early in February, but Regan recognized bougainvilleas growing at the sides of the porch. They would provide masses of intense color later in the year. Some green bulb shoots were starting to come up, promising even more color in front of the main plantings and along the entryway path.

Regan remembered there was a peek of the ocean from the porch, although it was too overcast to see it today. Building up a story would gain an ocean view. That's what Stephanie and Ed said they planned to do in time, once they got over the savings-draining shock of buying their first house, where, even with a downturn, entry-level houses on the west side of Santa Cruz still often topped six hundred thousand dollars.

The lockbox was on the garden water pipe. Regan

punched her personal code into her remote key, pressed the key into the designated slot in the lockbox, and waited. *Tink.* The bottom of the box dropped down revealing a key. She opened the front door and went inside, closing the door behind her.

It was force of habit rather than optimism that caused her to loudly announce, "Hello?" There was no response. Another habit, especially on a gray day like today, caused her to flip on lights.

Opening the front door pushed the pile of mail that had been deposited through the mail slot off to the side of the entry. She picked it up and put it on the little table left nearby just for that purpose, and during the time the house was for sale, to collect the business cards realtors left when they showed the house. A neatly printed tent sign remained on the table, still warning realtors: DO NOT LET THE CAT OUT.

She probably should have left then, but she didn't. Regan wasn't exactly sure what she was looking for — in fact, once she established the house was truly empty and Mr. Ansari really wasn't hiding in a closet — she felt blatantly nosey just for being there. She forced her guilt aside. There wasn't really anything else for her to be doing, and she needed to feel she was doing something.

I'll think of this as an in-lieu-of walkthrough since the Beltran's cancelled theirs, she told herself, pleased to be playing detective, keeping her pledge to Stephanie, and looking for clues to Mr. Ansari's whereabouts.

Even with boxes out and in the process of being packed, it was easy to see the house belonged to someone who was neat and well organized. Most of the non-essentials for day-to-day living were ready for the move.

The dining room was completely packed up with full boxes closed, labeled, sealed, and sitting on the dining room table. Three large paintings sat on the floor, resting against the walls. Someone had already removed the hanging hooks and done a perfect job of touching up the paint where it would have changed color behind the pictures. With no distractions, Regan could fully appreciate the coved ceilings and the soft patina of the hardwood floors that had come from years of wax and use.

"Great house you found for your clients," she congratulated herself out loud, another recognition that Mr. Ansari was not at home.

The living room was mostly packed as well. The only evidence that someone might still be using it was the weekly TV listings on an end table next to a well worn and comfortable looking lounge chair facing the still connected TV. Last week's TV listings, she noted.

The smaller bedroom was in similar condition to the dining room, but with boxes neatly placed on the stripped bed.

Some empty boxes were stacked in a corner of the master bedroom, but it was clear that packing hadn't been started and the room was still in use. The bed was neatly made. Slippers protruded from under the bed, ready to receive feet before they touched the hardwood floors, which would be chilly in the middle of the night, especially at this time of year.

Clothing still hung in the bedroom closet. It seemed to

be arranged by outfit, and there seemed to be many outfits. Regan saw the roots of Kaivan's clotheshorse ways in his uncle's closet. Suitcases, neatly folded extra blankets, and clear plastic boxes filled with more clothing and accessories were stacked and squeezed all the way to the ceiling on the shelf above the clothing rod.

Had Mr. Ansari been her client, she would have had him thin out the closet contents because, even though it was generously sized, the closet was so tightly packed it looked small, a turnoff for many buyers.

Yet, if Mr. Ansari had gone away, even more items usually must have been crammed into the space, she reasoned, since he would have taken at least one suitcase and some clothing with him if he were going on an outing for any length of time.

A large heavily-carved chest of drawers caught her eye. She peeked in the top drawer, feeling very guilty as she did so. A walkthrough, even this ad-libbed one, never involved going through a homeowner's personal possessions. There was really no way she could justify such an invasion of privacy, but she did it anyway, reminding herself why she was there.

"I'm looking for clues to Mr. Ansari's whereabouts. Who knows what I might find if I poke around," she told the vacant house.

Carefully folded socks, tee shirts, and boxer shorts filled the drawer to overflowing. It was so full, she had to compress the drawer's contents with one hand as she closed it with her other hand. Mr. Ansari certainly would have needed underwear on any kind of trip he took, but it

57

didn't look like any was missing from the overstuffed drawer; at least she couldn't imagine how the drawer could hold any more than it already did. Curious, she thought.

In the bathroom, a ceramic container held a toothbrush and a tube of toothpaste. An electric shaver rested in its charging unit, a tiny green light indicating it was fully charged. Unless Mr. Ansari had separate travel toiletries, it seemed odd he hadn't taken those things with him.

A plastic pill dispenser labeled for each day of the week sat next to the sink. Pills were still in it for all the days of the week except Sunday and Monday. It looked like Mr. Ansari had missed his regimen of medications beginning on Tuesday. When had the Beltrans signed off? Last Wednesday? No, it was last Thursday. According to his medication dispenser, if Kaivan was right and Mr. Ansari had left town, it must have been sometime on Monday.

Although she wasn't sure if Mr. Ansari was unprincipled, she doubted he was impolite. If he left on Monday, he certainly would have made it to Las Vegas in plenty of time to call Kaivan and explain that he was going to miss his appointment, rather than leave his favorite nephew stood-up in front of everyone at the escrow company.

A small pharmacy of yellow plastic medicine bottles sat out on the counter, probably the source of at least some of the pill dispenser's contents. She poked and twisted the bottles to read their labels. Regan recognized some names and purposes: Norvasc was for lowering blood pressure, Vicodin would be for pain, and Xanax was a sleeping pill. She recognized Dilantin and knew it was for seizures. Was

Mr. Ansari an epileptic, she wondered? There were other medications she wasn't familiar with at all.

Regan went to the kitchen next. The cupboards were mostly empty, their contents packed; although enough pots, pans, and dishes remained for simple meals. She opened the refrigerator, which according to the purchase contract, was going with Mr. Ansari when the house sold. Some eggs, butter, jam, and condiments remained, and there were a few carefully wrapped leftovers well past their prime.

It was apparent the contents weren't being replaced as they were used. That was a good sign; it meant the refrigerator was being prepared for a move.

As she closed the refrigerator door, she noticed a DO NOT RESUSCITATE order posted on it. The order was duly signed by Mr. Ansari and witnessed by Kaivan Nasseri on January 13th and by Eleanor Rosemont of 1219 Royale Street on January 14th, less than three weeks ago. The physician's name mentioned for primary care was Dr. Shepard.

The order wasn't just taped to the door. It was precisely centered and outlined in wide blue tape. It almost looked like it had been framed, so carefully and securely was the outlining tape placed around the document. The DNR order looked like it had been prepared for the move, too.

Mr. Ansari was clearly getting ready to vacate and planning to leave the house in beautiful condition for its new owners. Regan decided he wasn't trying to do something underhanded, like Rickie Longland and her deceitful father.

That was a relief of sorts. She erased all the potential

negatives she held from her impression of Mr. Ansari.

He was, however, still missing — and the grant deed remained unsigned.

Regan noticed two pet food bowls on the floor near the back door. One was labeled *Chat Aliments*, the other *Chat Eau* — the escape-artist cat's food and water bowls. Both were very empty, long since licked and lapped clean. Given the size of the mail pile at the front door, it seemed clear Kaivan had been letting himself in through the back door when he came to check on his uncle's whereabouts. The cat's bowls were so near the door, he would have practically tripped over them every time he came in. And, if this cat was anything like her cat, it was hard to imagine a hungry feline wouldn't greet him demanding food and water, especially a cat that was bold enough to warrant a warning sign for realtors.

Surely Kaivan knew his uncle had a pet and would have fed it on his regular visits during his uncle's absence. She wondered where the cat was.

"Cyrus, dear, is that you?" a female voice called out.

A bright yellow cap poked through the opening back door. An arresting head and a petite elderly woman followed it. She was hunched over, which made her seem even smaller than she was, and judging from her fragile appearance, she was at least in her eighties.

During her younger days, the woman must have been very proud to be a redhead, since she was clearly railing against the white hair her age would have dictated. She seemed to be trying hard to maintain her distinctive coloring, but she had gone too far and produced an intense carrot mane, unlike any that grew naturally on a human head. The effect was startling, and Regan hadn't heard the key in the lock, so she was already surprised.

"Oh, you're not Cyrus," the woman stated with disappointment in her voice. "I saw the lights come on and thought he might be back."

"No, I'm the real estate agent for the couple buying Mr. Ansari's house. I came by to see how he was doing with his move preparations," she said, relieved she had that excuse in mind to explain her actions.

"Well, he was progressing very well until early last week, but I haven't seen him since last Monday night and I'm quite worried about him." She pressed her lips tightly together and gave her carrot curls a slight shake.

"His nephew thinks he's gone out of town on business or maybe to Las Vegas to celebrate the sale," Regan suggested.

"Nonsense," the woman exclaimed. "He would have brought Harry to my house if he was leaving town, even overnight."

"Harry is…?" Regan started to ask.

"My cat," the woman declared. "Well, at least he used to be," she smiled. "He's named after my late husband, you know. I called him that so I wouldn't feel so crazy when I forgot my husband was dead and said 'Harry, look at this' or 'Harry, what about that'," she chuckled.

"But Harry took to Cyrus and would curl up on his lap whenever he came over for tea. One day Harry just left with him when Cyrus went home, and decided he'd rather live here. After that, I'd come to Cyrus' house for tea most every day to visit my cat." She emphasized 'my.'

"Whenever Cyrus was going out of town, he would bring Harry back to me. 'Eleanor,' he would say, 'I need to be away for a few days, so we'll have to skip our chats, but you can talk to Harry while I'm gone'.

"That cat would carry on something awful until Cyrus came home." She twiddled two of her fingers to pantomime running feet, "And then he'd zip right back here. I've never seen a cat do that. They usually have a bit of dignity and indifference, but not my Harry." She pursed her lips. "I believe he is really a dog in a cat's body," she added conspiratorially.

Regan remembered the witness name on the DNR taped on the refrigerator. She gestured toward it.

"Are you Eleanor Rosemont?"

"Yes — and Cyrus' dearest friend. That's what he told me when he asked me to sign that sorry thing. I hated to do it. It made me think too much about what was coming, but one must take care of things like that before it's too late," she sighed.

A memory surfaced and clicked into place in Regan's mind. Dr. Shepard. One of her friends had suffered a bout with cancer last year. Dr. Shepard was the name of her oncologist.

"Is Mr. Ansari ill?"

"He's more than ill. He's dying, poor dear. They told him he only has a little time left and most of it won't be pleasant."

Regan's mind raced, full of images of Mr. Ansari collapsed in some remote location. That would explain his leaving Kaivan dangling at the escrow company. Then she had a flashing vision of Mr. Ansari, unable to bear the thought of future suffering, with a gun to his head, bracing to squeeze the trigger and end it all, while he could still control his fate. Maybe that was the plan he alluded to when he called to ask if escrow was going to close on time.

She immediately chastised herself for having an overactive imagination. It didn't seem likely Mr. Ansari could have gone far when his car was still parked out front. So much for her remote location theory.

And from the look of his house, Mr. Ansari appeared to be too orderly a person to end his life impulsively. He would have signed the necessary documents so the sale of his house could proceed, arranged for Harry's care, and said goodbye to his dearest friend and confidant and to his family — especially to his favorite nephew.

Her spying had accomplished one thing: it laid to rest some of her wilder imaginings. But most of Regan's questions remained unanswered, and what Mrs. Rosemont told her made her ask several more.

7

Regan called Kaivan from her cell as she drove away and got him on the first ring, an unprecedented occurrence. "Kaivan, Hi. Any news about your uncle? I'm planning irritating nuisance calls at least twice a day until you tell me he's turned up and is ready to sign off."

Kaivan laughed. "Nothing yet. Didn't I promise I'd let you know immediately when I heard from him?"

"You did, but I'm fighting worry-mode here. I talked to the Beltran's mortgage broker this morning. He thinks he can sing and dance a bit and keep the mortgage available until near the end of next week, but we really need a wrap by next Wednesday at the latest. If the loan doesn't fund by then, the lender will pull it.

"Besides, Stephanie called this morning. Their landlord has new tenants lined up. They absolutely have to be out by a week from Saturday. They'll have nowhere to live after that. She's so close to her due date; I don't want to put her through trying to find another place to live. We've got to find your uncle and get his signature so escrow can close."

It sounded a bit melodramatic to suggest a hospital as

the possible location for the missing Cyrus Ansari. Regan was reasonably certain that Kaivan would have made sure his uncle wasn't an unconscious and unidentified patient somewhere. But it couldn't hurt to plant the suggestion in case he hadn't thought of it.

"The Beltran's schedule changed and they cancelled the walkthrough we were going to do last week, but I went by your uncle's house this morning to do one on their behalf. I noticed a Do-Not-Resuscitate order on his fridge. His next-door neighbor came by while I was there. She says she hasn't seen him since last Monday. Is there anything about his health you want to tell me? He couldn't be in a hospital somewhere, or worse, could he?"

"Lots of people have those things around, especially after Terri Shiavo. You really are a worrier, aren't you?"

It was a response she didn't expect, and a question she chose not to answer.

Another thought came to mind: "Could his being gone have anything to do with the plans he mentioned when he called me last week?"

"The plans he mentioned? Um...no, I don't think so..." Kaivan hesitated and then added decisively, "No, I'm sure it doesn't."

"Humor me, Kaivan. Let's start planning for what happens if he's not back by Friday."

"Tell you what, if he's not back by then, I'll start worrying, too. OK? We'll deal with it then, if we have to."

"Kaivan, you are way too relaxed about this for my liking," she exclaimed.

"I learned to be like that from my uncle. Lighten up.

He'll be back." Kaivan laughed again, an easy reassuring laugh. "I know him."

"All right," she agreed reluctantly. "You have until Friday then — Friday morning — not all day Friday," Regan added quickly.

"Oh, one more thing. When I went by the house this morning, I noticed empty pet food bowls. It looks like your uncle has a cat, but I couldn't find one. Do you know where his cat is?"

"Let's see now. A worrier. Pushy and tenacious. And concerned about the sweet little kitty, too," Kaivan kidded lightheartedly. "I have his cat. I was feeding him every time I went by to see if my uncle was back, but after a few days, it just got easier to bring him home with me."

"Back to worry-mode, Kaivan. Wouldn't your uncle have taken him to the next-door neighbor if he planned a trip?"

"No, no. That cat's tough. He can take care of himself. My uncle just leaves extra kibble out for him if he's going to be away. Uncle Cyrus expects me to drop by every couple of days, anyway. If he's away, he knows I'll come by more often to kind of check on the house, so he knows I'll watch out for Harry, that's his cat's name, if he's gone for a while. That's the arrangement we have.

"Look, I've got another call I need to take." Kaivan spoke rapidly, "I promise I'll let you know as soon as I hear from my uncle, and if I don't by Friday, I'll call you and we'll come up with plan B. Gotta go, bye."

"Friday morning," Regan tried to say before Kaivan was off the line, but he disconnected before she could get the words out.

She was left stymied by his quick getaway. She had other questions for him. She wanted to follow up with something like, "Are you sure about the cat?" Eleanor Rosemont said Mr. Ansari always brought Harry to her when he was going out of town. Why wouldn't he have done that this time?

It occurred to Regan it didn't matter that she hadn't had the opportunity to ask the question. Kaivan and his uncle didn't really have an arrangement about the cat. Kaivan had just lied to her. Well, maybe lied was too strong a term, she backpedaled. But he hadn't exactly told her the truth. Why would he bother to make up a story like that?

He danced around the DNR order, too. Mrs. Rosemont knew Kaivan's uncle was under a death sentence. If she knew, Kaivan knew. Why wouldn't he acknowledge his uncle was ill?

Even his faltering about his uncle's plans didn't feel right. Either he knew what the plans were, or he didn't. Why the hesitation? What was that about?

She understood why Kaivan hadn't given her a heads-up about his uncle disappearing for a while. Realtors were like everyone else; most tried to avoid confrontation, and all hoped for miracles. He might have skipped calling her with such news, hoping his uncle would turn up and spare him that unpleasantness. She knew all about trying to avoid disagreeable phone calls.

But the cat, the DNR order, and Mr. Ansari's plans — those weren't thorny questions or ones likely to have caused discord. He could easily have answered each of them with a simple, truthful response. If he had said, "I don't know why he didn't take Harry to his neighbor's house — yes he's ill, and yes, I've already checked the hospitals — and finally, I really don't know what his plans are," her level of anxiety would have been no higher than it was now. Why was he unwilling to be candid?

Instead of alleviating her apprehension, his furtive responses increased it, and made her wonder if he was aware of something about his uncle's disappearance that he wasn't admitting.

Regan drove to her next appointment, exasperated by Kaivan's lack of plain response, asking the disconnected phone line, "What's going on, Kaivan? What aren't you telling me?"

8

Regan was anxious to talk to Tom about Kaivan's small deceptions and seeming evasiveness. Those troubling red flags she sometimes saw, when no one else did, were in full flutter in her head. She wanted his input, which, unlike the intuitive reactions she often had, would be carefully reasoned. After he analyzed what she told him, maybe he would see things differently and be able to becalm those flags.

Tom was, as he reminded her often, rational. In the late '90s, he was a computer programmer who was so good at it, companies lined up for his services. He was able to negotiate his own hours and circumstances and all the equipment he needed to work from home. He even convinced one company to provide him with visual conference calling, so he didn't have to turn up in person at biweekly staff meetings unless he wanted social contact.

Then the stock market bubble burst, taking the exuberance, wealth, and jobs of Silicon Valley and so many of the flexible startups with it. Million dollar Christmas parties were replaced by outsourcing as companies tried to keep going. It became apparent his lifestyle was about to change dramatically.

"I'm ready for a change, anyway," Tom casually announced one night. "I don't want to go back to cubicle life, especially for less than I earn now, and I sure don't want to do the daily commute over the hill."

Going over the hill was the phrase used by Santa Cruzans to describe the twisty drive up and over the ridge of low mountains that separated coastal Santa Cruz County from Santa Clara County, where most of the companies that constituted Silicon Valley were located. When the road was constructed in 1940, the drive was usually a leisurely one, made by sightseers and beach-goers seeking respite from the heat of the inland valley. The four lane road now had to accommodate over thirty thousand commuter trips a day, but it hadn't been widened or straightened since it was built to better handle the load.

"I'm too used to my daily stroll down the hall to my office to accept that kind of routine. I like to look at houses almost as much as you do. Selling real estate might be interesting. I'm sure it's easy being a realtor. Why don't I get my license and we can be partners?" he questioned brightly. "Better yet, why don't I get my broker's license and we can start our own company?" Tom was on an animated roll. "I'll be the broker, the boss, and you can be my agent. You can work for me," he teasingly suggested.

"Oh no," she groaned. "New agents are trouble enough, but working under a broker without any experience? You'd be armed and seriously dangerous."

Tom made his fist into a gun and blew imaginary smoke

off his index finger, a huge grin on his face.

"I'd have to keep an eye on you every minute of every day. I don't think I could handle that and starting our own company at the same time." Regan wrinkled her nose, "Let's put off going out on our own for a while."

Tom did get his broker's license, but he hung it with an established brokerage, and joined all the newly minted California realtors, half of whom would be gone before a year in the business — burned out by such an easy job.

He was almost one of the dropouts. Initially, Tom tried to use the same mind set he'd used as a programmer. Price, condition, location, and square footage became his project definitions. He'd ask his clients to describe their needs, and then he'd design, or in his current situation, find a house that addressed their requirements.

Crisp logic like that worked well in programming but not always in house hunting, because most people bought homes, not houses, and what made a house feel like home was complicated and hard to measure in mere feet and inches. Tom decided being a realtor wasn't as easy as he had expected.

His frustration reached a peak one day, after he had spent most of it with buyer clients. He fumed into the office and slammed his lockbox key into its desk charger. "I don't know how you can stand this outrageous business. I've just wasted another day with clueless people."

If there'd been something handy to kick, he would have kicked it.

"I showed Christa and Joe exactly what they said they wanted. Now their criteria seem to have shifted again, but neither of them bothered to tell me that," he exploded.

"They really have no idea what they want. They don't buy what they should. They change their minds every day. Worst of all, I don't think they're completely truthful with me. They expect me to be honest and dependable," he muttered. "Why can't I count on the same from them? I'm going to tell them to find another realtor and stop wasting my time."

Regan had met Christa and Joe. They were nice people. Regan hadn't seen subterfuge or dishonesty in them. Tom had added them to the top of his list of future dinner invitees, an unmistakable indication of how he felt about them.

"They probably just haven't fallen in love yet," Regan said.

"Fallen in love? What does being in love have to do with buying a house?"

"Sometimes everything. You have to consider what the process must feel like to them. What they're doing is kind of like getting married. If they make the wrong decision, it's going to cost them a lot of money and emotional upheaval to extricate themselves," she explained with a wry smile. "They're not in love yet, so they're afraid of making a mistake."

Regan paused for a second, "No," she added, "they're terrified of making a mistake. Family and friends are circling, telling them what to do. You're telling them what to do. They're trying to decide whether or not to follow your advice — you — someone they hardly know, someone their family and friends are telling them to be wary of, all

74

the time hoping you know what the heck you're doing. And they're also hoping you aren't about to take horrible advantage of them. You know, a lot of people think we realtors can trick them into buying something they don't want, and that doing so is what we live for," she laughed.

"I don't think most people relish being in a situation like that." Regan shrugged, "Sometimes it amazes me clients can commit to anything. But love can change all that.

"Come on," she tried to cajole him out of his disgruntled mood. "You're good at having fun. In some ways this business is kind of like theater or performance art. Learn to enjoy the entertainment value in it," she said, full of merriment. "You just have to decide how much drama you're willing to put up with before you get paid."

"Some drama's OK. I like zany, even neurotic people. But my client base seems to start at the deeply troubled and rapidly decline to the pathologically damaged," he said, still peevish. "Why don't you come across people like that?"

"I get my share of them. I got a call today from a man who asked if it was enough of a buyer's market that he could hurt people. I thought I misunderstood him and said it was an excellent time to find a great buy. He said again he didn't just want a good buy, he wanted to inflict pain, and I don't believe he meant that metaphorically. He made it very clear he was looking for a victim and wanted a realtor willing to help him do exactly that — hurt someone.

"I didn't even say goodbye to him," Regan cringed. "I just quietly pressed the off button on my phone and hoped he'd move on once he realized we were disconnected."

"That guy sounds disturbed enough, he probably meant to call me and dialed your number by mistake," Tom smirked.

"I doubt it. He probably figured you were too nice a guy to help him out, and wanted someone," Regan gnashed her teeth as she said the word, "*nasty*, like me, to do his dirty work."

Tom snickered. "Ah, yes, my notoriously vicious Regan."

"As for the honesty part, people will tell you their truth every time — they just won't always do it with words. In fact, what they say can sometimes be a distraction.

"Your job description, Mr. Broker," she added his title deferentially but through a smile, "may have a lot in it about knowing inventory and legal requirements, but it's critical you learn to hear what people are really telling you. Find out what matters most to them. What you'd do in their place, or what you think they should do, is irrelevant."

Tom was dubious. "I know you buy that stuff, but I'm not sure I do. It all sounds a little psycho-babbly to me."

"It's not. Any time you doubt that, remember the protea house. It's a great example of what I mean," Regan said.

Before the recent downturn, there had been a long wild seller's market. At the height of it, she had helped some clients get a house they wanted. Her clients could afford the asking price of the home but not much more. When she previewed the house, she discovered the sellers were avid gardeners who had a true passion for growing Hawaiian proteas. They told her the unusual flowers were their babies. They hated to move and leave their collection behind, but they had to relocate because of a job transfer. They didn't think the proteas would transplant well, and the weather where they were going wouldn't support the exotic plants.

When Regan realized there were going to be multiple offers for the house, she knew the bidding war likely to ensue could quickly push the price beyond her clients' reach. Her buyers loved the property, so she called the sellers and planted some seeds of her own.

"My clients are gardeners, too," she told them. "Would you be willing to talk to them about your unusual plants? Growing proteas sounds complicated to me. I want them to understand what would be involved in maintaining your garden in case they are the people lucky enough to buy your home. They may decide the job is too much for them and not make an offer, but I think it would be dreadful if someone who wasn't committed to the task of properly caring for them, wound up owning your proteas."

As she drove her hopeful buyers to meet with the sellers, she reminded them to be especially interested in the proteas. She knew that would be easy for them because the garden was what attracted them to the house in the first place. Her clients took her advice, asked plenty of specific care questions, and let their genuine enthusiasm show.

Her clients offered as much as they were qualified to spend for the home — something she let the sellers know. Regan was sure some other agents had written higher offers. Still, she wasn't surprised when the owners accepted her clients' bid. The sellers believed they could trust her buyers to continue nurturing their proteas, so they sold the

77

house to them.

When she told Tom the details of how she got her offer accepted, he shook his head in amazement. "Why didn't they take a higher offer? They could have made more money on their sale."

"Because the most important concern for them wasn't money, it was the future of their proteas, their babies."

"They didn't act according to their own self interest," he protested.

"Maybe not according to their financial interests, but they knew what their priorities were and took care of them as best they could. Their behavior just seems perplexing to you because you don't share their values.

"Listen to people. Let them tell you what they fear, hate, desire, and what they love — especially what they love. That knowledge will explain why they behave the way they do."

Tom stayed in the business and learned. His approach was still logical, which enabled him to work well with sellers. He could explain the realities of pricing and skillfully deliver news they needed, but sometimes didn't want to hear. He solved their problems.

But Tom never learned to like working with buyers as much as Regan did. She loved the detective work involved in finding what a buyer wanted, and had the ability to remember details about people and properties. She appreciated subtleties.

Eventually their skills evened out and they figured out how to cooperate and use one another's very different strengths. Tonight, that meant when Regan thought she saw red flags, she'd ask Tom, "Am I right? Are they waving?"

She'd probably even ask him, "Wildly? Or just a little bit?"

🏠🏠🏠🏠🏠🏠🏠🏠🏠🏠🏠

Tom got a new listing that afternoon, a handsome home in Bonny Doon, just a couple of miles farther out into the country from where they lived. Regan was focused on the marketing they intended to do for the property and put the issue of Kaivan's uncle out of her mind while they ate dinner. They were almost finished with after-dinner cleanup before their conversation lulled and her questions about Kaivan's misleading answers wriggled their way back into the forefront of her thoughts.

"I'm having a red flag moment," Regan said, without segue. "I think Kaivan is keeping something from me." She quickly filled Tom in on the latest about the missing uncle, concluding with the conversation she'd had with Mrs. Rosemont about the DNR and the cat.

"He seems to be, I don't know, stalling, hedging maybe," Regan said, as she finished drying the last serving bowl and put it away.

"If he's playing for time, doesn't that mean he thinks he can take care of whatever's wrong, given a little wiggle room?" Tom asked. "That sounds like a good thing, like everything should sort itself out if you and your clients are patient."

"I think there's more going on than just a realtor-stall. There's something he's not telling me."

"It seems to me that the root cause of your concerns about Kaivan is that he and the neighbor told you two different stories. So," Tom asked, "what about the neighbor? How sure are you she's not the one misleading you? Remember I met Mr. Ansari at that Chamber of Commerce mixer a year or so ago. From what you've told me about her…what was her name again?" Tom asked.

"Eleanor Rosemont."

"Eleanor Rosemont doesn't sound like the type of person he'd have as a pal. You said she invited you to stop by for tea when you met her at Mr. Ansari's house, right?"

"Uh-huh," Regan replied.

"There you go. She might just be a lonely old lady looking for some attention or company. She might be telling you tales, trying to make herself seem more important in Mr. Ansari's life than she really is."

"I don't think so," Regan objected. "I don't think she's the needy type at all. She's one sharp lady — a bit unconventional, certainly, but that makes her interesting. I liked her immediately. She's one of those people who wouldn't bat an eye no matter what you told her. I'm looking forward to taking her up on her offer of tea."

"No, I think you're wrong. I could see Mr. Ansari enjoying her company. Besides, she used a key to open the back door, so Mr. Ansari must have given her one."

"Maybe." Tom waved his index finger, indicating an ah-hah moment. "Or, maybe Mr. Ansari kept an extra key near the back door; she saw him stash it, and knew where it was."

"She greeted me as 'Cyrus, dear' when she thought I

was him. She'd hardly call Mr. Ansari 'dear' if she didn't know him well. You're being so cynical," Regan scoffed. "And you haven't even met the woman. I think you'd like her, too."

"I'm not being cynical exactly, but I will let you call me skeptical, if you want."

"OK, I'll agree to that, but only if you pay attention to my intuition on this one," she negotiated playfully. "That's fair, isn't it?"

The lightheartedness of her challenge vanished. "Really though, Tom, something isn't as it seems." Regan turned to face him, hands on hips. "I've got a hunch about this one."

"One of your hunches," Tom whistled.

"Don't start." Regan rolled her eyes and tried to sound offended. "Mrs. Rosemont is telling me the truth. Kaivan isn't. He's being evasive and deceptive over such silly little details. He didn't need to make up a story about the cat. He's hedging all right, but not to buy fix-it time. There's another piece to it; I just don't know what it is. That's what worries me."

Regan rested one arm across her midsection to support her other elbow. Her hand was at her chin, her index finger extended to tap against her lips. "You know how I am. Sometimes I just get a sense — a little breeze fluttering around the edges of a deal, almost like a slight atmospheric change that…well," she squirmed a bit, "sets off one of my little red flags. Kaivan's behavior is doing that to me, now. I may not know why just yet, but I see waving red."

Tom was too rational to believe in intuition, but he was also too savvy to deny Regan did have some sort of radar

81

he lacked. She often seemed to know something was amiss before anyone told her. He'd watched her hunches turn into reality often enough in the business they shared.

If he believed in it, he might have said she had a sort of precognition, but he didn't believe in it. He understood her apparent prescience could be explained easily enough without invoking anything as unscientific as sixth sense. He recognized that sometimes she simply picked up on things which remained unnoticed by him and most other people.

For a few moments, Tom considered what she said. Then he put his hands on her shoulders and pulled her close. "Logic tells me you're making more out of the DNR and the cat story than you ought to," he said.

"Is there a 'but' coming?" She looked up into his deep blue eyes.

He nodded. "But — even though I'm not particularly troubled that Kaivan's and Mrs. Rosemont's versions don't jive, I do see a problem. Your uneasiness is what's important here. You want me to say 'don't worry about those inconsistencies, ignore your feelings about them', don't you?"

"I do."

"Sorry," he apologized. "I can't say that this time. You don't get blindsided very often. I have a great deal of respect for your hunches, even if I don't like admitting that I do," he smiled. "Your gut feeling might be right on this one as well."

The red flags in her mind fluttered madly.

Regan phoned Kaivan several times on Thursday, but never reached him. She decided he must be screening for her squeaky-wheel calls; that was why he didn't answer or return her messages. Friday morning she picked up her phone to call him with her ultimatum. The phone rang in her hand. She looked at it, pressed the *talk* button, and put the phone to her ear slowly, in that state of slightly startled disorientation that happens during such coincidences.

"Hello?" She asked tentatively.

"Hello, Regan."

She recognized his voice immediately and didn't say "Hi" or offer any of the usual pleasantries. She greeted him pointedly with, "I hope you have good news, Kaivan."

"Have you seen today's *Sentinel*?"

"Not yet. You caught me before I picked up the newspaper."

"There's a story on the front page about a body found near Steamer Lane," Kaivan's voice sounded tired. He didn't add anything else.

"I read about a teenager who disappeared after a party

last week up near Davenport." Regan spoke quickly, wanting to move on and get back to her point. "It was presumed he…" she said, before an awakening realization stopped her. He wouldn't be calling to discuss the latest news on a missing teenager. "Oh, Kaivan, do you think…could it be your uncle?"

Regan heard a deep inhalation of breath and a long quavering sigh. There was a protracted silence before Kaivan said, "I know it is. The police called last night. They said a surfer found him just before sundown. My uncle's body was at the back of Toilet Bowl, in one of the caverns undermining the cliffs by the lighthouse. He was washed so far in, he couldn't be seen from above. It took some surfer getting really flushed for him to be found."

Toilet Bowl was a rocky cove next to Steamer Lane, one of the most popular surfing areas in Santa Cruz. Sometimes surfers missed the run at the Lane and were forced into the Bowl, but more often they jumped in as a shortcut to the Steamer Lane breaks or for the thrill of getting flushed, the term local surfers used to describe what happened to them in the swirling currents inside the cove.

"He'd been in the water for quite a while, maybe ten days or more they think, and in some very rough surf. They told me I wouldn't be able to identify him, not to even try. They said no one could for sure — except," Kaivan's voice broke, "except his wallet was still in his pocket…after all that happened to him. He always wore pants that had a button loop to close the pocket flap over his wallet. It was a little idiosyncrasy of his, I don't know, maybe left over from Iran. He thought that button would stop pickpockets.

His wallet was still in his pants pocket and his driver's license could still be read. How could that paltry little button have stayed on when his body was so…" Kaivan's anguish was palpable, "damaged?"

"I'm so sorry, Kaivan."

"You were right about him being sick, Regan. He had been diagnosed with a brain tumor a couple of years ago. He had the whole treatment battery: surgery, chemo, and radiation. His doctors were really optimistic; they thought they got it all. But last September he started having headaches again. They did some tests. The tumor was back, and this time, they said it would eventually kill him.

"After his house sold, he was going to move to my parent's house and live in a little attached unit they have. We figured we could all help take care of him.

"He'd already had a couple of dizzy spells and was taking Dilantin to hold off the seizures that his doctors said would probably start soon."

Regan had a fleeting image of the Dilantin prescription bottle she had seen among Mr. Ansari's medicine collection.

"I think he must have walked to the ocean, planning to watch the sunset from out on the rocks where Woodrow Avenue dips down low and comes into West Cliff Drive. He probably climbed out to his favorite spot. He always said that location was the perfect place to watch the sun melt into the sea. He'd made the climb there so many times. Getting out to his favorite rock was easy, not really a climb at all, almost like just continuing a walk. But I think this time he must have gotten dizzy, or even had his first

85

seizure…" Kaivan's voice trailed off.

He was silent for a time. Regan couldn't think of anything to say to make the situation better, so she was silent as well, waiting for him to regain enough composure to speak again.

"The police talked to me a lot about suicide. They seemed to think that's what might have happened, but don't believe them. Please don't believe that. I know Uncle Cyrus wouldn't commit suicide. His death must have been an accident." There was a long pause again. At last Regan could hear Kaivan take another deep breath.

"So here's my plan. Plan B." His voice had recovered, he was in control again, no longer pleading for her to accept his reality.

"You've seen the preliminary title report, so you know my uncle had the house in a trust. He made me the successor trustee; it's up to me to decide what happens to his estate. He also left the house to me. Talk to your clients. If they still want to buy Uncle Cyrus' home, I'll sell it to them for the same price and terms that my uncle agreed to, as soon as the estate is settled. It shouldn't take very long because everything is in order.

"In the meantime, they can move in on schedule. They'll probably lose the loan they have lined up, so they can just live there rent-free until we can close the sale. That should more than make up for them having to start over with a new loan."

"That's very generous, Kaivan."

"I promised your clients would be OK. None of this is the Beltrans' fault. My uncle was a big-hearted and fair man. I know he would have wanted me to work things out this way."

Regan went by Stephanie and Ed's apartment that evening. She didn't want to tell them about Mr. Ansari's death over the phone; people often had uneasy reactions to death. After her father died, she and Tom listed her family home for sale. One week later, the next-door neighbor's house came on the market, too. Her parents were original owners in a subdivision of houses just outside San Francisco, just like the neighbors were. The houses looked a bit different from the outside, but the materials used on the inside were the same, and they had identical floor plans. Both had been impeccably maintained.

The real estate market was in a frenzy at that time, and both houses had multiple offers over the asking price, but her parent's house sold for thirty thousand dollars more than the house next door. Much as she and Tom wanted to say the price difference was because of their superior marketing or negotiating skills, they both knew the difference was because the man next door had died at home, a fact that by law had to be disclosed, and her father had not.

Regan wanted to be with the Beltrans when she told them about Mr. Ansari's death to see how they reacted. Whatever their response, she would be supportive.

Neither Stephanie nor Ed said anything as she told them what had happened and explained Kaivan's offer. As Regan spoke, they looked at one another every so often. At one point, Stephanie reached out and took Ed's hand, but mostly they maintained perfect poker faces.

Finally Ed said, "I don't know, I'm not superstitious. I mean, I don't believe in ghosts or anything like that, but this feels kind of creepy, you know? Maybe we should find something else. We could stay with my family for a while if we need to. What do you think, Steph?"

Stephanie absentmindedly put a hand on her very large belly and gently caressed it. "I think we should buy the house, honey. It's not like he died there. He took such good care of his place; it must have really been important to him. And it seems like we might make Mr. Ansari's family feel happy if we brought new life to his home. I think there was love in the house, enough to cancel out anything negative there. We looked for a long time. We really like the neighborhood and the house. I think we should buy it."

"Could we think about it overnight?" Ed chewed his lip.

"Of course," Regan said.

Ed glanced at Stephanie, a little look out of the corner of his eye, as she continued to stroke her stomach. He still held her other hand in his. "Oh, no, I guess," he squeezed her hand as a small smile started at the corners of his mouth, "I guess, yes, let's buy it." He shrugged and shook his head. Stephanie threw her arms around his neck, and it was settled.

🏠🏠🏠🏠🏠🏠🏠🏠🏠🏠🏠

On Saturday, several of Cyrus Ansari's family members came by 1215 Royale Street and took the pieces of furniture and remembrances they wanted. Kaivan stopped by and took a few things. Many items were put out on the curb with a sign that said FREE. Voracious bargain hunters, students, and people looking for items to sell on eBay, swarmed the area and carried off their favorite finds. Kaivan found some UCSC students looking to earn some quick cash, and had them take what was left to Goodwill on Mission Street.

Stephanie and Ed brought things over bit by bit as they came to paint the baby's room and prepare it for its new occupant. They would be able to make their move as scheduled, well before they had to be out of their apartment for the new tenant.

The Beltrans were thoughtful people. They took a picture of the baby's room after it was set up, and enclosed the photo in a condolence note for Mr. Ansari's family. Stephanie told Regan she didn't know where to send the card, and asked if she could see that the family got it. Regan promised she would.

There were several Nasseris in the phone book, so she decided to consider Kaivan the family spokesperson, and take the note to him in person. She also had a white camellia bush and another card from Tom and her for Kaivan's mother.

Regan knew where Kaivan lived a few years ago, but heard he had moved recently. She checked the phone book to see if he had listed his address with his phone number. He had. The address was a prestigious one.

Regan confirmed the brass house number matched what she had written down as she parked in front of Kaivan's house. It was an impressive place.

His house was located only a block off West Cliff Drive, the street that ran along the ocean's edge. But beach goers, roller-bladers, bike riders, and walkers didn't frequent his sidewalk like they did the wide sidewalk of popular West Cliff Drive, so his location was quiet and he enjoyed good privacy.

The street where he lived defined the back boundary of Lighthouse Field State Park. Since no houses were built along West Cliff Drive in front of his house, the low grassy mounds of the park were all that kept Kaivan's house from being ocean-front property. Nice, she thought — all the benefits of a close ocean view without any of the beach traffic drawbacks.

His house was pale gray stucco, large and very modern. There was an austere elegance about the property. Expanses of glass wrapped around the upper level on the ocean side of the house. The windows hinted at a reverse floor plan with living spaces on the second story to maximize what must be a spectacular ocean view.

There wasn't much of a front yard. The house took most of the lot, but what yard there was, was planted in dramatic grasses of varying heights and hues that did well in the salty air, inescapable this close to the ocean. The light breeze off the water made them wave softly, producing a soothing rustle which Regan enjoyed as she walked to the front door.

The walkway was paved with diagonally-cut and precisely-fitted granite squares that continued up the three broad stairs that led to the front door. It was an expensive treatment that added to the sophisticated look of the house.

She couldn't tell if he was home. Kaivan's BMW wasn't in the driveway, although this close to the ocean, anyone who cared about his car would garage it, and she knew Kaivan took good care of his cars. Having a late model perfectly polished black BMW was as much a part of his signature look as his well-cut custom clothing.

There weren't any lights on in the house that she could see, even though it was dusk going to dark when she arrived. Perhaps Kaivan liked dimmer light than she did, or perhaps he was inside, sitting in the fading daylight, sipping a glass of wine, and watching the sun get ready to take its nightly dip into the ocean. That's what she would be doing, if she lived here.

Regan juggled the camellia and cards to one side and rang the doorbell with her free hand. The bells chimed a more distinctive tune than the typical 'bing-bong' of most doorbells. The auditory first impression of the house was as urbane as its visual first impression.

No answer. She waited a minute and rang again. After another minute, she decided no one was home. She debated whether or not to leave the plant and cards near the door, but decided against it. Leaving condolences that way would be too impersonal. She'd have to try again another day. She turned, walked down the stairs, and headed toward her car.

Regan had only gone a few steps when she heard a faint sound at the entry that caused her to turn back toward the house.

Kaivan had opened the front door, but hadn't turned on the entry light or called out to her.

"Oh, Kaivan, you are here," she said, returning to his porch.

Regan might not have recognized him if she had run in to him on the street. It wasn't his clothing — she didn't expect him to dress in designer suits at home — but his manner lacked all the brisk confidence and charm he usually worked so hard to project. He didn't greet her, invite her in, or even make eye contact. He stood very still in the dimly lit doorway, his eyes downcast, focused on his shoeless, stockinged feet.

"I just found a suicide note," he said. He bit his bottom lip. "I brought some of my uncle's stuff back here. It was on his computer."

"Oh no, Kaivan," She hugged him impulsively and awkwardly with the arm not holding the camellia. She almost dropped the plant and its container. But he didn't return the embrace. He let his arms stay at his sides and didn't accept her comfort.

"I guess the police were right," he said in a small, defeated voice.

10

Depending on her mood, Regan either liked to make interesting, often complicated dinners, or she wanted one of the frozen pizzas they kept on hand.

Since there were no stores in Bonny Doon, Regan planted lemons, a kaffir lime, basil, thyme, rosemary, and heirloom tomatoes, and kept an array of offbeat specialty items in the pantry. Still, her recipe books always seemed to call for an item she didn't have, and it took a good forty minutes to make the round trip to town and back — too long a trip for a missing ingredient.

Her solution was to stop using recipes. Instead, decisions about what to have for dinner began by taking inventory of what was on hand, and then figuring out how to combine the available items in an edible way.

Remoteness had forced her to become a creative and resourceful cook. She prided herself on usually being able to make a decent meal out of whatever was in the refrigerator, the pantry, and growing in the garden.

Tonight, she was in the mood to cook, but tonight her routine was going to be different. Tonight, Regan was going to use recipes and follow them exactly. She shopped carefully before coming home, making sure she had exotic ingredients like fish sauce and palm sugar to create authentic Pad Thai, and snake beans for the fish cakes she planned to serve.

Regan hoped that concentrating on the recipe details would keep her from thinking about how sorry she felt for Kaivan. He so wanted to believe his uncle hadn't taken his own life — the suicide note must have been a devastating discovery for him.

The main reason she departed from her usual meal improvisation, however, was that Sandy and Dave were joining them for dinner. As clever a cook as she had become, not all spontaneous meals were a success. Tom was always tolerant of her failed attempts, but she didn't like to experiment too much on non-family, even long-time good friends like Sandy and Dave.

There was a predictable routine when the couple joined them for dinner. Ebullient Sandy, who had worked with Tom early in his programming career, was always enthused about something new in her life and would lead the conversation during dinner. At some point after the dishes were cleared, Sandy, who didn't openly admit to being a smoker, would slip outside 'for some fresh air'.

Her mother had died of lung cancer, but even after watching that happen, Sandy still couldn't quit smoking. She reproached herself for her failure and wanted company when she indulged. Tom had successfully kicked the habit some years ago, or at least had gotten down to being a pack-a-year man. As soon as Sandy stepped outside, he

would cheerfully announce he better keep her company —
maybe talk programming — and follow her out to the patio.
Most of his infrequent cigarettes were bummed from
Sandy. Regan and Dave would stay inside, talking and
pretending they didn't know about the smoking going on
outside.

Tonight, the predictability of the dinner customs should
have been comforting and distracting. Instead Regan was
on edge, anxious for dinner to be over so Sandy and Tom
would go outside and she could talk to Dave alone.

Dave was a former Santa Cruz cop who had taken a
bullet to the head some years ago. Miraculously the bullet
hadn't penetrated his skull, but it had shattered the occipital
bone around his right eye, causing dozens of minute bone
fragments to penetrate his eyeball. There were far too many
for any ophthalmological surgeon to remove, regardless of
how skilled he or she might be. Dave's eye couldn't be
saved. He had a prosthetic replacement that had been
cleverly attached to the muscles of his remaining eye, so it
sympathetically tracked the left and right movements it
made, mirroring the normal scanning of two sighted eyes.

Dave had a gracious sense of humor about what had
happened to him. He pretended to have never heard it
before whenever someone said he had such a thick skull
even a bullet couldn't impress him, or some variation of
that childish jest.

Because of his impaired vision, he couldn't remain an
active duty patrolman after the shooting, but he didn't want
to take early retirement. He had too much energy for that
and genuinely enjoyed police work. He fought hard to stay

on the force and had sort of succeeded.

The City of Santa Cruz was going to have to pay him disability anyway, so an unusual deal was struck. For a little more money, he agreed to stay on as an ombudsman, keeping the police force and Santa Cruz residents speaking to one another — something that required real skill in progressive Santa Cruz, a community where many local residents had bumper stickers that read KEEP SANTA CRUZ WEIRD, and police were often regarded as adversaries who interfered with citizens' enjoyment of their lifestyles, rather than as protectors of their lives.

Dave no longer wore a police uniform. As part of his new duties, he sometimes had to appear on TV to answer news media questions. With that in mind, he had devised his own consistent, recognizable style. Having decided Hawaiian shirts made him look approachable and seemed suited to a Santa Cruz persona, that's usually what he wore.

Mostly, his job required spending some time every day at the station house, answering citizens' questions and complaints, handling public relations, doing some overflow paperwork, and anything else that needed doing. He also managed to know everything any Santa Cruz cop knew, or suspected, was happening in the community. That wasn't part of his job description — that was just Dave.

Tonight, while Sandy and Tom smoked, Regan planned to ask Dave what he had heard about the body found in Toilet Bowl a few days ago. She hoped there might be something he could tell her that, despite Mr. Ansari's suicide note, would ease Kaivan's heart.

As soon as Sandy and Tom made their disguised exit,

Regan suggested, "Come on, Dave. Grab your beer and let's go into the living room."

"What's on your mind, Regan? You've been all squirmy and fidgety tonight," the observant Dave asked, as he settled into a leather chair.

"I'm that obvious?" Regan snickered. She kicked off her shoes and curled her long legs under her on the sofa. "I was hoping you could tell me what the authorities think about the man found in the ocean last week," she began.

"I'm surprised at you, Regan. You usually don't want me to talk about bodies," Dave said, taking another sip of his beer. He used the mocking banter that so often punctuated their conversations. "But if you like floaters, we've got plenty to talk about. Last week was a big week for them. You want to start with the old guy in Toilet Bowl or the kid that went in near Davenport? He washed up the day after the Toilet Bowl guy, you know. I can tell you all about both of them, if you want."

"Don't you dare." She held up her hands in front of her chest in a defensive mode to stop him. "No, no, I haven't suddenly developed a macabre interest in people whose bodies are found in the ocean. Don't tell me anything about the Davenport boy."

"So, you want details about the Toilet Bowl guy then?"

Regan nodded. "He's an exception. I met him once, when I presented an offer for his house. He was lively and full of enthusiasm," she said, her voice filled with poignancy. "He accepted my clients' offer. Escrow was scheduled to close shortly after he went missing, but he didn't make it to his appointment to sign the transfer documents, so it didn't happen.

"I know his nephew, Kaivan Nasseri, too. I worked with him a few years ago, and we've done some transactions together since then and kept in touch. He was the listing agent for his uncle's house. We were working together on that when his uncle disappeared. I like Kaivan and feel sorry for him. He seems devastated by his uncle's death."

"Yeah, well, everything was pretty grisly. The guy had been in the water for a while and nibbled on a lot before he hit the beach. And you know how Toilet Bowl works. He'd been rolled against those jagged rocks in the cove when he was already softened up a lot." Dave spoke casually, seemingly unaware of how his gory description was affecting Regan, but he was having fun with her sensibilities and was delighted with the way his words were affecting her eyes, which narrowed as she winced against the image he was creating.

"Yeah, he was pretty gross. By the time he washed up at the back of the Bowl, you couldn't tell much about who he was from the remains. Even fingerprints were pretty useless." Dave rolled his tongue over the outside of his upper teeth to hide a mischievous grin. "He was in worse shape than the decapitated sea lions that surfers usually find in Toilet Bowl."

Regan swallowed involuntarily. "It must have been awful for his nephew to try to identify him, from what you're saying about the body."

"Oh, he was way too far gone for that. What do you think? We'd make somebody try to ID a floater? No way," Dave shook his head and pressed his lips together. "We wouldn't do that. Besides, we got real lucky with the old man's wallet."

Dave had slipped into what Regan called cop speak, throwing in "we" and "us" as he spoke, like he was an investigator actively involved in the case.

"It was still in the old guy's pocket. We just had the nephew in to look at his uncle's driver's license and clothing. Once we were pretty sure who the deceased was, we were able to confirm his identity with dental records."

Dave took a sip of beer. "Odd thing, we thought at first, that no one filed a missing person report. From what we could find out, no one he knew had seen him for at least ten days before he washed up. Now, usually when somebody's missing that long, people get worried. We thought someone who knew him, someone in his family maybe, would have filed since he'd been gone so long."

Dave stopped his mild teasing as he began telling Regan how the police reasoned in their investigation. "But your friend said no one missed him right away, not until after he skipped an appointment. Probably it was your signing appointment he missed, right?" Dave asked.

"Probably," Regan agreed.

"Yeah." He paused for another sip of beer. "Then your friend said no one was particularly worried about the deceased 'cause he took off from time to time and didn't always tell his family he was going. That made some sense. The old guy was an adult and could do what he wanted. But ten days...that's a long time to go away without telling anyone your plans.

"Your pal's mother, the dead guy's sister," Dave noted

Regan's slight nod indicating her awareness of familial connections, "she said the deceased had some out-of-town visitors. Now they were real interesting. It seems a couple of guys arrived from Iran about the time the old man was last seen. They told the sister that their family and her brother had been involved in some way in the old country. They said they had some important unfinished business they wanted to see him about. They told her they went by the deceased's house pretty regularly, and his car was there, but he didn't answer his doorbell."

Dave gave the tip of his nose a quick rub with the side of his index finger. "Family says the Iranians waited around for the better part of a week for him to get back from wherever he went. According to the sister, they were kind of nuisances, insulting, too. They implied the deceased was hiding out.

"You know, we kind of wondered about that, as well. We got the sense the family, maybe considering who these guys were, thought the deceased was doing just that and weren't worried about him because they didn't really think he was missing.

"According to the dead guy's sister, very suddenly the Iranians said they had to give up and fly home before their airline tickets expired. The sister asked them if they wanted to leave a message or a phone number where her brother could reach them in Iran when he got back, but they didn't leave either one.

"We were interested in those guys for a while, you know, kind of curious what sort of unfinished business they might have had with the late Mr. Ansari. We sure wanted to talk to them for a while, but we weren't able to track 'em down."

Dave finished his beer and put the bottle on the coffee table. "The more we thought about them though, the less we cared about them, because some other interesting questions came up."

"Those men sound pretty significant to me," Regan said. "What other questions were the police trying to answer?"

"First one was, if the family did think the old man was hiding out, after the Iranians flew home, why didn't they get worried about him when he still didn't surface? Why didn't one of them report him missing then?"

Regan didn't say anything, but she nodded slowly.

"We made another round with family members, asking that question. That's when your friend told us the old man probably fell in the ocean because he was sick and got dizzy a lot — maybe even had a seizure," Dave said.

"Now, you know, we didn't feel good about that statement. Something sure didn't seem right. Once the family knew the deceased hadn't been hiding out, how would it work if everyone knew the old man was ailing, but no one would worry if he was missing for a week or more? Sick old man isn't seen by anyone for several days — I'd be worried.

"And wouldn't they be keepin' better track of him? I mean, he shouldn't even have been driving if he was dizzy or anything like that. His family seems pretty tight. They would probably have been carting him around, right?"

"Did his family know about his illness?" Regan asked. "Kaivan was aware of it, but maybe Mr. Ansari hadn't told anyone else in his family about his health."

"We asked that question. Word was out. So we figured maybe someone a little closer to home might have been involved in his disappearance. Maybe someone in the family wanted to get rid of him, or there was, you know, a little family conspiracy thing happening. Maybe that's why no one filed a missing person's report.

"Sex or money," Dave shrugged, "that's where we usually start an investigation. That's where they usually end up, too. The deceased seemed kind of old for the sex part to be the motive, unless he had some sort of a past or a secret lifestyle," Dave snickered, "that was catching up to him.

"But the family said 'no way'. They all agreed that he was a nice conservative old bachelor. And they all seemed to like him and respect him, too. It wasn't like he was some sort of pervert they couldn't leave alone with their kids.

"So we kind of ruled out sex. Then we took a quick look at finances to see if anyone in the family would benefit from the old guy's death, you know, who would be better off with the deceased buried than with him still kick'n? That's always a good question to ask.

"There weren't any hefty insurance policies, nothing like that. Seems he was mostly retired. He still had a finger in lots of business pies with family members, but he wasn't involved much anymore. If anything happened to him, family members would just take over completely and maybe get a little more income. Nothing significant.

"But his nephew…mister fell-in-the-ocean theory," Dave paused, nodding up and down, "…well now, that's a different story. He gets the house you're selling all to himself. The deceased owned it free and clear, and between that and some other assets the old man had, your guy's going to get six hundred, seven hundred K at least. We've seen people helped to eternity for a lot less than that."

"You mean the police think he was murdered?" Regan asked incredulously. "Are you saying you think Kaivan might have killed his uncle for six hundred thousand dollars?" She made a face. "That's crazy. His uncle was like a father to him."

"Like I said, leaving out people who wind up in the wrong place at the wrong time, it's usually sex or money that gets someone killed. Oh, and it's usually someone they know who does the deed. So that's what we were looking at.

"Your Mr. Nasseri was definitely a person of interest, especially when the deceased's family said your buddy was the one who pushed the idea that they didn't need to be worried because the old guy was probably just out of town, partying or something. Sure, we weren't ready to charge him with anything yet, but we were quietly investigating, you know, kind of watching him, asking around a little."

Regan was completely stunned. Kaivan a suspect in his uncle's death? That wasn't at all what she expected Dave to say. She returned her feet to the floor, her relaxed pose gone.

"I can't even think about Kaivan the way you do, Dave. He's a good guy." She frowned and shook her head, "Kaivan has plenty of his own money. I bet he's a millionaire in his own right. He's a very successful realtor who does a lot of business. He has a nice car and an impressive house near the beach. Besides, if he wanted money, why wouldn't he just wait to inherit? His uncle wasn't just sick, he was dying."

She leaned toward Dave for added emphasis, "Did the police know that?"

"Yeah, we did. Your buddy told us about his uncle having a brain tumor. We talked to the old guy's oncologist. He probably had five, maybe six months or so, tops."

"Well then, why would you even think Kaivan might have killed his uncle?"

"You mean besides the financial incentive?" Dave asked. "Well for starters, because he tried way too hard to convince us the old man accidentally fell into the ocean. Me thinketh the lady protesteth too much," he mangled Shakespeare. "Only in this case, it was the guy. He told us the old man liked to climb out on the rocks near Woodrow to watch the sunset and must have slipped. I mean, he really insisted that's what happened, like it was awful important to him to end our investigation right there.

"We didn't buy it. Remember, we were having that unseasonable warm weather at the end of January. Lots of people were out walking on West Cliff and looking around, especially around sunset. The spot your pal said was where his uncle liked to go is highly visible and very popular. The uncle probably had to share his perch with some other sunset watchers. Someone would have seen him go in, if he'd fallen like his nephew said. Old guy, fully clothed, takes a header into the ocean? Everybody has cell phones;

somebody would have called it in. More likely, somebody would have caught it on cell phone video and posted it to *YouTube*," Dave added sarcastically.

"Kaivan told me the police were asking him if he thought his uncle might have committed suicide," Regan said. "I don't think he was having an easy time accepting that his uncle might have done that, and yet even before he found the suicide note, he might have suspected his uncle had taken his own life. I think Kaivan's theory about his uncle falling was his way of making the death an accident in his own mind. I'm sure that's all it was.

"If Mr. Ansari didn't accidentally fall into the ocean, if he did commit suicide, couldn't he have gone into the water some other time," she asked, "maybe late at night when no one was around to see him?"

"Sure he could have, but that still leaves a problem," Dave said. "We get a lot of predictability about where to expect floaters to wash up. Usually when someone goes into the water in town, they either surface nearby real soon, or in a week or two near Aptos or even Manressa Beach. Predictable. That kid you don't want me to tell you about went in up the coast near Davenport a week ago Wednesday. When and where he turned up fit the pattern real well. Predictable. Nope — based on where Mr. Ansari showed up, with the way currents work, February storms, and how long he'd been in the drink, we think the old guy went in up the coast, too, maybe as far up as Waddell Creek.

"But his car was still at his house. Now we know he didn't walk there; it's fifteen, twenty miles up the road.

105

"As I said, we're still investigating. We wanted to know how the uncle could get that far away from home without driving. Yeah, he could have hitched a ride or even taken the bus to Waddell Creek, found someplace quiet and jumped in," Dave's tone oozed sarcasm, "but it's not likely.

"So for starters, we wanted to talk some more to the nephew, you know, at least ask your friend if he drove his uncle to some private place so the old guy could make his exit into the drink. That would make your pal an accessory to suicide, which is a felony.

"But I gotta say, some of us still continued to like the nephew for more than an accessory, if you get my drift," Dave squinted his good eye, hinting at conspiracy. "Maybe he did more than just drive. Maybe he pressured his uncle to hurry things along, maybe even hurried things along himself.

"Consider the suicide note your friend found on his uncle's computer," Dave said. "It was a short one. I looked at a printout of it enough I can remember exactly what it said. Let me quote it for you. It read '3:00 p.m. January 29th. I've decided to end my life now, before things get worse. Please forgive me'.

"Deceased put the date and time in it, but didn't address it to anyone or end the note with his name. It didn't say 'Cyrus' or 'your loving brother' or anything like that. It didn't sound natural.

"And a computer's a crummy place to leave a suicide note. The computer could have been given away, sold, erased, or even tossed. There's no guarantee anyone would read a suicide note left on a computer.

"Most suicides treat the note they leave as something real special. They want it found. Short note like that, we'd expect the old man to get out some nice paper, take a pen, write it, sign it, fold it," Dave acted out each step as he told Regan what might be done with the note, "maybe put it in an envelope and leave it where someone was sure to see it.

"It would have been more typical if he addressed it to somebody special, too, like his nephew, or his sister, or at least put someone's name on the envelope. Suicides usually decide who they want to find their goodbye note.

"Thing is, with a computer you don't have to try to forge a signature," Dave said with authority. "And the nephew found the suicide note on the computer right after we asked him to come in for another little chitchat. That seemed pretty convenient to some of us: no note until it was needed."

Regan started to protest.

"But," Dave held up his hand, stopping her, "you'll be relieved to know we did a discrete check of Nasseri's finances, part of our quiet little investigation. Looks like you're right about the guy having some bucks behind him. The money motive looks weak, and you're right about him inheriting. So with there being a note, even if it was conveniently found and on a computer...well," his mouth turned down at the corners.

Regan thought Dave seemed disappointed.

"Well, we're not closing the file just yet, but the nephew probably didn't do the old guy in for his money."

"Why aren't you closing the file?" Regan was incensed. "You have no good reason to think Kaivan murdered his uncle. There's no motive. What about those men you mentioned? Maybe their unfinished business was something sinister. Maybe Mr. Ansari *was* hiding from them like his sister thought, but they caught him…and…" Regan sputtered, "and once they finished with him, they said their tickets were expiring and flew back to Iran.

"Or, they could have killed him and acted like they couldn't find him…like they thought he was still alive. They could have been creating an alibi for themselves that way, couldn't they, you know, going through the motions to make people believe Mr. Ansari was still alive after they killed him? They could have driven his body up the coast and dumped him in the ocean. That would account for his car still being at his house."

Dave sat back in his seat, not even trying to interrupt Regan's rant.

"You've jumped to some awful conclusions. I think you owe Kaivan an apology. Do you police ever apologize when you've made a mistake?" Regan asked with icy accusation in her tone.

"I said probably," Dave replied, "and no, we're not big on apologies. Your buddy might have some serious debt we don't know about yet — gambling, drugs, or something like that, or there may be some completely different motive we haven't thought of yet. Your pal may have a deep dark expensive secret hidden away somewhere," Dave couldn't resist adding.

Sandy and Tom, their nicotine need satiated, came in and were greeted by a tense silence. Dave sat with his arms folded tightly across his chest and one leg crossed over the other, ankle on knee. Regan was in a similar pose, but with her legs crossed at the knee, a more feminine version of the same aggravated posture. Dave was studying the mantel; Regan was engrossed with the stitching on a needlepoint pillow.

If he chose to be observant, Tom would have been able to hear the silence, read their body language, and gauge how their conversation had gone. But Tom and Sandy were cold after all their fresh air, and he was concentrating on lighting a fire in the living room fireplace.

They had coffee and wedges of the dense homemade cheesecake Regan had prepared, and talked about the HO scale trains that Tom planned to set up in the barn, now that it had been remodeled and was rainproof.

Quickly putting aside his differences of opinion with Regan, Dave brought them up-to-date on his research for the book he was writing about Roman soldiers. But Regan couldn't let the exchange with Dave go. She remained a distracted hostess who missed much of the rest of the night's conversation.

Their evening ended sooner than usual because her distance and lapses of attention were taken by all to mean she was tired. Sandy and Dave thanked them for dinner and said goodnight by ten o'clock.

Their friends' car hadn't even cleared the parking area in front of their house before a still-irritated Regan began telling Tom all about her exchange with Dave. "I can't believe the way local law enforcement comes to idiotic conclusions and treats people," she huffed. "Can you imagine how Kaivan must feel? His uncle is dead, probably a suicide, which must be painful enough for him to accept, and now the police are as good as telling him they think he was involved in the death. The police even told him they think he might have murdered his uncle for his money."

"Police are trained to question any deaths that happen under unusual circumstances," Tom shrugged, "and it sounds like there are still some unanswered questions about Cyrus Ansari's death. Why don't you think it's possible that Kaivan was involved? Why couldn't he have done what the police think he did?" he asked evenly, using his usual calm reasoning to counter Regan's indignation.

"He couldn't have harmed his uncle because he loved him. I don't think the police considered that. They thought murder for money, period. How very convenient and how very trite that is. I don't think they spent much time looking beyond their pet theory. They aren't even following up with Mr. Ansari's visitors, and they seem suspicious, if you ask me.

"Dave even seemed a little disappointed that Kaivan wasn't penniless — I think because that inconvenient little fact thwarted his theory. But I know Kaivan, even if he was destitute, he'd never kill his uncle for money. Money just isn't that important to him. Certainly it's not as important as his uncle is," Regan said emphatically.

"You worked with him several years ago and have done a couple of transactions with him. Do you really know him that well?" Tom queried. "Maybe money means more to him than you think. Having all the realtor status symbols sure seems important to him. Doesn't he proudly sport a Rolex?" Tom asked, like a skilled prosecutor who had just put the question of the defendant's guilt to the jury.

Having a Rolex or any other very expensive watch was the height of excess and uselessness as far as Tom was concerned.

"All you need in a watch is reliability. You can get that for fifty bucks," he had said many times.

"Doesn't he drive a BMW and live in a big house with an ocean view?"

"You drive a BMW, and we live in a big house with an ocean view. Does that make us people who would be likely to kill someone? Of course not," Regan answered her own question. "We would never consider killing for any amount of money," she retorted, "especially not someone we cared about."

"True, although you know I have considered killing people for other reasons," Tom said.

"I know," she twisted her mouth into a disparaging comment, "like when they cut you off on the freeway."

"Maybe a few of those drivers do deserve to die," he grinned. "But I was thinking of the truly dangerous, the truly evil — people like the Dreaded Cheryl," he said, referring to one of his early clients, and using the dubious title that he and Regan had given her.

"Now there's someone the world would be better off without. What a way to earn a living: having tradesmen make repairs to that fixer-house she bought, and then, rather than paying them for their efforts, suing them in small claims court for fabricated damages. The insolence of that woman. Not only did she get work done for free, she made those poor guys pay her, to boot.

"She hurt an awful lot of our neighbors before moving away. The worst part of it is, she's probably up to her old tricks in another town by now. If she stayed here, maybe I would have killed her just to protect the community," he said with affected sincerity. "I bet no jury would have convicted me. Why, I might even have been labeled a hero once her full history was known.

"Let's hope she tries to sue a wild-eyed vigilante like me wherever she's living now, and gets her just come-uppance. The world wouldn't miss her." Tom's level of agitation rose as Regan's subsided.

"Tom, that's a terrible thing to say," Regan used all the political correctness she could muster.

"No, it's not," he said, smiling just a bit. He coaxed roguishly, "Come on, admit it, you agree with me, don't you?"

"No...well...maybe just a little, but only because I know you're not serious." The tiniest corresponding smile flitted across Regan's mouth.

Tom managed a perfectly straight face. "What makes you think I'm not serious?" he protested.

"OK," Regan smiled at him, "we'll pretend you are. But...you can't compare Kaivan, killing his favorite uncle and taking his money, to you saving the world from someone like the Dreaded Cheryl."

"All I'm saying is there are other reasons to kill someone besides money, never mind what Dave says. Let's say you're right about Kaivan, and money isn't an issue with him, especially since it sounds like he wouldn't benefit financially if his uncle died prematurely.

"What about Mr. Ansari getting up the coast without a car? It does seem like someone had to be involved in his death, and mysterious Iranian henchmen aside, Kaivan does seem like a good candidate.

"Play along here for a minute. Assume the police are wrong about the reason, but not the man. If money wouldn't motivate him, what do you think would?" Tom asked.

"If anything…" Regan thought for a moment, reaching for the right pronouncement. "If anything, and I know this sounds kind of corny, but I'd label Kaivan a bit of a gallant, and say something like honor would inspire him. I think that's one reason why the possibility that his uncle committed suicide troubles him so much. He might consider it dishonorable or even shameful," Regan said. "I think he could act out of love, too."

"OK." Tom nodded, formulating his thoughts. "OK, then suppose Kaivan had only praiseworthy motives. What would he have done if his uncle asked for help to commit suicide? If Kaivan loved his uncle as much as you think he did, even if it was repugnant to him personally, he might still have helped him.

"Haven't you ever thought about what you'd do if you were diagnosed with a life-ending illness that promised your death was going to be protracted and painful, or even worse, rob you of your personality?"

"I try not to think about things like that," Regan answered.

"I can't say I'm as mentally disciplined as you are, then. I have. What would you do if I was dying and asked you to

113

help me end my life? I'm not big on sin or eternal damnation. I might do that, you know. Would you help me? If you did, you'd have to realize it would be important that the authorities believed my death was an accident — for your protection." His tone had grown genuinely serious now. "Could you keep that kind of secret?

"You might not even be able to tell my sisters what we had done. You might well need to tell them I had an unfortunate mishap to preserve my reputation in their eyes, if you thought such a thing mattered to me, or to spare them added grief."

"Now I'm not going to get any sleep at all tonight. Thank you very much," Regan said.

"As long as you're going to think about this all night, I've got another idea for you to mull over," Tom continued. "Let's assume for a minute that Dave is right about the money motive."

Regan agreed with a very reluctant, very softly pronounced, "OK."

"Let's just suppose Kaivan did need quick money for some reason and asked his uncle for a loan. I don't know — it's a down market — maybe Kaivan wanted to buy an investment property. Whatever. Let's say his uncle said no. Here's Kaivan thinking, if he could just get his hands on some fast cash, he could parlay it into a bunch of capital."

Regan interrupted him. "His uncle would only have money to loan him after escrow closed. His uncle disappearing when he did, meant there weren't any funds to be borrowed or taken quickly."

"OK, then this time, let's suppose Kaivan asked his

uncle if he could borrow the proceeds from the sale when they were available. You were within a week or so of closing, weren't you? Let's say, just for the sake of argument, he got upset when his uncle said no. Maybe they got into a quarrel that got physical. If the old man was frail because of his illness, maybe something accidentally happened to him. So Kaivan took him up the coast and disposed of him."

Regan was genuinely surprised by all the ways Tom put Kaivan in the middle of his uncle's death. "You have a more active imagination tonight than I usually do," she laughed a bit uncomfortably.

"I'm just suggesting you don't know Kaivan well enough to know what he could or couldn't do. Not really."

A flaw in Tom's reasoning occurred to her. "If your wild theory is right, how did Kaivan get his uncle to write a suicide note after he killed him?"

"The note was just on the computer, not a signed note, right?"

"Yes, that's right."

"Then why are you so sure it was written before he disappeared?" Tom asked. "Or for that matter, that it was written by Kaivan's uncle?"

"Because according to Dave, the note was dated the afternoon of the 29th. We can look on a calendar to be sure, but I'm certain the 29th was a Monday. I remember that, because that was the day I found out I didn't get the Ferguson's listing that I wanted so badly, and thought it was a terrible way to start the week.

"I also remember Eleanor Rosemont telling me the last

time she saw Mr. Ansari was Monday evening. That means he was seen alive after the note was written.

"You know how we realtors take notes on the computer and save email in case we have to document conversations? The date it was written is recorded as the create date and time. Even if 'someone',," Regan made little quotation movements with her fingers, "dated the suicide note the 29th at 3:00 p.m., but it was actually created on, say the 30th at 11:00 a.m., wouldn't the create date and time on the computer still say the 30th at 11:00 am?"

She didn't give him time to answer. "So, if the date and time the note was created was the 29th at 3:00 p.m., and I bet the police checked that it was, it must have been written by Mr. Ansari before he went missing," Regan deduced triumphantly. "You may call me Holmes, Doctor Watson."

Regan felt quite proud, not only of her logic, but also of her understanding of a computer function, especially since her usual computer expertise consisted of walking into Tom's office, looking frustrated, and doing a credible pantomime of tossing her laptop against a wall. "It's not working again!" she would complain, agitated almost to the point of weeping through all of this routine for added emphasis.

Tom's response was predictable. He would say, "Error Code 39 — Bad User on Device," and come fix whatever was wrong.

"I hate to dispute your brilliant deduction…"

"But?" Regan's certain triumph quickly gave way to disappointment.

"Well, that's basically true for received email dates, but

it's possible to change the create date for a document," Tom said. "You just change the date and time on the computer before you type the document. Then after you finish writing, you change the date and time back so it's correct again.

"I'm sure any reasonably competent investigator would think of that right away, and not put too much credence in the date and time for a computer document. That may be why the police are still suspicious of Kaivan. You couldn't call what's on the computer a solid piece of evidence," he said. "You certainly couldn't use it to establish a real alibi."

"You mean all those careful real estate notes we take are meaningless because they could be tampered with after the fact?" she asked.

"A good attorney could probably argue that the notes could be altered. But, as I said, that's not the case with received email. If I'm ever concerned that someone might say I didn't disclose a material fact in a timely manner, I email the disclosure to them and 'bcc' it to a friend.

"Remember that problem we had with the Penningham escrow? As soon as I got concerned about where it was going, that's what I did. In that case it was Charles who got a copy of the email. That way, if I ever need to, I can have him print it out with the date intact to demonstrate I haven't tampered with anything. It would become my way of documenting what I disclosed and when I disclosed it.

"Fortunately all the fuss came to nothing. But being the cynic that I am," he chuckled, "I've still asked Charles to keep the email just in case I ever need it. I like having insurance."

As she predicted, Regan didn't sleep well that night. One of her most useful talents was her aptitude for reading people. She relied on that skill every day in her work. Until Tom started tossing out his what ifs, she had been absolutely convinced she knew Kaivan well, and that Dave was annoyingly off base to suspect him of any involvement in his uncle's death.

But Tom's suppositions had shaken her. His conjectures had bewildered her convictions, turning them inside out and upside down. Now she wasn't at all confident of either her perceptive abilities or of Kaivan's innocence.

How could Tom, so easily and so completely, confound her self-assurance and her certainty, Regan railed, given how insightful she'd been recently with clients?

"We intend to sell the house ourselves," Jill Turley informed her when she called Regan two weeks before. "We don't have much equity in our house so we can't afford a realtor. We're pretty sure we can sell the house on our own; we just don't have anyone who wants to buy it lined up yet. We've done some research online and have a price in mind. All we want from you is confirmation that it's a reasonable price to ask."

After a bit of hesitation, Jill added, "and maybe for you to make sure we disclose everything correctly...oh, and possibly to give us some tips on how to make the house look good, and...and on negotiating, although we're not really worried about that part. What would you charge to do that?"

"Are you sure those are all the services you'll need?" an amused Regan asked.

"I think so...umm, maybe we could use a little help with advertising, too," Jill replied, missing the irony in Regan's question.

Regan's people-reading skills kicked in immediately. Even over the phone, she could tell these were folks who couldn't afford not to hire a real estate agent. They didn't feel comfortable selling their house, didn't know how to evaluate strangers — people-reading again — and were concerned they might make a mistake that could leave them vulnerable to a future non-disclosure lawsuit.

Then of course, there was the advertising. She chuckled to herself softly enough that she knew Jill hadn't picked up on her amusement.

Regan explained she couldn't phone in a value; she needed to see the house before estimating its worth. Jill invited her to come by, meet her and her husband, Scott, and have a look.

It turned out her over-the-phone assessment had been correct. The Turleys quickly realized that, too, and hired her to sell their house.

To Jill and Scott's delight, two offers over the asking price arrived the first weekend the house was for sale. The offers were virtually identical, so they turned to her for advice about which one they should accept.

"I'd take the first one presented," Regan said without hesitation. "Let me explain why. Your next-door neighbors stopped by the open house today so I had a chance to meet them. They're lovely people, very gentle and..." Regan searched for the right words to explain her sense of them, "well, they seemed rather spiritual."

"That's a good description of them," Scott agreed. "We like them a lot, and want them to have good neighbors when we leave."

Regan nodded. "That's why I'd take the first offer. I met the woman who made the second offer; she came to your open house today as well. She said you'd want to sell to her because she was a great friend of your next-door neighbors, and that they would be thrilled if she moved in here. She also said she wasn't thinking about buying a new home, but had just fallen in love with your house, and had to make an offer.

"Now, that all sounds great..." Regan paused for emphasis, "but I don't think it is."

"I don't understand," Jill protested.

Regan explained, "The sense I got of offerer number two is that, even though she does know your neighbors, they're casual acquaintances at best, not what you'd call great friends. I bet your neighbors might even discourage you from selling to her, if you asked them their opinion.

"I also think she made her offer impulsively — not to say your house isn't one people might fall in love with," Regan laughed. "In fact, I think that's what happened with the first-offer people, but I just think this particular woman is changeable. She could fall out of love with your house as quickly as she fell *in* love with it. I wouldn't expect her to stay on track all the way to a sale.

"Take the first offer. It's a safer one for you and your neighbors."

Scott's expression said he wasn't convinced.

Jill's look was even more skeptical. "You really think you could get all that from a one-time conversation?" she smirked. "Let's make a call and test your theories," Jill said, as she reached for the phone and pressed her neighbor's speed dial number.

She got right to the point as soon as they answered. "James, I'm calling because we got an offer on our house today from your friend Susan Hayer. We're trying to decide if we should take it," she said in clipped tones. There was a long pause. Finally Jill said, "Uh-huh. Uh-huh. Yes, of course we do. No, we won't. No, don't worry, James. OK. Bye-bye.

"Now, really, how did you do that?" Jill had a bemused expression on her face.

"What did he say?" Scott asked eagerly.

"Well," Jill replied in a gossipy tone, "James said they do know her, but she's not a friend. They don't particularly like her. He said she's very assertive and kind of hyper," Jill offered with a restrained smile. "James asked if we cared about them. He said if we did, to please not sell to

122

her," her restraint gave way to a full-blown laugh, "because he thought that woman would make their lives a living hell."

The next morning Susan Hayer retracted her offer, saying she had been overly hasty and wasn't sure she liked the house well enough to buy it.

There hadn't been anything mystifying or even particularly shrewd about Regan's predictions. Susan Hayer's speech patterns had been highly agitated as she flitted around the house. She never finished a thought or listened to Regan's answer to a posed question. Her behavior made Regan uncomfortable. It was a good bet she would irritate the rather serene, thoughtful next-door neighbors, as well.

And she wasn't so much taken by the house as she was by the fact that someone else wanted it. Buyer number two wasn't committed, just competitive.

Most damning, though, was the reason she gave for selling her last house. She said the neighborhood had become unenlightened and had turned against her. Throw in a little megalomania and a touch of paranoia for good measure; that ought to make life interesting for the Turley's favorite neighbors.

Regan hadn't used any extraordinary means to forecast the woman's actions or to gauge the neighbors' likely reaction to her. She just paid attention and read Susan Hayer. That was the crux of what was troubling her about Tom's challenges.

The point was that Regan did pay attention — that's why she was so good at reading people. And she'd had lots of time to understand who Kaivan was. She didn't want to think she could be so wrong about him, that she could have missed so much.

She knew Tom was raising questions mostly as a devil's advocate, but his last "let's suppose" troubled her even more than his inadvertent questioning of her knack.

Suppose Kaivan really did need money for some unknown reason. He might have all the trappings of success, but no access to ready cash.

Real estate was often a feast or famine business. An agent might hit a dry spell and have no sales close for months. Then he'd bring home several commission checks in rapid succession — checks that were already earmarked for catch-up — checks which would disappear in a day to cover the credit card debt accrued from making mortgage and car payments, meeting daily living expenses, and paying quarterly IRS taxes, and all the other business expenses that were due, even when there was no income to cover them.

Many realtors who made an overall excellent yearly income didn't manage it well enough to smooth out the peaks and valleys of their paydays. Some found themselves always behind and near financial disaster. All it took was a slowing market, like the one they were experiencing right now, for some agents to fall into the abyss. Was it possible Kaivan had swirled into one of those nasty cycles and was living dangerously near the edge?

A middle-of-the-night idea occurred to her. Since she wasn't sleeping anyway, she got up, went into their office, turned on her computer, and logged onto her favorite title company website. She entered her password, and had immediate access to all sorts of public records, courtesy of the title company.

She entered "California" and "Santa Cruz" in the state and county boxes, and "Kaivan" and "Nasseri" in the first and last name boxes, and then clicked on the SEARCH button. His name was unique, not like looking up William Jones. Only his properties came up, so she didn't have to sort through a list to find out what he owned.

He showed up as the sole owner of his home as well as three other houses. Regan copied the parcel numbers onto a piece of paper and put it in her purse.

She was going to see Arlene tomorrow about a new escrow; she might as well take care of a very different type of business then, too. With Arlene's help, she just might be able to blow up Dave's hypothesis and sweep away Tom's what ifs. By tomorrow night, Regan might be able to banish all of her uncertainties about Kaivan and about her abilities in the people-reading department.

She rolled her head in a tired circle and yawned. She had a plan of action; it was going to feel great to put her misgivings behind her.

Regan shut down her computer and went back to bed, and this time, to peaceful sleep — peaceful because she was careful to keep herself from asking two important questions. The first was: what if Tom and Dave really were right that Kaivan needed money? The second question, which required more effort to suppress, was potentially even more troubling. The second question she didn't dare ask was: what if her investigation incriminated Kaivan?

A couple of Regan's clients, the Atwoods, had made a low offer on a starter house in the Seabright area on the east side of Santa Cruz. The sellers were already in contract to buy a new home as soon as they could sell theirs. They hadn't had any offers for their property during the four months it had been for sale, and the owners of the house they wanted to buy were getting restive. They were what realtors call "motivated". They accepted the Atwood's offer with only one counter, a simple change of the date escrow would close, to make it concurrent with their new home purchase.

Regan had phoned in all the needed information to get everything started with her favorite escrow officer, Arlene Smith.

Now she needed to turn in the buyer's deposit check to make the escrow official. That was what she planned to do today. That, and ask Arlene for some private information about Kaivan.

Regan wouldn't have attempted to get this particular kind of help from just any escrow officer. Collectively they were usually staid people who followed rules. If she had asked most of them to do something slightly inappropriate, not illegal certainly, but outside their comfort zones, their replies would have involved some stiff rejoinders about "tight company policy" and "not breaking company regulations".

But Arlene wasn't like that. Regan always thought that enjoying the outlandish was a freeing exercise. It limbered you up to bend rules. And she knew Arlene appreciated the absurd as much as she did.

She learned about Arlene's suppleness during the Albright to Davidson escrow. The Davidsons were repeat clients who had taken an early retirement, sold their Santa Cruz home, and moved to Oregon, where they expected to enjoy nature and reading, their two passions in life.

When they left Santa Cruz, the Davidsons overlooked the fact that their adult children remained and would soon start producing adorable grandchildren capable of changing their definition of contentment. It wasn't long until they decided to move back to the Santa Cruz area. Regional home prices had skyrocketed during their absence, so they were only able to return to a condo, albeit a spacious and attractive one that Regan found for them in Scotts Valley, one of the four incorporated towns in Santa Cruz County.

Their escrow progressed smoothly, a little too smoothly to be in line with her expectations. The listing agent was new, doing her first sale. Regan knew from experience that a lot of things usually went wrong when an agent was a beginner. New licensees had book learning, but not enough hands on experience to know how to take control of a deal and head off potential trouble.

Sure enough, just three days before the sale was to close, Arlene called to say the condo had gone into foreclosure. That was a huge problem. Depending on the lending institution involved, undoing foreclosure proceedings could be more complicated than reversing death.

When a seller's agent was taking a new listing, they needed to probe a bit to make sure the homeowners were current on their mortgage payments. If they weren't, a properly handled sale might forestall foreclosure and bail out the seller, but only if the listing agent took immediate action to guide the client through an intricate sequence of steps.

Obviously, this seller's agent hadn't asked the right questions.

To make the situation more problematic, Regan's clients were already on the road from Oregon with everything they owned following them in a moving van.

Regan and Agent Newbie — in her mind Regan had started calling her that — worked for the same company. As soon as Arlene told her what was happening, she tracked down her colleague and asked her why she hadn't addressed the potential foreclosure early on.

"My seller, she ees a neighbor," Agent Newbie, a recent émigré from Portugal, explained in rapid fire, heavily accented English. "I knew she was late een her mortgage. What was she supposed to do, I ask you? Her husband was foolin' around; he walked out on her for some lettle twenty-two year old." Agent Newbie indicated her disgust.

"Everyone knew about eet. I couldin' make eet worse by asking her nosey questions, could I? She would be upset eef I asked her these thins. You understan' thees don' you?" Agent Newbie accompanied her explanation with animated gestures that culminated in a palms-up shrug.

The condo owner's predicament got a full measure of Regan's sympathy — the agent's explanation, not so much. Agent Newbie had avoided asking hard, necessary questions, and then compounded her lassitude with poor judgment by deciding to play a game of extreme ostrich, hoping no one would notice the late payments — especially not the bank they were owed to.

"You have to take care of things like this," Regan stressed. "Now the bank has started foreclosure and foreclosures don't just go away by themselves."

Agent Newbie crossed her arms and her legs defiantly. "That ees what you thin', but how do you know thees for sure? I thin' sometimes they maybe do," she said as she closed her eyes and wagged her head with the same headstrong certainty that a fifteen year old girl might inflict on a parent.

Their mutual broker-boss set up an emergency problem solving meeting in his office and invited several seasoned agents and the house attorney. He tried to make it an occasion. He began the meeting with a clap of his hands. "Let's everybody brainstorm," he declared with vigor. "I'm sure we can solve this little glitch. And while we're at it, let's make our agent look good and make sure everyone gets paid."

Lessons learned during years of experience were all

ignored by Agent Newbie, who greeted each suggestion with a dismissive wave of her hand or a negative shake of her head. Her behavior regressed from that of petulant teenager to a determined two year old.

Finally, Agent Newbie covered her ears and stomped toward the door. She whined as she went, "You all thin' this is my fault. You are all peekin' on me. Why do you all wan' to peek on me?" Persecution turned to defiance as she reached the door. "Leave me alone. I know what I'm doin'. I don' wan' to hear another thin'," she said, slamming the door behind her as she flounced out of the room.

The broker bought Agent Newbie's wounded departure. "I guess we shouldn't have ganged up on her like that," he suggested. "She's a sensitive person and not too sure of herself yet. We didn't help her, we just made her defensive."

It was irritating that their co-worker had made such a mess. Everyone involved in the sale was going to have to spend time cleaning it up. They all went to work; they all pulled strings. But Arlene pulled more than most, and the problem got resolved in record time.

Nine days later, Regan, Arlene, the broker, a bank representative, the seller, and the buyers were back at the title company with revised documents and an escrow successfully salvaged and ready to close.

The seller was signing a carefully worded contract amendment when the conference room door opened with such force that it slammed into the adjoining wall. Agent Newbie was back.

Her entrance was so dramatic all eyes locked on her. All

ears listened keenly, almost expecting a trumpet fanfare to sound her arrival. She paused theatrically in the doorway with one eyebrow raised menacingly and narrowed her eyes until they became mere slits, ready to fire beams of contempt at anyone who dared challenge her right to center stage.

Clearly, Agent Newbie thought looking down her nose at the assembled group empowered her. She struggled to do so — quite an undertaking for such a petite woman. Even though the signoff participants were seated and her three inch stilettos leveraged her height, she had to throw her head back at an extreme angle to accomplish her goal.

She held her ground momentarily, chin in the air, chest thrust forward, and spine bowed in an unnatural curve. For several seconds she remained a motionless figure except for a slight wobble in her pose — her balance under constant challenge as the height of her heels and her skin-tight floral-print skirt worked against her exaggerated posture.

Without warning, Agent Newbie's frozen stance became riotously animated. She cuchi-cuchied into the room, propelled by a series of rapid, mincing steps, high heels clacking rhythmically, hips gyrating under quivering flora, hands held high above her vigorously shaking head, waving like the hands of a wild-eyed sinner at a revival meeting.

She pooched her lips into a perfect circle. "Don' sign anythin'! Don' sign anythin'!" she shrieked at the seller. "Eet says here you will pay the buyer's actual added expenses." She waved a copy of the amendment, "I don' know what thees word 'actual' means. Don' sign anythin' till someone gets me a Engleesh to Portuguese deectionary."

Title company employees gathered just outside the glass-fronted conference room to catch her performance, enthralled as Agent Newbie continued to careen around the room, shouting her demands.

One of the spectators grinned and elbowed a compatriot. He took the opportunity to add to the spectacle by softly intoning the pulsating melody of a conga line: "Da, da, da, da, da, DAH."

The show continued until the seller rose to her feet and stammered, "P-p-please. Sit down and be quiet."

Agent Newbie was too fired up to sit, but she stopped her histrionics so abruptly, the vocalist got caught in the middle of a "da", and had to slink away to escape an evil-eye squint from the stifled prima donna. Escrow company employees followed his lead and hastily scattered.

The remaining audience was momentarily dumbfounded into silence.

Then Regan got the giggles.

She pretended to cough, but without conviction. She realized at once how mediocre her deception was — it made her laugh even harder. She waved her hand in front of her face and tried again. "Need…uhh…water."

She fooled no one.

Escape was the only remaining option. She dashed from the conference room, red-faced with swallowed laughter.

Something must have been in the air, maybe the smoke left over from Agent Newbie's smoldering performance, because Arlene, struggling to maintain her own properly sober decorum, discovered she too, was overwhelmed with coughing, and had to flee for water as well.

"Arlene," Regan squealed when the escrow officer joined her in the break room, "Did you leave those people sitting there? You can't just leave the room. You're in charge. That's shocking form," she chortled. "You're so bad!"

"Stop it!" Arlene snorted. "I'm bad? You left first. Some advocate for your clients you turned out to be. Don't make me laugh any more. My side already hurts."

The two usually composed professional women left their abandoned clients to fend off the farce that was Agent Newbie for a good five minutes. They struggled to keep from looking at one another, because every time they did, they were seized by renewed spasms of laughter.

Ever since then, Regan considered Arlene a kindred spirit, someone she could count on for more than prim proficiency. That was reassuring right now, given what she wanted her to do.

Regan went to Arlene's cubicle and found her on the phone with a customer. Arlene motioned for her to sit down and silently mouthed, "One more minute."

"Here's the deposit check for the Atwood's purchase," she said as soon as Arlene was free.

"Great." Arlene entered some numbers on her computer and printed a receipt for the check. "I've ordered prelims already and notified the listing agent of the escrow number. I think we're all set." She handed the receipt to Regan.

"I have kind of a favor to ask," Regan said, pulling the

note paper with Kaivan's parcel numbers out of her purse. "I would like to tell you these are listings I have coming up, and that I need information because of that, but you'd know that wasn't true as soon as you started looking them up. I'll let you know now, I have no right to ask you to do this, but I sure hope you'll help me. I need to know the current mortgage balance on each of these properties, and I need to know quickly and quietly." With that, Regan handed the parcel numbers to Arlene.

"Who owns them?"

"Kaivan Nasseri."

Arlene rolled her eyes. "I'm not even going to ask why you want to know. Call me in a couple of hours. I should have what you want by then." She threw up her hands, cuchi-cuchi style, and shimmied them on either side of her head. "And don't tell anyone I did this for you. Don' tell anyone," she chuckled.

That evening, Regan was delighted to let Tom know his most disturbing wild theory was just that. Arlene had produced Kaivan's outstanding mortgage balances as promised, and Regan had done a cursory drive by the houses involved.

Even without seeing them from the inside, she could tell Kaivan had considerable equity in his properties. Each house had only one relatively small mortgage. He had probably bought them some time ago, well before the market went up crazily. He hadn't refinanced as his equity increased to take cash out, like so many people had during the recent market surge.

135

They were huge potential piggy banks with bolted foundations. If he needed money in a hurry, he could easily and quickly add an equity line of credit on any one of them. Should he ever need serious capital, he could sell one. He had room to price any of his properties aggressively enough to move it quickly, even in a slow market. No need to ever ask his uncle for a loan or argue with him about money.

If Mr. Ansari had asked Kaivan to help him end his life, she felt sorry for the burden he must be carrying. If that was what had happened, doing so would have created a personal risk for Kaivan, and might have gone against his particular sense of morality. She admired him for having the courage to perform that act of kindness and love for his uncle, in spite of what were likely his own misgivings.

The police could continue to investigate. Dave could even find a secret vice Kaivan might have. It wouldn't matter. They would no doubt come to the same conclusion she had about his finances.

If it did turn out he had been involved in his uncle's suicide, in liberal Santa Cruz, the authorities would probably let Kaivan and Mr. Ansari have their respective peace, felony or not.

13

Ed called a couple of weeks later to tell Regan that Stephanie and their baby boy were doing well. Regan had a gift ready for them, and asked when she could come by to meet their new son. They settled on a little after one o'clock the next afternoon.

The baby was awake and making newborn mewing sounds when Regan arrived. Stephanie let her hold him, sharing her treasure. Ed sat on the arm of Stephanie's overstuffed chair, his arm casually around her shoulder, a huge smile on his face. He was clearly delighted with his family. Interesting what Ed's body language said, Regan thought. He seems so relaxed the way he's sitting, but he could instantly spring to his feet to protect his family if the need arose.

The visit was pleasant but short. Stephanie was still tired from a long labor. Of course, they admitted, having a newborn cut into their sleep. When the baby decided to take a nap, Stephanie announced she wanted to do the same thing. Ed was stifling a yawn as Regan said her goodbyes.

"I'll let myself out. I still remember the door has an odd

little idiosyncrasy: I need to lift up slightly to close the door all the way."

"Not anymore," Ed said proudly. "I fixed it."

"Wow, new house, new baby, and you managed to take care of details this soon. I'm impressed," she laughed.

Regan was barely halfway down the Beltran's front walkway, when she heard a sharp rap on the window from the house next door. It was loud enough to make her stop and turn. Eleanor Rosemont was at her living room window, motioning for Regan to come over. She nodded, but continued down the path to the sidewalk and then turned up Mrs. Rosemont's walkway toward her front door, which by then was open.

"Mrs. Rosemont, how are you? Have you met your new neighbors yet?" Regan asked, when she got within comfortable earshot.

"I have. Such a darling young couple. I'm very pleased with Cyrus' choice of neighbors for me." Mrs. Rosemont's tone was wistful. "He was looking out for me and being a great friend, as usual, when he picked them."

The elderly woman spiritedly waved an arm, "Come in, come in. Please. May I offer you some tea? I have so much I'd like to talk about."

Regan accepted the offer, and Mrs. Rosemont led her through the house. The living room walls were lined with rows of similarly-framed black and white photographs. From the changing hem length on the women's clothing and varying hairstyles on both sexes, it was clear they were taken over time, but all were from some years ago. She recognized Mrs. Rosemont gradually aging in them, and the same handsome man, always in a military uniform and always standing next to her, doing the same. Some of the other people in the photographs looked vaguely familiar. She had probably seen their faces in news magazines and on TV. She did recognize Dwight Eisenhower, out of military uniform and wearing a suit, in a photo that must have been taken after World War II, possibly during his presidency.

Regan slowed her pace for a closer look at some of the other pictures. The prominently-nosed countenance of Charles De Gaulle and the unique faces of Golda Meier and Anwar Sadat shared the spotlight with Mrs. Rosemont and the smartly-postured military man. Regan paused for a closer look at one photo in particular, when she recognized Queen Elizabeth II. The Queen, in fancy dress and full tiara, was posed facing Mrs. Rosemont and her ever present soldier, who were also dressed formally and in the process of curtsying and bowing.

Mrs. Rosemont noticed her falling behind. "Ah, our rogues' gallery," she chortled. "My husband was British military. His profession guaranteed we would never be rich, but it did provide for quite an interesting life. We were fortunate to be stationed all over the world and met some of the...hum...what should I call them?" Mrs. Rosemont screwed up her mouth, and her head swayed to and fro, fiery curls bobbing, as she searched for the perfect phrase to describe some of the world's leaders. "Local influentials," she said at last, conveying something less than total esteem for some of the pictured figures. "We found the time we spent in Iran, Iraq, Egypt, and several other Middle Eastern counties most intriguing," she smiled.

Their progress through the house led into a room most people would use as their dining room. It held a small table and a couple of welcoming and comfortable looking wing chairs, their upholstery well worn with use. The walls were lined with a myriad of bookshelves. Clearly Mrs. Rosemont preferred a library to formal dining.

The trek ended at a fine wooden table in the kitchen, small for a dining room table, but generously sized as kitchen tables went. It was pleasantly set with a lace tablecloth and fresh flowers in a glistening crystal vase. The kitchen chairs matched the formality of the table and were upholstered in floral chintz, which, like the fabric on the library wing chairs, was softened by years of use.

"Do you mind if we take our tea in the kitchen?" Mrs. Rosemont asked.

"Not at all," Regan replied, "tea is welcome anywhere, and you've created such a charming setting here."

The compact working portion of Mrs. Rosemont's kitchen was arranged galley-style. The sink was on the back wall, under a lace-trimmed window which overlooked the backyard garden. A white tile-topped island, with an inset cook top, formed the other galley side and separated the work area from the eating area. The kitchen was tidy and devoid of counter clutter, possibly because there wasn't much counter space, or Regan thought, more probably because of the woman's innate orderliness.

Mrs. Rosemont took a small enameled kettle off the stove — it appeared to be the one exception to her empty surface policy — and carried it to the sink. She filled it with fresh water, returned it to the stove, and turned on the burner.

Mrs. Rosemont had a three-step kitchen ladder open and set up next to the sink. It was made of lightweight molded plastic, with a handrail on the left that followed the angle of the steps. She used the handrail to move it to the next cupboard over.

"Let me help you," Regan offered.

"No, no, please. You have a seat, dear. I'm not good at having a helper. I know where everything is, and my 'buddy' here," she patted the handle of the stepstool, "more than makes up for my stature." She nimbly climbed up the first step, opened the cupboard, and began her process of removing a teapot, cups, and saucers.

It was hard for Regan to watch without helping. Each item required a climb up, then down the stepladder, since the elderly woman always kept her left hand on the rail, and only had her right hand free to retrieve items from the cupboard.

"This is how I get my exercise," Mrs. Rosemont chuckled. "Not too many of my contemporaries use a 'Stairmaster' regularly, like I do. I've never had a bit of trouble sleeping, and I believe I owe it to my regular workouts. Near the end, poor Cyrus said he needed medication to get to sleep. I told him it was probably his conscience that kept him up nights. Of course it was his illness, but I used to rib him anyway, and told him that one week with my 'buddy' and he'd be sleeping like a young man again."

Mrs. Rosemont swiftly moved the step stool to the next

cupboard over, and with two more climbs and descents, produced a small wooden tea canister in the shape of an apple and a blue and white sugar bowl. "Do you use milk in your tea, dear?" she asked, as she started up again for the creamer.

"No, thank you — just a bit of sugar," Regan replied.

"You should have milk in your tea, you know. It's good for your bones. I always have milk in my tea."

Considering Mrs. Rosemont's pronounced stoop, the irony of that statement made Regan smile, but she was careful to change her expression before Mrs. Rosemont finished her climb down and turned toward her.

"You probably think I look fragile and have osteoporosis, don't you. Not so, not so. I'm delicately built, but my posture is due to a war injury. During World War II I was a WASP. I flew our fighter planes from the factory, here in California, to the east coast for transport to the front. I had a crash landing in one of them. I'm actually a very sturdy person," she smiled proudly.

Regan felt something press against her leg. "Meow, reow."

"Harry, don't be fresh. Leave that young woman alone." Her words were stern, but her tone was indulgent.

"So, this is Harry." Regan bent over and stroked a huge gray cat with golden eyes. "Nice to finally meet you, Harry. I thought you were staying with Kaivan."

"He was, but as I told you before, Harry is my cat. It wasn't too difficult to persuade Kaivan to bring him home to me. Harry still goes over to Cyrus' house sometimes to look for him." Mrs. Rosemont pursed her lips and shook her head sadly. The movement caused her flame colored curls to bounce slightly. "But you should see how Kaivan and Harry get on," she added, her mouth reforming in a smile. "Now, Harry requires Kaivan to come by and visit him here. In time, they may grow to be as close as Harry and Cyrus were. I sometimes think that cat prefers Iranian men to me. Perhaps Harry was a Persian cat in a former life," Mrs. Rosemont laughed heartily at her own joke.

"How is Kaivan doing?" Regan asked. "I haven't talked to him in a couple of weeks. I know his uncle's death really troubled him."

"Indeed," Mrs. Rosemont said. She put a cup and saucer and a dainty silver spoon in front of each of them. She poured milk into the delicate blue and white creamer and placed it on the table together with the matching sugar bowl. She measured three spoonfuls of tea into a small container, counting as she did, "One for you, one for me, and one for the pot." Then she returned the apple canister to its place in the cupboard.

Her tasks temporarily completed, she sat down across the table from Regan as she waited for the water to boil. "It's more than missing Cyrus that's weighing him down, you know. There's so much more to it than that," Mrs. Rosemont sighed. "I don't believe Kaivan knows Cyrus told anyone but him about his past, so that young man must feel secure with the decision he made and with what he did, but life is more complicated than that. One sees things. Secrets are very hard to keep, you know, especially when they involve so much passion."

The kettle sounded, and Mrs. Rosemont got up to finish

her tea preparation. She swished some boiling water in the teapot and emptied it into the sink before she added the tea leaves and the rest of the water.

Eleanor Rosemont made tea in the British manner, like Regan's Irish grandmother had taught her to make it. That was something Mrs. Rosemont must have learned from her time in England or in British outposts and kept as part of her regular routine.

Finally she brought the teapot to the table and sat back down. "We'll just let that steep for a bit," she said. Mrs. Rosemont folded her hands in her lap and became very still. It seemed to Regan that all of Mrs. Rosemont's natural color faded, making her artificially colored hair even more intense. Her manner of speaking became subdued, unhurried, and very intimate.

"Cyrus came to me several months ago," she began, "and said he had a great confession to make and a great joy to share. It was a private matter he told me, as I'm telling you. He said I would know the correct time, if it might need to become more than that, as will you.

"Before he came to Santa Cruz, he met a young married woman in his old country. They fell in love and committed the sin of adultery. He begged her to leave her husband and marry him, but she refused. She had children with her husband, a daughter and a young son; and according to the customs of that country, if she left her husband for another man, she would have to leave her children as well. As much as she loved Cyrus, she couldn't give up her children.

"They reluctantly ended their affair, Cyrus said, when they accepted they didn't have a future together. Their families were intertwined socially, however, and though they tried, it was impossible for them to keep from crossing paths from time to time. When Cyrus could no longer stand seeing her with her husband, especially as it became apparent she was pregnant, he fled Iran and joined his relatives living in Santa Cruz.

"His love for her was never extinguished and he never married. He also never told anyone of his great love affair, for fear of damaging her reputation and causing discord between their families."

Eleanor Rosemont pronounced the tea ready and poured it through a silver strainer into their cups.

"Then some months ago, he received a letter from her, the only one he had ever received," Mrs. Rosemont continued. "She told him she was a widow now and ill herself. Her daughter was grown, married with children of her own. Her eldest son had converted to Islam, and as can be the case when young people become fascinated with a calling at just the right age, he had become quite fanatical in his newfound religion. He had managed to convert her younger son, as well.

"Then he had done the unthinkable and unforgivable. He had gone into Iraq, where he became a suicide bomber. She had been shown a videotape of him saying farewell to his family. In it, he was full of confidence that his martyrdom, as he called it, for his Shi'ite brethren would ensure his place in paradise.

"As a traditional Christian however, his mother believed he was doomed to an eternity in misery for his terrible and impenitent crime. Her heart was absolutely shattered. But she had an even greater torment. She now lived in constant fear for her younger son because he worshipped his older brother and was becoming more and more involved with the same radical group that had destroyed his brother's life.

"She told Cyrus that the youngest boy was his son, not her husband's, as she had led everyone to believe, and begged him to find a way to save their child from the danger that he would eventually come to share his brother's end.

"Cyrus had written back immediately, saying he would come to Iran as soon as he was able. He made travel plans, but before he could carry them out, his cancer became active again.

"The next letter he received was from his son, who said his mother had confessed everything to him and told him who his real father was.

"The boy admitted he had slapped his mother when she confessed her sin, cursed her, and left her house. When he returned some days later, he found his mother had suffered a heart attack and was near death. He felt responsible for her condition and begged her forgiveness. His mother made him swear at her deathbed that he would renounce his new connections and return to his Christian community.

"He agreed and promised her, if his father came for him, he would go to America with him. According to the boy, his mother had died a happy woman, and he was ready, even eager, to meet his father and keep his promise.

"Cyrus was devastated by the loss of his one true love, but you have never seen anyone so thrilled to discover he had a child. He began collecting the necessary paperwork to bring his son home. He still couldn't bring himself to tell his family about his past, but the treatment he was undergoing for his brain tumor made him very weak and ill, and he was concerned he might need help on his journey.

"He thought his nephew, Kaivan, might understand. They had such a special bond, and Kaivan had become very much the American man. Cyrus hoped his nephew wouldn't be burdened by old country mores and family expectations, so he reluctantly confided in him and asked for his help."

Mrs. Rosemont poured them more tea. Regan sat very still, mesmerized by her story.

"But Kaivan refused to help his uncle. He even questioned the boy's paternity, and referred to him as Cyrus' alleged son, which broke the poor man's heart. They argued about the boy a great deal. Once, I even saw Kaivan come out of Cyrus' house in a rage. When Cyrus attempted to follow him, Kaivan angrily shouted at his uncle that he was a naïve old fool, before he drove away. Of course, I never let anyone know I had witnessed that dreadful episode.

"Cyrus was frantic for a while after that. Finally, he made the decision to stop treatment for his cancer. He didn't hold out much hope it would help him anyway, and he was willing to risk shortening his life if it meant he could meet his son and bring him to America before he died. His strength and endurance did improve for a time, once he abandoned chemotherapy and radiation treatments, and he purchased a plane ticket to Iran.

"He was due to fly there on February eighth, and was literally counting the days until he would meet his son." Mrs. Rosemont smiled as she talked about Mr. Ansari's anticipated trip, truly sharing it seemed, some of his bittersweet joy.

"Two weeks before his scheduled departure, however, he had a small seizure and a fall. Cyrus no longer thought he could travel alone, and implored Kaivan one last time to go with him to Iran. But Kaivan still refused." Mrs. Rosemont dropped her eyes and bowed her head. "What Kaivan did to his uncle was heartless and shameful. It's his guilt that is causing him so much pain now.

"After Cyrus disappeared, I found his passport together with plane tickets and some very official looking papers for his son in a packet on his dresser. I have them here," Mrs. Rosemont motioned to the top drawer, one over from the sink, "in my junk drawer where I keep all my odds and ends.

"The plane tickets have expired of course, but the travel visa for Cyrus' son is good for a few more weeks. I have stressed how important it was to Cyrus to bring his son home. Kaivan resisted at first, but I can be very resolute," she smiled defiantly. "At our last visit, I told him what Gandhi said about the raising of an orphaned child. I believe that has convinced him.

"Kaivan needs to atone for what he did to his uncle. The next time he comes to visit Harry, I intend to give him Cyrus' packet and send him on his way. Then, maybe Kaivan can be at peace."

One thing was certain: Regan could indeed be at peace. She drove home, feeling a sense of quietude for the first time since Arlene had called to tell her that Mr. Ansari had been misplaced. Kaivan hadn't helped his uncle when he most needed him. That didn't increase his esteem in her eyes, but now she had an explanation for Mr. Ansari's death that had nothing to do with Kaivan.

Cyrus Ansari had a past. That changed everything.

She had steadfastly defended Kaivan in public and insisted he hadn't murdered his uncle. But, when she wasn't being his outspoken champion, maintaining her inner conviction about him was still something she had to do consciously. Without vigilance, she felt a bit uneasy about him.

That was, of course, because of her two favorite men. Tom continued to regularly bring up his much beloved treatise that the police were professionals, with experience in guilt or innocence that she lacked.

And Dave. Dave reminded her relentlessly that, even though the authorities hadn't discovered any proof he was involved in his uncle's death, he and several of his fellow officers still believed Kaivan had killed his uncle for his money.

"Killed him for his money." The phrase repeated itself in her head like a tune she couldn't stop humming, like an earworm. But Dave's jingle had another part to it, didn't it? "People usually get killed for *sex* or money."

Now Cyrus Ansari had a past, a past which included an adulterous sexual liaison that produced a child.

If Mr. Ansari had been murdered, it seemed to her that

his visitors with *unfinished business* loomed larger and larger as possible guilty parties.

It made sense. Mrs. Rosemont had called Cyrus Ansari's old love a traditional Christian. Perhaps she made a deathbed confession — she might well have wanted to unburden her soul before dying. Or the boy could have fled to a relative's house after he mistreated his mother and tearfully told them his true heritage. The Iranian men's mission might have been revenge in the name of the cuckolded husband or for the disgrace they believed Mr. Ansari caused their family.

If they killed him, there really wasn't anything to be done about it. Dave had said the authorities lost track of the men once they returned to Iran. Strangely, if they escaped punishment, that didn't seem to matter much. What did matter to her, was that she now saw a motive for Mr. Ansari's death that clearly didn't involve Kaivan in any way — not even as a reluctant participant in a merciful suicide.

Mrs. Rosemont said the subject of Mr. Ansari's son was private. Regan would respect that request unless the authorities started to harass Kaivan. If that happened, she'd explain to Mrs. Rosemont that it was time to share Mr. Ansari's story.

Perhaps if Dave still wasn't convinced of Kaivan's innocence by the time the police were ready to close their file, she might share the story of Mr. Ansari's son with him. It might make Dave feel better, too.

For now, Regan decided, she wouldn't even tell Tom about Cyrus Ansari's son. It was indeed a private matter.

With a great sigh of relief, she determined the subtly nagging question of Kaivan's possible complicity in his uncle's death had been answered. It was over as far as she was concerned.

Regan called Kaivan the next day. "I wanted to know how you're doing, and how the settling of the estate is going."

"I'm doing much better, and good progress is being made with the settlement. I kind of miss the cat, though." He sounded like he was smiling as he said it, and she assumed he must be in better spirits than the last time she saw him. "I thought he should live with my uncle's neighbor, Mrs. Rosemont. Harry started out as her cat, after all."

"Yes, I know. And Mrs. Rosemont must be right about him preferring Iranian men to her." Something clicked in Regan's mind as she said it, and though she didn't know why, she wished she hadn't. She moved on quickly.

"I stopped by your uncle's house yesterday to see the new baby. Did you know Stephanie and Ed Beltran had a little boy?"

She was about to mention her tea with Mrs. Rosemont and ask Kaivan if Eleanor had finally convinced him to bring his uncle's son to Santa Cruz. She realized in time she shouldn't. Unless Kaivan chose to bring it up, it was best not to let him know Mrs. Rosemont had told her about the boy.

That's what her momentary discomfort was, she realized. She didn't want Kaivan to know she and Eleanor had been talking about him and his uncle. That's what it was that troubled her about her cat comment.

What Mrs. Rosemont told her about Mr. Ansari's son added to her understanding of a man who was obviously beloved and highly regarded by his family. What's more, it put her mind at ease about a friend. She felt certain that was Mrs. Rosemont's intent. But it might seem to Kaivan like they had been gossiping about private matters. Being a realtor had taught her it was often best to play her cards close to her chest and leave some things unsaid.

"They seem very content in your uncle's home," was all she added.

🏠🏠🏠🏠🏠🏠🏠🏠🏠🏠🏠

There were some papers that Stephanie and Ed needed to sign. Although Kaivan was letting them stay in Mr. Ansari's house rent-free until the estate was settled, they still needed to initial a lease agreement that specified landlord and tenant responsibilities. The lease amount was filled in as zero dollars per month, and Kaivan had agreed to maintain the homeowner's insurance, but the agreement needed to have a termination date and state that Stephanie and Ed were going to pay for electricity, water, and their cable connection. Regan wanted a formal purchase agreement in place as soon as possible, too, this time between the Beltrans and the estate of Cyrus Ansari.

Stephanie and Ed were going to be signing a stack of papers once again. She called to ask if she could bring them by the house.

"I'm also looking for an excuse to see the baby again," she said, after she explained the call to Stephanie.

"You don't need excuses. You're welcome to see him any time you want," Stephanie said. "Isn't that right, pumpkin," she added, as she slipped into baby talk to her infant. "He's already grown. Wait 'till you see. Say 'Hi' to Regan, say 'Hi'."

"Are you rubbing his cheeks like I told you to?" Regan laughed.

"What? I don't remember you saying that. Why should I rub his cheeks?" Stephanie asked.

"Because little boys turn into men so quickly, you need to enjoy how soft their cheeks are while you still can. When you look back, it will seem like only a couple of years before he's grown and has a scratchy beard growing on those little pink cheeks," she laughed again.

Stephanie laughed, too, "Not my precious little boy, he's not going to become a big rough man," she cooed to the baby.

"Is there a good time in the next few days, when both of you can be there to sign everything?" Regan asked.

"Ed's days off this week are tomorrow and the next day. How about day after tomorrow at eleven, maybe?"

"Perfect, see you then," Regan signed off.

155

🏠🏠🏠🏠🏠🏠🏠🏠🏠🏠🏠

Regan arrived exactly at eleven, two days later, parked in front of the house, collected her briefcase, and walked up the path to the front porch. The day was sunny and clear. She remembered there was an ocean peek, as realtors would call it, from the porch. Regan never missed an opportunity to look at the ocean. She rang the doorbell, and as she waited for the Beltrans to answer, she turned to see what ever-changing color the water was today.

The water was aqua, Regan decided, and where a puffy cloud drifted overhead casting a shadow, something approaching pale indigo.

She heard a click and turned to see a tired-looking Ed opening the front door. The baby was wailing in the background. Stephanie was walking back and forth, patting him on the back, but to no avail.

"Come on in. Sorry for the confusion. We've pretty much been up all night," Ed said.

Stephanie looked even more tired than Ed. "I don't know what's happened," she said. "He's been such a good baby."

"Disrupting their parents' lives is what babies do," Regan quipped. "It's their job. You just got exceptionally lucky for a while. He figured now that you're all caught up with sleep and rested," Regan said, making sure they knew she was saying it tongue-in-cheek, "it's time to shake things up a bit.

"We'll need a table for these," Regan said as she patted her briefcase.

Ed wordlessly led the way to the kitchen.

It seemed that some portion of most real estate transactions took place at a kitchen table. Regan had been in Beltran kitchens twice before, first in their rented apartment, and then when Regan had stopped by to see the baby. Both times they had been squeaky clean and tidy. That wasn't the case today. Pots and pans filled the sink, and Ed had to remove the remains of breakfast before Regan could put her things on the kitchen table. The baby continued to cry the whole time Ed was tidying up.

They finally all sat down, Stephanie, still patting the baby's back, next to Ed on one side of the table, and Regan across from them. She brought the first set of documents out from her briefcase. All five pages of the lease agreement were new to the Beltrans and required explaining.

As she spoke, a large gray cat with golden eyes brushed against her leg. "Harry, is that you? Are you visiting?" she asked the cat.

"He's here again?" an exasperated Stephanie squealed. "How did he get in this time?"

"He must have snuck into the garage when I came home last night and opened the garage door. Then, when I went into the garage just now to put some clothes in the washer, he must have slipped into the house through the kitchen door," Ed said. "That's the only way for him to get in that I can think of. That cat's really tricky and very persistent," he added.

"He's all right as cats go, I guess," Stephanie explained, "but we don't want him in our house anymore. We're really more dog people and want to get a puppy as soon as the baby gets big enough.

"Anyway, he belongs to Mrs. Rosemont again," Stephanie said. "She told us how the cat had adopted Mr. Ansari, so we understood him coming over for a while. It was kind of amusing at first. He'd sort of throw himself against the kitchen door, over and over, sort of like he was knocking, until we opened it to let him come in and look around. After a few minutes, he'd leave again."

Ed took up the complaint. "He pretty much stopped coming over for a while, and we thought he was getting over looking for Mr. Ansari. But the last couple of days, he's been impossible." Regan could hear the agitation in Ed's voice. "I mean he's just been at the kitchen door all the time, complaining and sneaking in every chance he gets. He doesn't want to leave. I've had to sort of push him out a couple of times. Look where he scratched me once." Ed held up his arm for Regan to see recent claw marks. "Then he'd just stay on the back stoop and meow. I felt bad for him. He seems really upset, but he just shouldn't be our problem, especially not right now."

The baby continued to wail, showing no signs of slowing down, and Stephanie looked like she was about to join in, too.

"You know what? This doesn't seem like a great time for us to go over these papers," Regan said.

She took the remaining contracts out of her briefcase and put them on the table. "You've seen most of these before. I've filled in all the line items on the purchase contract just as they were on your original offer. The only change is substituting Kaivan's name for the Cyrus Ansari Trust. I brought a copy of your original offer; I figured you might not have easy access to it, what with moving and all," Regan smiled.

"You'd be right about that," Ed said.

"You can compare the copy with this new contract. Make sure I got everything exactly right, and then just sign and initial in all the places you did the first time. Read over the lease agreement, too. You're both smart people. The contract is fairly long, but most of the paragraphs are crossed out because they don't apply in this unusual situation. It's pretty straightforward. I've marked everywhere you need to initial or sign with a yellow marker. If there are any parts you have questions about, just circle them.

"Neither of these contracts needs to be worked on today. Take your time and call me when you've finished. I can come by again and answer any questions you have.

"In the meantime, come here, Harry," she scooped the cat up in a quick motion, "Let's go back home, see your owner, and tell her you can't be such a nuisance."

"Thank you so much," Stephanie said. "We do like Mrs. Rosemont and don't want to hurt her feelings, but that cat is getting really annoying."

Regan wiggled the shoulder strap of her briefcase into place and cradled Harry in her arms, feet in the air, like a baby. He didn't seem to mind, but she wasn't sure how long he'd be content to be carried, so she cut across the lawn from the Beltran's front door to Mrs. Rosemont's front door.

All the houses in this area sat on fairly standard Santa Cruz city lots, generally fifty feet wide by one hundred feet deep, which put them pretty close together. Even though the lots were similar, the houses weren't. They had all been built at different times.

Mrs. Rosemont's house probably dated from the mid 1950's. It was a wide shiplap wooden ranch style house, popular with the families of soldiers back from World War II. They were easy and relatively cheap to build, and went up all over California as the baby boom generation began arriving. It was about the same size as Mr. Ansari's house, but it was broader, with the garage, living room, and dining room across the front, and the kitchen, bedrooms, and bathroom in the back.

Although it lacked the unique curb appeal of Mr. Ansari's house, it did have the same ocean peek from the front porch. But Regan didn't take time to enjoy it, because Harry was becoming restless. She rang the doorbell and could hear it loudly announcing her presence. No answer. She waited just a moment and rang again — still no answer. Finally, she decided to try the kitchen door. She didn't think Mrs. Rosemont was hard of hearing, but it was possible she had difficulty with certain pitches. Perhaps she was in the kitchen, behind the garage, and hadn't heard the bell.

There weren't any tall plantings between Mr. Ansari's house and Mrs. Rosemont's house, only a low row of flowers. That wasn't the case on the kitchen side of the house. Either Mrs. Rosemont or her other neighbor had planted a row of pittosporum that ran the full length of the property line, from the curb to the end of their back yards. The plants must have been there for some time and were tall and dense, providing complete privacy on that side of the house.

Regan walked around the garage and along the narrow walkway by the pittosporum to the kitchen stoop. She knocked on the door and called, "Mrs. Rosemont? Eleanor?" Again, no answer. Harry had just about had enough of being carried and began squirming wildly and hissing at her.

She tried the kitchen door and wasn't at all surprised when it opened. She hadn't locked her back door when she first moved to Santa Cruz and lived in town — no one seemed to. Tom had been shocked to realize that, when they started dating. He lived over the hill in Palo Alto at the time, where everyone locked their doors, all their doors, all the time. Most people did now, even in Santa Cruz, but many older, long-time Santa Cruz residents never got into the habit of doing it.

She decided to take advantage of the unlocked door, deposit Harry inside, and leave her card with a note on the back, asking Mrs. Rosemont to call her so she could explain that Harry needed to change his ways.

"In you go, Harry," she said as she dropped him onto the kitchen floor and closed the door behind them before he could escape. He tried to get behind her and out the cat door in the bottom of the kitchen door, but she blocked it with her foot. There was a metal slide resting next to the cat door. She bent over and slid it into place, sealing Harry inside. Seeing he was trapped, he tore out of the kitchen and down the hall. "You're a wily one, aren't you?" she called after him.

She tugged her briefcase in front of her, lifted the flap to open a pocket on the outside where she kept business cards, and pulled one out as she walked toward the island that held the stove. The next little briefcase pocket over produced a pen.

The first thing she noticed when her distractions ended wasn't the mass of flame colored curls just visible on the floor between the sink and stove-island. What she noticed was the rust-colored smear on the white tile at the corner of the island. Regan hadn't even gotten to the point of thinking it odd to find such an unsightly smudge in an otherwise spotless house — curiosity was all she had time to register as she moved closer to the island — before she saw her friend lying on the floor.

"HUOH!" she gasped and found she was unable to release her breath.

Mrs. Rosemont lay on her back. Her pale blue eyes were open, staring but not seeing, covered with a milky film that made them seem a ghostly white. Her lips were parted, as if she had one more story to tell. She seemed even smaller than Regan remembered.

Her right hand held a handle and enough of a cup that Regan knew what it had been. The rest of the cup was shattered on the floor beside her. Another piece of china was smashed near her left hand. A drift of white partially covered the shattered piece. It had been Eleanor Rosemont's fragile blue and white sugar bowl.

Regan's breath, which she had been involuntarily

holding, came out at last. She might have screamed then, but she couldn't take in enough air for more than a whimper. Her breathing came as small pants and quick little pushes of air: "huh-huh-huh-huh."

Regan struggled to pull her cell phone out of its briefcase compartment, but her hands were suddenly so cold her fingers wouldn't do what she asked of them. She couldn't hold onto the small device. The phone dropped to the floor and bounced once, toward Mrs. Rosemont's head.

Some of the bright carroty curls appeared covered with rust — like the smear on the kitchen island. More was on the floor under her head. Not rust, Regan realized. Blood. Old dried blood.

She started to shiver. She bent down, staying as far from the body as she could, and very slowly reached her hand toward her phone…fingers rigidly extended…stretching …shaking…trying not to look at Mrs. Rosemont, as her fingers moved ever closer to mortality.

Regan wasn't afraid of the dead. She didn't avoid cemeteries or fear the dead could harm her. It was just that she didn't like to see dead people, or even worse, accidentally touch one of them.

But she had to retrieve her cell phone which now rested perilously close to Mrs. Rosemont, millimeters from the edge of the cold blood under her head.

The chill that invaded Regan's fingers spread throughout her body so that her movements were no longer fluid or natural. As Regan's trembling fingers stiffly wrapped around her phone, the back of her hand brushed against some of Mrs. Rosemont's hair.

Regan's icy skin burned suddenly, as if it had been seared by the flame-colored hair.

This time the scream did come, but not loudly or shrilly. It was more of a wail for the dead.

She managed to hold onto the phone and to stand, bracing herself against the stove-island, while a wave of dizziness swept past. It was a full minute before she could dial 9·1·1. She knew what to say to bring the police. Her words were precise but came out through sobs.

"This is Regan McHenry. I'm at the home of Eleanor Rosemont. I don't know the address, but it's the green house next door to 1215 Royale Street. She's dead. Please send help."

A woman's slightly nasal voice asked, "Are you hurt, ma'am."

"No, I'm OK." She held her lower lip in her teeth and took a deep breath. She turned away from Mrs. Rosemont's body to regain control and some composure. "I'm OK," she told herself and the dispatcher, "but I've just found her."

"Help is on the way, ma'am. Is the person you found breathing?" the voice on the phone asked.

"No, she's dead."

"Are you certain of that, ma'am?"

"Oh, God." She closed her eyes to try to stop the tears that were coming again. "Yes, I'm quite certain," Regan said.

"I'm going to connect you to officer Bellingham now, ma'am. Please remain on the line."

In a few seconds, the whiny voice was replaced by a deep masculine one. "This is detective Steve Bellingham.

The 9·1·1 dispatcher informed me you have discovered a body. Is that correct?"

"Yes."

"What is your location?"

"I told the dispatcher," Regan said.

"Tell me, please, and also tell me your name."

She was in a kitchen with the dead body of a delightful old woman she had come to like very much. Detective Bellingham's tone wasn't the least bit sympathetic. In fact, this all seemed about as exciting and unusual to him as getting the details he would need to write her up for speeding.

Regan realized she knew his wife, DeDe. She had taken aerobic dance classes from her a few years before. She had even met Detective Bellingham. He was a pleasant man who smiled easily, not at all like this dispassionate voice on the phone.

He knew what he was doing. He had taken control of a woman who could easily have become hysterical, and was calming her down. Regan was incredibly grateful to have someone who knew what to do…someone to take charge of her, at least until he got to the final question of their interview.

"Can you stay right where you are until I arrive?" he asked.

"Do I have to?" she asked, like a child being told she had to go to bed.

"Yes, you do," he said. It was good he hadn't given her any options.

"Then I guess I can," she replied in a tiny voice.

165

"One more thing," he said before ending the call, "don't touch anything."

Regan badly needed to sit down. But now that she had been admonished by Detective Bellingham, she decided she shouldn't disturb the kitchen chairs. Instead she walked over to the kitchen door and leaned against it.

It was as far away from Mrs. Rosemont as she could get, and the stove island blocked her view of the body, as it had when she brought Harry home. That helped somewhat.

She began noticing things she hadn't seen before when she was distracted with Harry and her briefcase. The top cupboard next to the sink where Mrs. Rosemont kept her teacups was partly open. Mrs. Rosemont's 'buddy', as she called her stepstool, was at a slightly odd angle but still upright below it. The tea canister was on the counter and open, and the kettle was next to the sink, ready to be filled.

Harry bounded back into the kitchen, rushed at her and stood upright against her leg, his sharp little claws going through her pant leg and hurting her. He meowed insistently.

She noticed his food and water bowls at her feet, near the kitchen door. They were in a similar place to where they had been at Mr. Ansari's house when she went through it looking for him, and in a similar condition — very empty. "That's why you've been such a pest," she said to the cat, discovering it helped her to talk to him. "There's been no one here to feed you. You're hungry and thirsty, aren't you?"

Surely the police wouldn't mind if she fed Harry. She would be careful to remember anything she touched and tell the police what she had done. That wouldn't interfere with their investigation, would it? No, she decided. She could feed Harry.

But to get Harry water, she would have to see Mrs. Rosemont again. She steeled herself against that for a moment or two before she picked up Harry's water bowl and took it near the sink. Harry maneuvered around her ankles, meowing pleadingly. She had to be very careful where she stepped. Mrs. Rosemont's left arm was thrown out toward the sink, but by stretching, Regan could still reach the faucet handle and turn on the water without disturbing poor Eleanor.

Having to see her body again made the shivering return.

"I've now touched the coldwater handle of the faucet. Make a mental note of that," she told herself out loud, as much to distract her mind from Eleanor's stare as to remember what she had done. It did help. Having to pay careful attention to what she did and noting it in detail, calmed her. She put the filled water bowl down in its original spot.

Next she looked around for cat food. There was a tall pantry cupboard set away from the rest of the kitchen, near Harry's bowls. "That's where I would keep your things," she said to Harry, who was frantically lapping water from his bowl. He had no comment.

Regan gingerly opened the door of the cupboard, adding another mental note about touching the door handle. "Good guess," she congratulated herself. Litter and cleanup equipment were on the bottom shelf. Cans of cat food were stacked within easy reach, one shelf up.

She took out the first can she reached. Harry seemed to understand this process and knew he was about to eat his first meal in, what might be, several days. His meows reached a new level of song. "I need a can opener, Harry, and I don't see one here."

She realized she would need to go near Eleanor again.

Regan started with the drawer farthest from the left side of the sink and as far away from the body as she could be. She was able to open it without looking down and seeing Mrs. Rosemont.

"Mental note to self, that's the third handle I've touched." She carefully pulled the drawer open. Scotch tape, a screwdriver, a small hammer, some pencils and a pad of paper, rubber bands, several corks, matches, and an assortment of other mismatched items filled the drawer. But there wasn't a can opener.

She closed the drawer and tried the next one over. Silverware was neatly arranged in a caddy. Around the holder she noted sharp knives, a bottle opener, and finally, the can opener. She removed it carefully, leaving the drawer open.

She took the tool to Harry's bowl, squatted down, and started to open the can of cat food. Harry went crazy the minute the opener pierced the can and he recognized what was coming. He tried to push his nose into the can before the lid was completely severed. "Harry, wait a minute. No, Harry."

Regan dropped the can opener and tried to pull the lid up to free his food. He lunged at her hand at just the wrong moment, and her finger caught the lid's jagged edge.

Her blood was redder than Eleanor's by far, but far less disturbing.

She quickly dumped the cat food into Harry's bowl and put her bloodied finger into her mouth. She thought about leaving the opener right there with the can, but decided it was better to return it to its proper place and close the drawer, since that was how it had been when she arrived.

Regan picked up the can opener with her uninjured hand and returned it to the drawer.

She was getting better at not looking at Eleanor.

It seemed like a very long time before the kitchen door opened and Detective Bellingham and another officer came in, but it probably had taken them less than ten minutes to arrive. The second officer finished putting on latex protective gloves before he bent over Mrs. Rosemont. "No pulse," he announced as he touched her neck.

Regan stared at him perplexedly; it was incredibly clear to her there wouldn't be one. Why was he telling her what she already knew?

"The deceased is a female, aged late seventies to mid-eighties. Body temperature is consistent with ambient air temperature, with no evidence of rigor. Lividity is set," he added more details before Regan realized he was talking into a microphone clipped to his shirt. He must have a recorder in his shirt pocket.

There were protocols to be followed, she realized, and this was the first of many activities that would help determine why Mrs. Rosemont had died. But it was painful for her to hear terminology which reduced such a level-headed, intelligent, and engaging woman to a mere corpse to be impassively studied.

"Please, can I leave now that you're here," she begged.

"Let's go sit in the patrol car outside, while I take a more complete statement from you," suggested Detective Bellingham.

As soon as they stepped outside, Regan took a deep breath. The outdoor air was such a relief, it felt fresh and warm. Alive. Poor Eleanor.

The Detective asked her why she went to see the deceased — there was that word again, that cold, clinical, final word — and she told him the tale of the cat bothering the next-door neighbors.

He told her the investigating unit would look for signs of a forced entry. They needed to know if she had broken or forced anything to get in. She told them about the unlocked back door.

"Did that seem unusual to you," he asked, "you know, an elderly woman who lived alone, not locking her doors?"

"Not at all. I'm a real estate agent and see that all the time. People often don't have keys for some of their doors because they never lock them or only twist the latch to lock them from the inside at night before they go to bed."

"You said you knew the deceased. How well did you know her?"

"I just met her recently, but I would say we had become friends. I sold the house next door and met her because of that. We've had a couple of conversations and she invited me in one time. We had tea." She didn't add they had even shared secrets.

"Did you touch or move anything after you found the body?"

Regan didn't know what kind of expression swept across her face, but Detective Bellingham quickly said, "I mean, after you found your friend."

"I did." Confession time, Regan realized. "But I paid very good attention to what I touched so I can tell you about it."

The detective closed his eyes, little more than a prolonged blink, inhaled, and exhaled very loudly. "What did you do?" he asked slowly.

"Well, Harry was starving." Detective Bellingham looked puzzled.

"Harry's the cat," Regan clarified. "He was getting really frantic to be fed. I guess it had been…a while…" her voice trailed off.

"Anyway, I decided I better do it before you got here. I didn't want him running around searching for food, disturbing…things. I remember exactly what I did and what I touched.

"First, I picked up his water bowl and got as close to the sink as I could without disturbing anything near Mrs. Rosemont. I held the dish in my right hand and turned on the cold water tap with my left," Regan demonstrated as she talked. "I put the water bowl back down where it had been and opened the tall cupboard next to the back door. I was careful to only lightly touch the handle. I took out a can of cat food.

"It wasn't one of the pop-top kinds, so I had to find a can opener. I opened the first drawer nearest the kitchen door, again being careful to only lightly touch the bottom of the handle, but there wasn't a can opener in it, so I closed it and tried the next drawer over in the direction of the sink. I found a can opener, took it out, went back to Harry's bowl, opened the can, dumped it in his bowl, put the empty can on the floor by the bowls, and returned the can opener to the drawer and closed it. I cut my finger on the cat food can lid, but I'm sure I didn't get blood on anything other than that," she said, holding her finger up for the detective to see her wound.

"Except for the can on the floor and the cat's bowls being full, everything looks just as it did when I came in," she concluded.

"Oh, and I put the cat door in," she quickly added. "But I did that before I saw her — before I found Eleanor ...her...body," Regan braved the word.

Detective Bellingham was busy finishing the notes he had been taking as she spoke.

"What's going to happen to Harry, now?"

"Animal control will take Harry to a shelter," Detective Bellingham said. He seemed amused that he was now referring to the cat by name. Regan guessed he didn't call cats by their name, especially when he was working.

"I'll take him home with me tonight, instead of letting him go to the pound, if that's OK," Regan volunteered.

"Umm," he weighed Harry's importance for just a second, "Sure, you can go ahead and take him."

A quick search of the garage produced a cat carrier, and it was agreed that removing it wouldn't interfere with the police investigation.

Now that he had food in him, Harry was ready for a nap and didn't protest as Regan put him in the carrier.

On her drive home, with the cat carrier seat-belted next to her and Harry asleep inside, Regan mentally replayed the day. Tom said when something unpleasant happened to her she needed to tell people about it to dull the event's impact, its color. It was a diluting process for her, like mixing red paint with progressively more white paint. The mixture started out intensely pink, but as more white paint was added, the pink faded until, even though the color was still there, it had been reduced to a mere tinge, an acceptable background color.

He had a theory about how many people needed to hear Regan's stories and how detailed her tales needed to be to make them fade. A mildly troubling event, something like a disloyal client who had their realtor cousin write an offer on a property Regan had shown them, required a simple conversation, told in broad brushstrokes: one cup of white paint, two cups of white paint. As soon as she told someone what happened and how bad it made her feel, she could dismiss it from her mind.

At the other end of the event spectrum was something

big, like being in an automobile accident. An incident like that took numerous debriefing sessions to recede. One gallon of white paint, two gallons of white paint. Finally the right hue appeared, and she got over it.

Regan wasn't sure how many times she would have to speak about finding Mrs. Rosemont's body before she could move on, but she was pretty sure it would be many, many times. It would take untold gallons of white to dilute the red of Mrs. Rosemont's blood.

Regan always started the process by talking to Tom, and tonight he was going to have to hold her while she went over every detail of what happened in Mrs. Rosemont's kitchen.

The evening was gorgeous. The sun had fallen below the horizon, but the sky was still dazzling. The setting sun colored the bottom of the few wispy clouds over the bay various shades of orange, lavender, and crimson against the acute blue of the sky. It was the time of year when the air was crisp and still, and so clear they could make out the streets in Pacific Grove, thirty-three miles across Monterey Bay. They sat outside on a two-person slide swing. Regan curled up against Tom with her feet on the swing, seeking his warmth and protection against the shaking she feared would return as she began her tale.

Tom had his arm around her, and they each held a glass of Pinot Noir. He kept refilling her glass before it was empty, so she wasn't sure how much wine she had drunk so far, but she knew it was more than the one glass she allowed herself most nights. Tonight, she would have welcomed the disconnect that came with excessive alcohol, but so far she didn't feel any effects from her wine.

Tom pushed against the brick patio to keep the swing moving slowly and rhythmically, his long legs making it easy to do so. She found the gentle motion soothing, reassuring. It was only 62 degrees outside, but just three days ago there had been a light fall of snow, followed by pea-sized hail. After that snap of cold, this much warmth felt like summer. They had a blanket ready to wrap around them though, because there wasn't any residual warmth in the air. Once the sun set, the temperature would drop rapidly.

Tom knew his role in all this. He was to listen without interrupting. As they talked, or rather as Regan talked and Tom comforted her, the sky darkened and lights began to twinkle on around the edge of the bay where towns merged with the water.

Regan had reached the point in her blow-by-blow recounting of her ordeal where she was trying to find a can opener for Harry's cat food.

"I opened her junk drawer, but she didn't keep her can opener in it." She stopped abruptly. "That's right," she said, straightening up and unwinding to face Tom.

"The first drawer I opened was Mrs. Rosemont's junk drawer; I'm sure it was because it had all kinds of odds and ends in it. But you know what wasn't in it?"

Tom recognized the rhetorical nature of the question and shook his head attentively but in silence.

"Mr. Ansari's papers," she said slowly, attaching great weight to each word. "The other day, when Mrs. Rosemont had me in for tea, she told me quite a story. It seems Mr.

177

Ansari had an illegitimate son living in Iran. Mr. Ansari didn't know he existed until very recently when the boy's mother, who was married to someone else when the child was conceived, wrote to tell him that he had fathered her youngest son.

"The woman, who was now a widow, died shortly after telling Mr. Ansari about the boy. He wanted to bring his son here, and I guess the boy wanted to come. Mrs. Rosemont said she discovered Mr. Ansari's passport, plane tickets, and paperwork to get his son out of Iran at his house after he disappeared. She said she took them all home and put them in her junk drawer. None of those things were in it today."

"She probably moved them, put them somewhere else," Tom said.

"I don't think so. She said bringing his son here was really important to Mr. Ansari. She'd been trying to persuade Kaivan to go to Iran and get the boy. She thought she finally had. She said she was going to give all the papers to him at his next visit. I got the feeling she was going to see him soon, maybe even later that day.

"She said something about him needing to make up for what he had done to his uncle. You see, evidently Mr. Ansari needed help going to Iran because of his illness, and asked Kaivan to go with him. Kaivan refused. According to Mrs. Rosemont, they'd had a big row about it.

"Anyway, she seemed to think if Kaivan finished what Mr. Ansari started, maybe even had the boy in his life in the same kind of relationship he had with his uncle, it would help him feel better about his loss.

178

"So here's to you, Eleanor," Regan said, elevating her glass. "You must have had your talk with Kaivan before you died and convinced him to bring his cousin to America. What a remarkable woman you were. Mr. Ansari was fortunate to have you for a friend," she said, before continuing her story.

Harry had been relegated to the garage for the night. He couldn't be left outside. They didn't want him running away, and local raccoons and the occasional passing coyote could pose a real threat to an uninitiated city pet; but they weren't sure how their cat would feel about a sudden houseguest, so they didn't want him loose in their house, either. If Kaivan didn't want Harry, they would begin the process of a proper introduction of the two felines, but none of them were up to it tonight.

They checked on him before going to bed. He had returned to the open cat carrier and was peacefully asleep.

16

Mrs. Rosemont's death didn't make it to the front section of the *Santa Cruz Sentinel*. The next day, a short single-column article on page eleven announced: Local Senior Found Dead. The brief story gave her name and age, which it turned out was eighty-six, and said Regan McHenry, a visiting friend, had found her in her Royale Street home. Police Detective Bellingham listed the probable cause of death as an accidental fall, but an autopsy was pending.

Regan made an early call to Kaivan, hoping she might catch him in person. No such luck. Either he had an early morning or a late night, she never knew which with him, but either way, he didn't pick up. She had to settle for leaving a message.

"It's my turn to ask if you've seen the *Sentinel* today." She winced as soon as the words were out of her mouth. How she hated answering machines. Once again she had blurted out something that didn't come out at all the way she intended, and now the callous and unforgiving machine would preserve her words.

181

That brainless message would make it seem like she was mocking the call Kaivan made to her when he told her about his uncle's body being found.

Since she couldn't go back, she fumbled forward. "Mrs. Rosemont is dead. I'm the one who found her. The police were going to send Harry to the pound, so I asked if I could bring him home with me, instead. I know you'll probably want him; I should have called you right away, but I wasn't thinking very clearly yesterday." And you still aren't, she thought.

"Anyway, I'll bring him to your house today, if you want me to. Just let me know when you'll be home…unless you're going to Iran right away…I mean…if you have to go there…if there's anything you have to take care of there for your uncle…and want me to keep him until you get back. Just let me know." She hung up — very dissatisfied with her whole message.

Kaivan called back almost immediately.

"You can keep Harry if you want to."

"You mean you'll be away for a while?" Regan said hopefully.

"No. I mean I don't want him."

Kaivan's tone was abrupt, almost angry. Regan credited that to her bungled phone message. It must have offended him even more than she thought it might.

"But Mrs. Rosemont said you came to visit him, and you two had bonded. Are you sure you don't want him?"

"I'm sure." Kaivan said definitively. "If you and Tom want him, he's yours; otherwise I'll try to find a home for him or take him to the pound myself. A pet doesn't fit in my lifestyle."

"No, that's OK, we'll keep him. We've been thinking our cat needs a playmate," she tried to move the conversation into a lighter, friendlier direction. "We've even been looking for one…"

"Great," he interrupted, still sounding irritated, "Gotta go." With that he hung up.

She could understand him being annoyed at her message, but why the change toward Harry?

Regan was left wondering why he bothered to visit a cat he didn't seem to care about, but she didn't have long to think about it. Her phone rang again, almost as soon as she returned it to its cradle.

She didn't recognize the number and it didn't have an identifying name attached to it. That could mean it was an inquiry about a listing.

"Kiley and Associates Real Estate; this is Regan," she used her business greeting.

"Is it now? This is Mitchell Carless, a voice from your past."

It certainly was. Had it been three years? More likely four, the way time passed. She remembered Mitchell as a teddy bear of a man. He was stocky overall with a large barrel-chested body and proportionally shorter arms and legs. He saw the world through small, dark shoe-button eyes that seemed to be set in a furry head, the impression caused by his dense short beard and tightly curled hair.

His taciturnity added to his teddy bear-ness. He sat quietly at office meetings, observing the goings-on like an outgrown plaything that had been relegated to a shelf, not yet discarded, but no longer cuddled.

The last time she saw him, he'd been a realtor for a couple of decades, who one day just announced he was done. He hadn't complained about being burned out or bored with the profession, and though he was never a superstar, he had a good business going and made a decent living without working terribly hard.

Regan remembered the day he quit. It was late in the afternoon and only she and one other real estate agent, a woman who was perpetually involved with important phone calls, remained in the office. Mitchell walked in carrying a large cardboard box and started emptying his desk.

"Mitchell, what's up? Are you switching companies?" she asked.

"Nope."

"But you look like you're leaving?"

"Yep."

"Are you retiring? Should we have a party?"

"No need. I'm just not doing this anymore." He unceremoniously picked up the box and headed for the front door, signaling the end of the conversation, such as it had been, and the end of their contact.

Regan returned to the present and answered him, curious about why he was calling after such a long silence. "Mitchell, it's been years, how are you?"

"I'm well. I saw the story about you finding a body and thought you might not be."

Direct and concise as always, Regan thought. She had never considered him to be big on empathy. They had been associates, never friends, and had never done a transaction together. His observation surprised her; it was not something she would have expected from him. She wondered if the call might somehow have more to do with him, than with his concern for her emotional state, but she said, "Thanks for thinking about me. I'm OK, really. It was distressing to find her. I'm over that now. I'm just a bit down because I liked her."

"Don't let what happened make you pack up and leave the business, like I did. You'll regret it."

"Is that why you quit so suddenly? Mitchell, you found a body? What happened?" she asked.

The usually unforthcoming Mitchell Carless poured out his tale.

"I was unhappy because I drew a Wednesday morning floor-time shift. You know how Wednesday mornings go; no one real ever calls on a Wednesday morning. I figured I was going to waste three hours of my life being nothing more than a glorified receptionist, answering phones and questions for people who couldn't reach their own agent. But this time was different. I got a great up-call from a lady who didn't have an agent.

"This woman wanted to buy a condo in the three-story complex on Atlantic Street, half a block from the beach. You know the ones I mean?"

"Yes, the green building, right?"

"That's right. She said she was an all-cash buyer and only wanted to live in that group of condos. We agreed to meet at the front door of the complex the next day, and I was jazzed because she sounded like a live one.

"There were three condos for sale, one on each floor. I set up showings from the bottom up. The owner of the top condo said he didn't believe in lock boxes, but he'd be there to let us in and then discreetly take a walk on the beach while I showed his property.

"We looked at condo number one and she said it was OK. We looked at condo number two and she didn't like it at all.

"When we got up to the top floor, I made sure we stopped at an observation window so she could see the ocean view from there. Then we went to condo number three. I knocked and knocked, but no answer. I was getting pretty ticked; and the lady, you know the type: artsy, sixty-ish, short gray hair, flowing clothes, and lots of beads, was getting antsy.

"I tried the doorknob on impulse and the thing was unlocked. I figured the owner saw us coming when we did the ocean-view detour, and left. So, in we went. She really liked the living room and the kitchen, and I started getting enthused. Gonna make a sale, the most expensive one in the complex, to boot; and I kind of backed into the bedroom, doing the walking-backward, pointing-out-the-features thing.

"She had a big grin on her face until she followed me into the bedroom. Then she looked kind of strange, so I turned around to see what she was looking at.

"The owner was spread eagle on the bed with the phone still in his hand. Turned out he must have had a massive coronary and croaked right after I made the appointment with him. He didn't even have time to hang up."

"Oh my golly, Mitchell. I bet you and your client were shocked," Regan empathized.

"Well, one of us was. I called 9·1·1 right away, and you know what they wanted me to do? They wanted me to wait with the body until they got there. Can you believe that?"

"As a matter of fact, I can. They told me to do the same thing when I found Mrs. Rosemont."

"I wasn't going to spend my afternoon with a corpse. My client was out of the bedroom as soon as she spotted the owner, and I figured she was off somewhere fainting or throwing up, which is what I wanted to do.

"Oh no, not her. She was sitting like a cross-legged Buddha on the floor in the middle of the living room, eyes closed and arms out to her sides, with her palms in the air. I thought she was moaning and I went to help her, but she said she was communing. Communing. What kind of crap is that?"

Regan had been holding the phone to her ear with her shoulder. With that image in mind, she had to keep the phone in place with her hand. She held her other hand over her mouth, pressing her fingers hard against her lips, grateful Mitchell couldn't see the smile spreading over her face. "Umm" was all she could manage. She hoped he would take that as a sympathetic comment.

"Umm is exactly right. She said she was telling the dead owner she loved his place, and was negotiating a fair price with him to offer his estate. Since she was so cozy with the owner, I figured she could wait there with him for the police.

"Man, what a whacked out way to make a living! I went back to the office and packed up. Enough crazies for one career."

"I literally don't know what to say, Mitchell." Regan's voice was choked with the demands of keeping from laughing.

"Well, I never told anyone about it, until now. I can tell you really care, and I appreciate that. I just wanted to let you know not to quit. I got freaked out by what happened. I over-reacted and told all my clients to find other real estate agents, 'cause I was done. They all did, and I couldn't get 'em back. I was too old and tired to start over in the business. Fire in the belly was out, and all that.

"Ever since, I wished I had just taken some time off instead. You do that. Give yourself some time to let your mind settle. Don't try to run away from the scene like I did. You'll get over it. Anyway, that's all I wanted to say."

"It was so kind of you to be concerned about me. I'll definitely think about what you've said."

"Good. OK then, goodbye."

Regan put the phone down and started to laugh. She continued to laugh as tears started to flow down her cheeks, but somewhere in the midst of her sobbing with laughter, she found herself just sobbing.

17

Regan had been carefully scanning the newspaper for a follow-up story on her friend's death for almost a week, but hadn't seen one. When she gave up looking and called Dave, she found out Eleanor Rosemont's autopsy had been completed two days before.

"I need to know why she died," she told him. "I have clients living next door in Cyrus Ansari's house who are very uncomfortable, because it seems to them like there's been too much death in the neighborhood. Detective Bellingham said it looked like a fall was the cause. I need to know if she had a heart attack or a stroke, or something like that before she fell. Anything other than natural causes and my clients are probably out of there.

"Besides, Dave, I liked her. And I'm the one who found her." Regan paused, then let out a deep breath. "I guess you police get used to seeing death like that, but I'm struggling with it. I don't think anything is going to erase my memory of her, the way she looked, but it would help to know it was just her time. Who can I talk to about the autopsy results?"

"You can talk to me," Dave was sympathetic. "You at your office?"

"I am."

"Kelly's Bakery is right across the street from you. Why don't I buy you a cup of coffee there in about an hour?"

"Thank you Dave, I'll take you up on that. But I'll buy the coffee, and I think we'll each need one of those little individual frosted cakes they do so well, too."

"Deal," he said enthusiastically. "See you in an hour."

Dave tossed in the remains of cake number one and was eyeing the second one on his plate. "How natural do the causes have to be for you and your next-door neighbors?" he asked.

"What do you mean?"

"Well, the cause of death was a blow to the head. The M-E — sorry, Medical Examiner to civilians like you — matched up the wound with the counter corner, so there's no question that's what did it. There wasn't any evidence of a stroke or heart attack, or for that matter, of foul play.

"Initial toxicology report said the old lady was loaded to the gills with Xanax. That's a type of sleeping pill."

Regan already knew what Xanax was.

"We found a prescription for them in her medicine chest with about half of them gone." Dave was back in his inclusive-investigator manner of speaking.

"Our theory is she took her nightly meds and then decided to make herself a nice cup of tea. The pills hit sooner than she expected, she got dizzy, lost her balance, and down she went…end of story. Does that count as a natural cause?"

"Maybe. I'll have to think about it, and tell my clients how she died, and let them think about it."

Stephanie and Ed felt better the more they thought about it. Regan did not.

🏠🏠🏠🏠🏠🏠🏠🏠🏠🏠🏠

After the slow season around the holidays and at the start of the year, Regan's work load was increasing. Normally, early spring, at least as it was defined in Santa Cruz, was one of her favorite times of the year as a real estate agent. She should be enjoying herself right now. The promise of new business offered interesting challenges, and she looked forward to advising clients about how to increase their property's value and marketability. Regan and Tom hadn't flipped a house yet, as buying, fixing up, and immediately reselling a house was called; but they were getting ready to try it, and working with clients seemed like a good way to hone the skills they would need when they did.

This was hardly a normal year, though. In the space of two months, she'd been one of the last people to talk to a murder victim, had a contract with a man who died under questionable circumstances, and discovered the body of a friend. One of her associates had started calling her "the grim reaperette", and jokingly asked if she put a disclaimer in her disclosure packet advising clients that working with her could prove hazardous to their health.

She didn't need to; her clients were fine. It was Regan's

well-being that was suffering. Since finding Mrs. Rosemont's body, she had talked with several friends and repeatedly with Tom about the experience, but it hadn't helped. All of her talking had not erased the horror of it, or even diminished the intensity of her distress.

Her final visual memory of Eleanor Rosemont was one she would rather not have locked inside her brain — but it was there and seemed determined to disrupt her sleep.

The same pattern repeated itself every night. She would fall asleep without difficulty, but her slumber wasn't restful; it was filled with the nightmare image of Eleanor lying dead and still, her skin and eyes faded to a chalky, icy white, her curls changed in color from a lively carroty shade to the color and texture of caked dried blood.

Yet it was more than the dreadfulness of the image that was causing her sleeplessness.

Life was a fragile gift, and Eleanor Rosemont had enjoyed the singular boon of having it bestowed for many years. She had likely enjoyed it to the fullest, given her adventurous life and the devotion between husband and wife that was obvious in Eleanor's photo gallery. Regan could mourn the end of a long productive life, certainly, but that wasn't all that was troubling her.

It also wasn't the irony, that after such a life, Mrs. Rosemont's end had been so quiet and ordinary. Death didn't have to match life. Just the week before, Regan read a news story about a brave soldier home from Iraq, who, having survived the worst of combat and roadside bombs, was killed in a traffic accident on the drive home after buying groceries.

What was causing her such sleeplessness, she concluded, was a question she couldn't answer. No, that wasn't quite right. What was troubling her so was a question she couldn't ask, couldn't even formulate.

Mrs. Rosemont's specter never attempted to communicate with her. It always lay still, in the same position the elderly woman was in when Regan found her, a tiny unmoving husk, with the shattered cup handle in one hand and the smashed sugar bowl near her other outstretched hand.

Her ghoulish nightly-dream intruder never asked her to consider anything, never posed a question. Eleanor's image only tormented her...and yet...and yet, her nightly visit must be happening for some reason.

But if she didn't know the question to ask, Regan lamented, how could being forced to see Mrs. Rosemont like that possibly serve any useful purpose?

Her nightly visions were not something she wanted to continue. She needed those horrible images to leave her alone. Regan tried to bury her nightmares, like Mrs. Rosemont had been buried.

Until she could figure out the question that was troubling her — the question she couldn't yet ask — work would have to be her answer. Work and time. *Stay busy, Regan*, she ordered herself as she struggled to stay diverted with the details of her occupation.

The Atwoods were firmly in escrow. There were several inspections to attend to and inspection results to be considered with them. It was discovered that the firebox in the furnace had a hole in it, potentially letting carbon

193

monoxide into the heating system. The sellers said they
didn't know about the hole before the home inspector
found it. No doubt that was the truth, because it was a
dangerous condition that could have put their entire family
at risk. Even so, they weren't eager to pay for a new
furnace. Her clients were disinclined to buy the house
without one.

A contract renegotiation appeared necessary to save the
transaction. Fortunately, the realtor for the sellers, Anne
Craigen, was a capable agent and a good friend of Regan's.
They worked hard trying to renegotiate the contract. But
the furnace wasn't just a minor issue needing resolution,
and things had quickly turned ugly. Both sides became
righteously intransigent. The sellers argued they had
already accepted a low offer and wouldn't give any more
concessions. Her clients, like all buyers in this slower
market, were ready to walk.

When Anne and Regan realized there was no way to
bring their clients together, they met for coffee and decided
a little agent cooperation was the easiest and most
expedient way to make the problem go away. All that was
needed was a new furnace box, since all the tubing to
deliver heat was in acceptable condition. A new furnace
cost fifteen hundred ninety-nine dollars, installed. A highly
energy efficient model could be purchased and installed for
seventeen hundred forty-eight dollars.

Anne and Regan decided on the energy efficient model.
The math was easy. Each wrote a check for eight hundred
seventy-four dollars, a reasonable investment for what they
accomplished. Escrow held together and both agents felt

good about helping Santa Cruz be a little greener. They earned their commission, made their clients happy, and were now free to move on to other business concerns.

Regan was grateful for the distraction that kept her mind busy during the day with an issue she could resolve.

Her nights still remained a problem. Her sleep was getting ever more troubled and fitful as the image of Mrs. Rosemont's body continued to make its regular disturbing appearance.

In a psychology class in college, Regan's professor had lectured about people who remembered things visually. They had an observable behavior they followed when trying to recall an event or place, he said. They would look up, usually to their right, as if they were looking at a suspended image of what they were trying to recall.

The professor could have been talking about her and the way she remembered things. Her memory didn't come in parts. She didn't string recollections together to form a whole. She saw the past intact again, like looking at a photo in an old album.

She could remember floor plans years after she had seen a house, and could often even remember how a house was decorated, sometimes right down to the color of the walls. It was easy for her. She simply retrieved the picture she had in her memory and looked at it to see the details.

That particular way of storing memories served her well in her profession. When it came to Mrs. Rosemont, however, it was causing her real misery.

Work and time, she gave herself a little pep talk after a particularly disturbing night. *Work and time,* she repeated like a mantra as she redoubled her efforts to impose control over her mind's eye.

Regan assembled a spring client-newsletter earlier than she usually did. It became another keep-busy task. In it, she targeted buyers, encouraging them that it was a buyer's market. The newsletter produced many more responses than she expected, and several of Regan's contacts asked her to find them a new home.

There were too many properties for sale to show all of them to her clients, so she was spending a lot of time alone in her car, driving from house to house, previewing. Her goal was to cut properties, eliminating all those homes that didn't make a serious dent in her clients' wish lists. The remaining "A-list" homes constituted the best values in their price range and became the ones that she would show.

Regan liked to listen to Ronn Owens or Gil Gross on KGO talk-radio, out of San Francisco, as she drove. They were both good interviewers. Authors pushing their latest books were frequent guests on the shows. Many of them wrote about politics, and she was an avowed political junky. She also enjoyed hearing the latest news and commentary on current events, and sometimes even guiltily enjoyed trashy celebrity gossip.

But recently, she was losing all ability to track what she was hearing on the radio. Mrs. Rosemont's memory was even beginning to interfere with her daytime concentration.

The likeness of Eleanor's small body lying on the floor of her kitchen, her lips parted, invaded her dreams as she slept, and increasingly, her consciousness during waking hours. It was becoming so intrusive that Regan told Tom she understood now what people meant when they said they were haunted by a memory.

Even more troubling was the unsettling knowledge — yes, it was a certainty now, it had grown from a feeling to a conviction — that Eleanor still had something important to tell her, something Regan, who was usually such a good listener, couldn't seem to hear.

She had spent her days and nights since having coffee with Dave, doing everything she could to avoid her memory of Mrs. Rosemont. But it had become clear that wasn't working. If she was going to have her self-possession back, she was finally going to have to look once again at the dead Eleanor, embrace her memory, and try to figure out what, beyond the obvious trauma of finding her friend as she had, was troubling her.

The finality of her decision made Regan bold. She would do it today, immediately, she decided.

And once she accepted what she had to do, the questions she needed to ask finally began to form in her mind.

18

There were two puzzles troubling Regan, two bits of information that were irreconcilable with what she knew about Mrs. Rosemont's death.

First, there was the Xanax.

Eleanor said she didn't take sleeping pills. She had been very clear about her stepstool exercise insuring she slept well, and specifically said she never needed anything to help her sleep.

And yet, Dave said the police found a half-empty bottle of sleeping pills in her bathroom medicine chest. Xanax — the same compound that, according to the Medical Examiner, overwhelmed her system and caused her fall.

Why would Mrs. Rosemont have stated so clearly she didn't take sleeping pills if she had a prescription and regularly took such medication? Her photo collection demonstrated that her earlier years must have been exceptional, but she didn't aggrandize her life. It seemed to Regan, a woman like that wouldn't feel the need to exaggerate her independence from sleeping medication, either.

Even assuming that the sleeping pill prescription had come after their tea together, she still would have felt uneasy about the number of missing pills.

Mrs. Rosemont would never have taken a handful of a new medication, especially one that specified one or possibly two pills per night. She was much too sharp for that. Yet the prescription was half gone. There hadn't been enough time between their tea together and Mrs. Rosemont's death for her to have taken so many pills.

And the sleeping pills were Xanax. That's what Regan had seen in Cyrus Ansari's bathroom. Xanax was pretty heavy-duty stuff. Given his cancer, Mr. Ansari may have needed something like that. But Eleanor? Her doctor probably would have started her off with one of the frequently advertised, newer sleeping compounds like Ambien or Lunesta, maybe even given her some of the free samples that doctors get from drug company reps, to see how she would tolerate the medication.

Regan pulled up in front of the last house on her preview list and parked. The house was at the end of a small lane off a short residential drive. No gardeners were mowing their lawns or watering their flowers. Good. There was no through traffic. There would be no sudden braking or horns sounding. Excellent. The house was vacant, so she was no longer on a strict appointment schedule.

She had time and privacy and no real likelihood of being disturbed. No more diversions. No more distractions. Regan turned off the radio and reluctantly, but determinedly, prepared herself to face the tiny specter of Eleanor Rosemont.

The sun shone cheerfully outside, casting a warming ray reassuringly through the window of her car. She wished she could have Tom help her through what would likely be a disturbing process, but this was a solitary task, one she had to finish alone.

"I can do this," she told herself quietly. She took a deep breath, closed her eyes, and exhaled slowly.

The photo-like picture of Mrs. Rosemont's lifeless body materialized in front of her. Unlike all the nights when she had worked so hard to push the image away, Regan tried to accept this vision and even welcome it. She sat in her car, hands on the steering wheel for support, and confronted her memory.

Mrs. Rosemont was again on her back on the floor, dried blood under her head and staining the top of her sweater and blouse. There was so much blood. In her right hand she clutched the handle of a broken cup. It had probably smashed when she fell against the counter. That part made sense.

What didn't make sense was the shattered sugar bowl near Mrs. Rosemont's left hand. That was the second puzzle that troubled her.

Regan saw herself back in the kitchen, stretching to turn on the water, trying not to disturb any of the scattered sugar as she filled Harry's water bowl at the sink; and recalled how terrified she had been that Harry would run through the sugar, disturbing its scatter pattern, something she thought might be helpful to the police in their investigation.

When Mrs. Rosemont had her in for tea, it made her incredibly uncomfortable to sit as the elderly woman repeatedly climbed up and down her stepstool to take one item at a time out of the cupboard. She never took her left hand off the stepstool handle during her ascents or descents, so she was never able to hold more than one piece of china at a time. Regan had to restrain herself from helping; it was clear Eleanor had her movements down to a routine born of long habit.

But if that was so, how had the sugar bowl been broken? If the elderly woman had taken the sugar bowl down from the cupboard and placed it on the counter and then somehow knocked it to the ground as she fell, the sugar would have been scattered away from the counter, toward Mrs. Rosemont. The scatter pattern was clear in her mind. The sugar was thrown from the broken bowl near Mrs. Rosemont's left hand toward the counter. How could that have happened if she wasn't holding the sugar bowl as she fell?

And yet, she was absolutely certain that Mrs. Rosemont wouldn't be on her stepstool, holding both a cup and the sugar bowl at the same time. She just couldn't see it in her memory so that it all made sense.

The sun had shifted enough that Regan's sunbeam had moved on, choosing to cast its comforting ray elsewhere. Its absence and her mental return to the death scene left her almost as chilled as she had been in the Royale Street kitchen when she found Eleanor's body.

Maybe now that she had what had been troubling her clearly in mind, though, she might not have to revisit that horrible place where a forever still Eleanor lay surrounded by blood. She fervently hoped that was true.

She opened her eyes and glanced at her watch, an old fashioned one that had belonged to her grandmother. The hands on it indicated she had been sitting in her car for almost an hour. She would have to think about all this again later — think about it, she hoped, not see it, which promised to be much less agonizing.

Regan took another deep breath, her way of compartmentalizing her thoughts and shifting to a new task. She needed to finish her tour if she was going to get to her listing appointment with the Bridgemanns on time. Regan opened her car door, got out, and walked up to the front door of the last house on her list.

She punched in the code to her lockbox key and aimed it at the corresponding box hanging from the front door. It was the latest model of lockbox, an aim-and-shoot type that didn't require physical contact between the lockbox key and the key-container box.

Not many realtors in Santa Cruz had them yet, but this type of equipment was very popular in Carmel; and yes, she thought as she looked at the FOR SALE sign in the front yard, this house was listed by a Carmel company.

She and Tom saw this type of lockbox regularly when they played hooky and went to the quaint, pricey community, their favorite quick escape destination, for a day trip.

To assuage their guilt for slipping out of town on a work day, they usually printed out a list of vacant homes with an asking price between three and four million dollars, and stopped by a few of them on their visit to Carmel.

They would tell one another they were doing research

and keeping abreast of what was available in that price range.

"You never know when you'll meet someone who wants to buy an expensive home in charming Carmel-by-the-Sea," Regan would say.

"Absolutely," Tom would agree. "Just because it hasn't happened yet, doesn't mean it never will. And it could happen at any time, so we need to be prepared."

They were knowingly deluding themselves, of course, and enjoying the living pages of decorator magazines, since vacant homes in that price range, in the high-status, upscale market of Carmel, would all be tastefully staged with the latest, trendiest designs and furnishings available. It was a fun game, made more enjoyable because they knew it was all part of having a stolen day off, a day of playing hooky.

When Regan opened the entry door, she was surprised to discover, although the house she was previewing was definitely a Santa Cruz property with a Santa Cruz asking price, the vacant home looked like a Carmel listing.

Home staging was becoming more and more popular in Santa Cruz in high-end homes, and local home-staging companies proliferated. Because the stakes were so high, high-end homeowners would spend whatever their real estate agent and stager recommended. Tastefully done, staging might easily net a tenfold return on every dollar spent to present a home in a favorable way.

As the market sagged, the practice was finding its way into more modestly priced properties as well, especially vacant houses that would otherwise look sterile and uninviting. Still, in homes priced just under a million dollars, like the property she was previewing, it was unusual to see a house so elegantly and completely staged as this one was.

Most low and mid-range sellers had a somewhat more modest fix-up budget and couldn't expect to gain as much from their investment, so homes were staged accordingly. In this price range, usually only the living room, dining room, and master bedroom were decorated. Even those rooms would often be only partially done. A few pieces would be added for color impact to give a potential buyer a sense of what could be, and how their furniture might be arranged.

But this home was flawlessly and completely staged with phenomenal attention to detail, with expensive attention to detail. This homeowner must have authorized a comprehensive staging at the behest of their Carmel agent.

The entire interior had been freshly painted a neutral beige so it looked clean and expansive. Then a few walls had been painted contrasting colors to give the rooms punch. A use had been assigned to each of the three bedrooms, and based on those uses, the house appeared to belong to affluent empty-nesters.

The master bedroom had become an elegant retreat. It was large enough to support a sitting area in addition to the king-sized pencil-post bed, which was mounded high with thick down comforters and richly embroidered pillows.

The focal point was a stager-added fireplace, likely the kind that burned sterno instead of wood or gas, and didn't require an outside vent. It was centered in a wall-mounted antique mantel which added visual weight. There was even a small fire ablaze in the fireplace. Of course it didn't really burn anything, the logs were ceramic, but Regan wondered how they managed to keep it lit for random previews and showings.

Two delicate long-stemmed glasses, filled with what appeared to be champagne, complete with tiny bubbles caught permanently rising in the fluid-simulating resin, sat on a small table by the fireplace. Sharing the table was an array of lifelike cheese and fruit on a wooden tray. The realistic tidbits looked like they were ready for nibbling.

A book, turned page-side down to preserve the reader's place, rested on one of the cushy chairs that flanked the table. Reading glasses rested nearby. A sumptuous throw was draped over a chair arm in case the reader needed more warmth than the small fire could provide.

The second bedroom was staged as an office, complete with sleek furnishings. It held all the latest electronic toys and a laptop open and turned on with a screensaver showing colorful tropical fish swimming in an aquarium.

On the desk, a copy of the *Wall Street Journal* was open to the stock market pages and several stock symbols were highlighted. Stock picks that were expected to do well? Regan chuckled. She resisted the temptation to see exactly which stocks the stager had marked.

The final bedroom had become an exercise room. The stager had added a small glass-door refrigerator, stocked it with designer bottled water, and placed an attractive bowl filled with energy bars on top of it.

Workout equipment was arranged in appropriate order so the exerciser could first work his upper body, move to the next piece of equipment for a leg workout, and finally mount a treadmill for a cardio-vascular workout. A fresh towel was looped over the handle of the treadmill, ready to wipe imaginary perspiration from the neck of its imaginary user.

But it was the dining room that truly dazzled her. Not only was the dining room table set, it had a theme; it appeared to be ready for twenty guests who came to participate in a bridal shower. She guessed that number had been chosen to show how spacious the dining room was, and the bridal theme had been selected because of the happy time and positive emotions it would suggest in the minds of potential buyers.

Amazing how real it all seemed. She had never seen anything so perfectly staged to evoke a mood. Unless told the house was vacant, a visitor would think it was enjoyably occupied by well-to-do, fit owners who kept a meticulously perfect house, had a comfortable, interesting, even romantic life, and had just stepped out for a second so as not to disturb the potential buyers, who could, if only they made a suitable offer, assume their very desirable lifestyle.

Regan smiled and shook her head. "Incredible," she said out loud. The house established a reality of lives for people who didn't exist, work that wasn't actually being done, and a party that wasn't really happening.

Her smile slowly vanished.

All the parts fit together to make up an event that didn't really occur either. Sleeping pills that weren't really taken. A dizzy spell that didn't actually happen. And a fall that couldn't have caused a sugar bowl to smash in Mrs. Rosemont's left hand.

Regan gripped the corner of the dining room table. She was finally certain Mrs. Rosemont's death could never be considered natural. The accident that ended Eleanor Rosemont's life had been staged as carefully as this house.

Her listing presentation at the Bridgemanns was a disaster. Most of Regan's business came from referrals and returning clients who needed her services as their lives and housing needs changed over time. She didn't do much self-promotion and consequently didn't get as many opportunities to go on listing presentations with new clients as some of the high profile names in town. She wasn't as practiced or as scripted as some of them were.

Even so, when she got face to face with potential clients, she usually did well. She was more interested in listening to what each client needed than in bragging about how many homes she sold in the past year and what level of recognition that entitled her to within her office. Most people picked up on that and liked her. If they didn't, well, she could always try flash, too, even though it seemed a bit disrespectful to her.

But tonight she couldn't connect or impress.

She'd met the Bridgemanns at an open house a few weeks earlier. When she read their names on her sign-in sheet, she saw they were Wayne and Ruth, her parent's names. Their conversation started with names and moved quickly to mutual liking. Wayne and Ruth Bridgemann called her a few days later and asked if she would meet them when they came back from visiting his ailing parents to talk about selling their home.

Regan was well prepared for the listing presentation, and the Bridgemanns already liked her. It should have been easy for her to reinforce their connection.

But not tonight.

Tonight, Regan could hardly think or breathe, let alone continue to build on the rapport she had established with the Bridgemanns. She stammered and paused her way through her presentation. They probably considered her distant, scattered, and not up to the task of getting their house sold.

And tonight they would have been right.

When she finished fumbling through her speech and perfunctorily asked for their listing, they told her they wanted to think about it. That phrase was often the kiss of death after a presentation.

Normally, she would have asked them what they wanted to think about, and tried to find out why they were reluctant to sign the listing agreement. It was called overcoming objections. If done properly, she could often get sellers to explain what was worrying them, address the issues involved, and lead them to signing a contract.

But tonight she was grateful for the opportunity to end their meeting. She said that was fine and left immediately, anxious for the solitude of the drive home and an opportunity to think about the way Mrs. Rosemont died.

By the time she started her car, Regan already believed Eleanor Rosemont had been murdered, and was afraid she knew who had done it.

There were no signs of a struggle at the house. Eleanor's murder wasn't a random act. She hadn't surprised a burglar, for example, who over-reacted and killed her. She knew the person who ended her life.

The autopsy had found no indication Mrs. Rosemont had been restrained or forcibly given Xanax. That meant she willingly took the sleeping pills that would render her unable to defend herself, or they had been given to her without her realizing it. Most likely, she didn't know she was taking them.

Since she might have questioned the medication in pill form, it had probably been ground into a powder, which could have been added to her food. No, Regan thought. It would have been put in her tea. The hefty amount of milk and sugar Mrs. Rosemont habitually added would have masked any odd flavor the pills might have caused.

Once she accepted that Mrs. Rosemont had been murdered, it was surprisingly easy to imagine how the killer had prepared to take her life.

He would have had tea with her, probably more than once, and used those other times to plan how he was going to make her murder look like an accident.

He would have asked if he might use her bathroom one of the times he visited, which would have given him an opportunity to discreetly open the medicine cabinet and read the names of her physician and the pharmacy she used, clearly printed on any prescription medications he found there.

Then he would have manufactured a fake label, easy enough to do with a computer, a simple graphics program, a printer, and easily purchased sticky labels, and put it on a real pill bottle. His creation would be ready to plant as part of his staging.

Once he had done his simple preparation, it would only have taken another invitation and a minor distraction to provide the opportunity to put the powdered Xanax in Mrs. Rosemont's tea.

Kaivan had been visiting Mrs. Rosemont, or rather, Harry, the cat he wasn't particularly fond of, regularly. Eleanor told her they had tea during those visits. He would know her habits.

Kaivan also had access to Xanax, even a partly used bottle, ready to have its label switched. His uncle's medicine cabinet would have been the source of the pills and their container. Regan had seen Xanax there during her walkthrough. It would have been easy for him to remove it from his uncle's house, as easy as it was for him to take his uncle's computer.

Mrs. Rosemont told Regan he was coming over again soon. She remembered Eleanor saying she planned to give him Mr. Ansari's paperwork and press him to go to Iran and bring his cousin back to Santa Cruz. Kaivan had everything he needed to stage her death; Mrs. Rosemont's invitation would give him the opportunity to carry it out.

After he committed his crime, he would have put the prepared container, which he probably carried in his pocket, into her medicine cabinet for the police to discover.

Using Harry as a cover, but more significantly, saving his uncle's pills and doctoring their label, would have implied some pretty clear planning, some real premeditation on Kaivan's part.

While she reflected on what probably happened in Mrs. Rosemont's house leading up to the elderly woman's murder, Regan had managed to drive across town from the Bridgeman's east side Santa Cruz home to the far west side of town without registering the road or the cars around her. Fortunately, she hadn't collided with any pedestrians, bike riders, or vehicle drivers who didn't know what a distracted danger was maneuvering through traffic in their midst.

She was safely past the west entrance to the university, the last road into UCSC, and the last stop-signed road she needed to cross on her way home. She was in the country now, well-known territory. At this time of night she might meet one or two cars at most, headed into Santa Cruz. Regan was so familiar with the rest of the road home, unless an unfortunate deer decided this was the night to test its luck crossing the road, she could almost drive on autopilot.

In the nighttime dark of the road, made even darker and lonelier by the towering roadside trees whose interwoven branches blocked any light coming from the waning moon, Regan imagined what the last few minutes of Mrs. Rosemont's life must have been like.

In her mind, she saw Kaivan, charming as ever, even though he knew what he was about to do, calmly chatting with Mrs. Rosemont and waiting for the effects of the drug to overwhelm her. He probably let her think she had convinced him to bring his cousin to America. Regan hoped he had given her this final small gift; she would have been so pleased to think she had caused her dear friend's last wish to be fulfilled.

As the drugs began to work, Mrs. Rosemont might have said she simply couldn't keep her eyes open any longer and needed to excuse herself and get ready for bed.

He might have said goodnight then, and gone out through the kitchen door, making certain it was unlocked as he left. He could have waited in the dark, unseen in the cover of the dense pittosporum bushes along the side of her property, until she was asleep, ready to slip back inside to complete his awful task.

No, that wasn't right. When she found her, Mrs. Rosemont was still dressed as she had been during the day, in a skirt, blouse, and sweater. Regan reset the scene.

Mrs. Rosemont probably did tell Kaivan she was getting very tired and tried to excuse herself. But he would have wanted to keep her where she was a little longer.

He knew it wouldn't be much longer.

He might have talked about Harry and how he would miss visiting him while he was away. Eventually she wouldn't have been able to resist the drug. Regan imagined Mrs. Rosemont putting her head down on her arm and drifting off to sleep at the kitchen table.

Finally.

Kaivan had probably already been noting what he needed to do, to make it seem like Mrs. Rosemont was making tea alone. If he hadn't, he would have done that now.

Two teacups would make the police ask who was with her when she died, so he would have washed their tea service and put one cup and saucer away as his victim slipped deeper into her drugged sleep.

He would have left just enough implements out to make it look like Mrs. Rosemont was about to begin her preparation: the kettle on the sink, ready to be filled, the tea canister next to it, and a spoon to measure out tea leaves.

High-beam car lights, coming from the other direction, ended her nightmarish vision and brought her back to the security of her car. Her heart was pounding. She couldn't allow herself to see Kaivan actually killing Mrs. Rosemont, but she thought she knew what would have happened in the next few minutes.

Kaivan would have picked up her tiny unconscious body and thrust her down so her head struck the counter edge with great force. Would he have been overcome by what he had done? Would it have been a struggle for him to set the stage so everything looked like an accident? Or would he have been detached, dispassionately analyzing what would make the scene believable?

He probably broke the cup next. They were such delicate cups, he must have been surprised when the handle remained intact. Would he have avoided her eyes as he put the handle in her hand and closed her fingers around it? Would he have even noticed her unseeing gaze, Regan shivered, or just been pleased that the handle hadn't broken, considering it a boon, something to make the staged accident look more real?

Then he must have decided her accidental fall would

look more convincing to the police if they thought both of Mrs. Rosemont's hands were full when she lost her balance, and he smashed the sugar bowl to make it seem that way.

Regan had built quite a crime scene in her mind and made Kaivan a murderer. But it worked. In fact, it was hard for her to come to any other conclusion.

What did they always say on those TV detective shows? Motive, opportunity, and means? Was that it? She thought so. Kaivan had the opportunity and seemed to be the only one with the means. But what was his motive? If he did commit such a terrible crime, he must have had a powerful motive for doing so. What could have caused him to decide Mrs. Rosemont had to meet such a pitiless fate?

Regan was almost home. She made the turn off Empire Grade Road. In another minute she reached their quarter-mile-long driveway, and could make out the first string of lights welcoming her home. Many Christmas seasons ago, she and Tom had bedecked the fence along their driveway with tiny white lights. They liked the effect so well, they left them up. Then they added additional strings to outline the low white fence and arbor that separated the front garden from the guest parking area.

The driveway fence lights were on an automatic sensor which turned them on as soon as it registered complete darkness, and turned them off three hours later.

The lights on the fence and arbor, near the house, could only be turned on from a switch inside. Whenever one of them wasn't home by dark, the other turned on the lights to welcome the anticipated spouse. The lights were their way of reminding one another they were home now and eagerly awaited by a loving partner.

Regan drove around a small curve in their long driveway and down the final incline. The brightly-festooned arbor and fence came into view. She was especially grateful to see the lights on tonight: they meant Tom was home, waiting for her. She was anxious to see him and tell him her theory. Maybe he could supply a motive.

Better yet, maybe he could find a flaw in her reasoning which would exonerate Kaivan. She wanted to be wrong — even though she was afraid she wasn't.

20

Tom was in the kitchen, sitting at the breakfast bar, reading the newspaper, a beer in his hand. Regan could smell pizza in the oven.

"Do we have a new listing?" he asked

"Probably not. I blew the listing presentation, big time."

"You sound like me, ever the pessimist about how I did. And you'll get over it, just like I do, when the sellers sign the listing agreement."

Regan got a soda out of the refrigerator.

"No, I really blew it." She was unequivocal. "Not only will they not be listing their house with me, right now they're also probably calling everyone they know, warning them to avoid me.

"Just before the listing appointment started, I decided Kaivan killed Mrs. Rosemont, so I was a bit distracted," she said matter-of-factly.

"Well, I guess so!" he exclaimed emphatically. It was good he had swallowed before she spoke, or he might have spewed out his last mouthful of beer. "And just why did you decide that?"

She explained why she believed Kaivan was a murderer of delightful elderly ladies. Tom didn't interrupt her with questions or say anything as she went through her thesis point by point, counting out each step on an extended finger for added emphasis. Regan finished her theorizing and soda at about the same time.

"Hum," he exhaled. "That's all pretty interesting." Tom paused for a moment. "But why did he do it?"

"That's what I haven't figured out, yet," a somewhat sheepish note crept into her voice. "Do you think we should call Dave and tell him what I have so far?"

She anticipated the answer Tom gave her. "Let's wait on that for a little while," he winked.

"You're right, I suppose," she sighed. "I can just hear him."

She shifted her posture and voice to Dave mode. "So you think the little old lady was murdered because you don't like the way the sugar bowl broke, and because she took the same kind of sleeping pills as the guy next door? Oh! Oh! And don't forget the accomplice, Harry the cat." She made an elaborate rolling flourish with her right hand and then threw both hands in the air. "Quick, somebody, call the DA."

Tom was laughing as she finished her impersonation, and so was Regan.

"That's a great impression you do of him."

"It is, isn't it?"

The buzzer sounded. Tom folded the paper, which he had given up all hope of reading, and put it down on the counter. He took the pizza out of the oven and began cutting it into wedges as Regan opened a prepackaged salad combo, lazy person's salad was her name for it, and dumped the contents into a glass bowl.

"Saying it out loud does make my theory sound kind of lame," she said, verbalizing doubt not heard in her voice. "But I believe that is the way it happened. I'm just going to have to find some real evidence to prove it."

Her voice sounded doubtful and her smile was tentative as she added, "I guess a motive would be helpful, too." Regan poured herself more soda and got another beer out of the refrigerator for Tom.

"Motive is key," Tom said. "Remember how frustrated you were with Dave and the police when they seemed ready to tie Kaivan to his uncle's death, with what you thought were only the flimsiest of motives? Kaivan may have had the means and the opportunity to kill Mrs. Rosemont, but why on earth would he do it?"

"I don't have an answer to that question, not even a bad answer," Regan said. "I just know," she hesitated, "well, feel, I'm right."

"Your hypothesis must have a fatal flaw in it somewhere. It seems to me you're trying to make something fit that has other easier explanations. The authorities certainly seem to think so. You see murder where they see an accident. Cars have four wheels, but not all vehicles with four wheels are cars, that sort of thing."

Tom's tone was somber, "Still, the weird thing about it is, if you are right about the pieces of your theory…well then…let's just say the mechanics of it hang together pretty well. On the face of it, your death scene drama

221

seems…plausible," he admitted reluctantly.

"If you accept that Kaivan did kill Mrs. Rosemont, it follows he's dangerous. And since we don't know why he did it — if he did it, and that's an awfully big if — he's potentially even more dangerous. He's kind of like a land mine that's waiting unseen, below the surface, ready to do a lot of damage unexpectedly. We don't know what pressure point might set him off.

"You can play private investigator if you want to, but just to be safe, you have to promise me you won't be alone with Kaivan while you do it, OK?"

Regan shrugged.

"But, and please don't take this the wrong way, sweetheart, I'm getting a little worried about you. I know how upsetting it was for you to find Mrs. Rosemont the way you did, and I know you haven't been sleeping that well. I think you ought to ask Dave if he has the names of some grief counselors, or people who help victims of crimes, whatever you'd call them. I think you should talk to one of them."

"Suppose I agree I won't eat or drink anything if Kaivan is within one hundred yards of me," she joked, deliberately trying to lighten both their moods. "I won't give him any opportunity to slip me a Mickey. Let me look into a couple of things, questions I have that need answers, things I should do that won't put me anywhere near Kaivan. After I do my research, if I'm still the only one who thinks he killed Eleanor, I'll back off my big murder conspiracy theory and start going to Black Helicopters Anonymous meetings. I promise."

🏠🏠🏠🏠🏠🏠🏠🏠🏠🏠🏠

Mr. Ansari's trust was expertly done. It was easy to move through escrow this time, since all the inspections had been completed before, and all the disclosures had been reviewed previously. Arlene was able to draw up a single-page directive to transfer all the documents and agreements that Mr. Ansari and the Beltrans had signed to the new escrow.

Stephanie and Ed were spared from re-signing the seventeen, often multi-paged disclosures required by the state, the four required by the city, and the six-page packet required as part of Kiley & Associates Real Estate.

Their mortgage broker put together a new loan package that didn't require their starting from scratch, either. The stock market took a newsworthy tumble the week before, affecting interest rates; and he skillfully locked the new loan at a rate one-quarter percent lower than their original loan. Stephanie and Ed were ecstatic.

"This is all great news," Ed beamed, once again seated at a conference table at the escrow company, this time for their second signoff.

"And the baby is sleeping through the night," Stephanie whispered, eyeing their son who was in his baby carrier, happily watching a string of bright plastic butterflies strung above his head that fluttered whenever he moved.

Regan produced a bottle of Roederer Brut champagne from her briefcase and handed it to them. "This is a long time coming," she said merrily.

"I bet we set some sort of record, you know, the longest sale you ever had," Ed laughed.

"A closing postponed from early February to late March? You're not even close," Regan said. "What happened with you wasn't just a minor blip, but it's no record breaker."

"It certainly isn't," Arlene chimed in. "Regan, did you know the transaction you've always said is your record for longest escrow, is also mine?"

"I didn't until just this second," Regan quipped.

"Let's see if I remember it all." Arlene paused to remember the facts. "The Buddhist group was buying a property on Mission Hill, near Holy Cross Church, right near the site of the original Mission Santa Cruz, from a very religious woman who had once been a sister, and whose sisters were all nuns. I mean her birth sisters, not her former nun sisters," Arlene waved her hand in front of her face as if to dispel any confusion.

"Well, anyway, the owner died during escrow, and we all thought her executer, who was a devout and very conservative Catholic gentleman, would never let the sale happen. He was getting a lot of pressure from the sisters — nuns, not sister sisters — who had been acquaintances of the owner, to let the church have the property.

"But the owner had told a friend of hers that she was happy about the sale to 'her little Buddhists.' She had planned on donating the proceeds to the church, so her will specified that, but she said she was glad the Buddhists would make her property a beautiful meditation retreat. The friend came forward and convinced the executor to honor the owner's wishes, so the sale went forward.

"It took quite a while though, about six months if I remember correctly. Is that about the way it went?" Arlene asked.

"You have a great memory, Arlene. Except for the required archeological investigation of the site, the historic preservation issues that had to be resolved, and the fact that the Buddhists' loan didn't work out the way it was supposed to — yes, that's about right," Regan chuckled.

"Oh my gosh," Arlene said, putting her hand over her mouth in mock horror, "you didn't tell me about any of that during escrow."

"You work on a need-to-know basis. Aren't you glad?" Regan added cheerfully.

Stephanie picked up the bottle of champagne. "I'm glad our escrow took so long to close. I can have some of this now that I'm not pregnant anymore. I thought our situation was so unique, but listening to you two, you do make it sound like a death in the middle of all this," Stephanie swished her hand over the documents, "isn't that unusual."

"I don't know, maybe one in every four or five hundred transactions, someone dies during it," Arlene guessed.

"This is the third one I've been involved in," Regan added. "No. No, it's only the second. In the other one I was thinking of, one of the owners was already dead. It was just that we found his ashes in the middle of the process," she said, a devilish grin on her face.

"It seems his widow put the urn under his favorite recliner chair and forgot about it, since she never used his chair. The housecleaner I hired to get the house ready for showing found it when she moved the chair to clean. I remember there was screaming involved, but the widow was very glad to have found her husband again." Regan laughed heartily.

Stephanie's eyes got very big. "Not really? You're just making that up, aren't you?"

Regan laughed again. "Maybe, maybe not," she said as she raised one eyebrow for dramatic effect. "I'll never tell." But of course she wasn't making it up.

The abbreviated paperwork was signed, and Regan and her group were just saying their goodbyes in the lobby when Kaivan strode in.

They hadn't had a direct conversation since Regan decided he must have killed Mrs. Rosemont. She had called him several times, steeling herself before each call to sound normal and friendly. Miraculously, or maybe because she called him very early in the morning, she always got his answering machine.

Since she knew she wasn't good at thinking on her feet, especially when she was hiding something and could be thrown by an unexpected phone question, she spent the next couple of days screening her calls to make sure his replies always went to her answering machine. Finally, he gave up playing phone tag and did what business they needed to do, via fax and email.

Seeing him unexpectedly made Regan catch her breath, but all realtors are actors, and she managed an even, "Hello, Kaivan," and a reasonable smile.

She couldn't control her cheeks though, and she was sure they flushed. She wasn't sure if her blush was because she felt guilty for suspecting Kaivan, or because of the rising anger she felt toward him, now that she believed he had killed Mrs. Rosemont. In either case, controlling inappropriately-timed high color wasn't one of her mastered skills.

To cover and to escape, she quickly looked at her watch, exclaimed she was already late for her next appointment, said a couple of hasty goodbyes, and dashed out the door. She pulled out her cell phone for effect as she went, pretending to be calling her next appointment to tell them she was running late.

Once outside, she held the cell phone to her ear and turned for a last wave at the assembled group. No one waved back. They were all too busy talking to one another to notice her. All except for Kaivan. He was staring at her. Staring hard.

21

For all her theories, Regan still had only guesswork and a somewhat fanciful stringing-together of purely circumstantial evidence to suggest Mrs. Rosemont's death hadn't been an accident. What she needed was some compelling support for her reasoning before calling Dave or Detective Bellingham with her murder scenario.

What she needed to do first, was find out whether or not Mrs. Rosemont's physician had given her a prescription for Xanax. It was an absolutely crucial point. If the medication had been prescribed, and Eleanor had misled her, her entire theory fell apart. Just like that. Done.

It would have simply been a curious coincidence that Mrs. Rosemont took the same sleeping pills as her next-door neighbor. And she would owe Kaivan an apology, at least a cerebral one.

If, on the other hand, she could confirm Mrs. Rosemont didn't take sleeping medication, well, it might not be time to talk to Detective Bellingham, but it would certainly be time to buy Dave some more coffee.

Regan didn't know who Mrs. Rosemont's doctor was,

but she had an idea how to figure that out.

Much as she hated the process, her plan was to revive the all-but-banished real estate practice of cold calling likely prospects.

Years had passed since she had participated in a cold calling session. At the Century 21 office, where she worked with Kaivan, there was an annual ritual of agents getting together on the first workday of the new year to call all the owners whose properties hadn't sold the year before and whose listing contracts were now past their expiration date, making it ethical for other realtors to woo them.

All the expired listings for the entire county were already compiled by the time the agents arrived at the office. The agents did a military count off: one, two, three, four, until each agent had a number. Then the pool list was similarly divided and the calling began.

The goal for the agents was to set appointments with the homeowners to pitch why they would be able to sell their property when the seller's last agent hadn't been able to.

The company provided donuts and coffee, and later in the day, pizza and soda to help create what they hoped would be a festive atmosphere, and more probably, to keep everyone a little buzzed on sugar and caffeine.

To help maintain everyone's enthusiasm during what could be a grueling process, agents were encouraged to yell out "I got one!" whenever a seller agreed to meet with them.

All the agents knew that properties occasionally didn't sell because the last agent did a terrible job of marketing, or because the listing agent was considered a pariah within the real estate community and other agents avoided showing their listings. But the preponderance of houses hadn't sold because they were overpriced. That, of course, wasn't what the frustrated homeowners wanted to hear.

The real estate agents asked scripted questions to make sure they heard all the other reasons the homeowners had devised to explain why their houses were still unsold. There were many excuses and complaints mentioned, but they always ended with "It was my agent's fault."

The calling agent's job was to encourage the would-be seller to grumble while they listened and sympathized. By the time the seller had finished venting, the agent would have plenty of information to exploit. After that, it was pretty easy to tell the homeowner how different an agent they were from that terrible, lazy, useless salesperson who hadn't worked hard at all for the want-to-be seller.

They'd start by empathizing, "I can certainly understand how frustrated you must be." Then the agent would explain, "One of the things I think is most important to get your house sold is (fill in the blank)." The blank, of course, was whatever the seller said their former agent hadn't done or hadn't done right. Pricing was never discussed over the phone.

Finally, the agent would politely say, "I know my plan will get your house sold. My whole company is committed to helping me do it. Could I come by and show you what I will do differently?"

If the seller said "yes", as soon as the phone hit the cradle, a huge "I got one!" would echo throughout the office.

Regan hated cold calling and had stopped doing it as her business grew and became mostly repeat and referred clients, but she knew how to make those calls if she had to. All she needed to track down Mrs. Rosemont's doctor was a list, patience, and a good script.

Regan got out the phone book and turned to the list of physicians. She started with doctors who specialized in family practice, geriatrics, and internal medicine. They were her expired listings, the most likely types of physicians to have seen Mrs. Rosemont.

Next, she planned exactly what she would say, even taking the time to write out her script and practice it until she didn't need it anymore. Confident she could make her questions sound natural and genuine, she dialed the first office.

"Hello, my name is Nora Rosemont. I hope you can help me. My mom has just had a stroke, and I'm trying to find out who her doctor is. We can't find any record of a doctor's phone number in her address book, and right now she can't tell us who to call, but I think I remember her saying her doctor was (fill in the blank). Is Eleanor Rosemont a patient there?"

She was all the way down the alphabet to Dr. Samantha Simpson before she got a hit.

"Just a moment please, let me check. How do you spell the last name," the sympathetic medical receptionist asked.

"R-O-S-E-M-O-N-T," Regan spelled slowly.

"Yes, she is Dr. Simpson's patient."

"Does the doctor have office hours on Saturday? I'm eager to speak to her in person. Would it be possible for me to come in and see her tomorrow for just a few minutes?"

"Doctor could see you at the end of the day. I'll schedule you for five o'clock, but you might have to wait if she's running late. Is that OK?"

"That will work very well. Thank you so much for your help." As she hung up, Regan resisted the urge to yell, "I got one!"

Doctor Samantha Simpson looked like she could have been a movie star if she hadn't become an MD. She had large expressive eyes, flawless creamy skin, long thick blond hair, and the widest, most perfect beauty-queen smile Regan had seen in a very long time. She was also extremely well endowed and not embarrassed to show off her ample cleavage. She wore the traditional white doctor coat, but had it partly unbuttoned to reveal a low-cut, stretch-jersey top in a bold red and orange print.

Regan focused on the friendliness of the young doctor's smile, deemed her open-minded, and made the decision to drop her daughter-stroke story line and tell Dr. Simpson the real reason she had requested a meeting. The truth was always so much easier to tell.

"Dr. Simpson, thank you for seeing me. I'll try to take as little of your time as possible and come right to the point. I lied to your receptionist to get in to see you. I'm not Eleanor Rosemont's daughter, and she hasn't had a stroke."

"Yes, I know that." The smile didn't lessen at all. "I do find time to read the newspaper and I know my patient's names quite well, so I know what happened to her. In any event, Eleanor was a memorable lady, not a person to be easily forgotten after a busy day. And she was childless."

If it was possible, Dr. Simpson's smile became even broader. "Why don't you tell me what this is really all about, and why you felt the need to tell such a big fib to get in to see me?"

"I became Eleanor's friend recently, and I'm the one who found her…" Regan hesitated for a second, "body. There were no signs of foul play, and her death appeared to have been caused by a fall, so the police thought it was an accident."

"But you don't? Is that it?"

"I don't know. That's why I'm here. I'm having doubts, doubts that you can lay to rest, if you can tell me about a prescription she may have been taking."

"You must know I can't discuss my patient's medical history with you." The smile faded ever so slightly.

"Yes, I know that." Regan acknowledged the statement, but moved right along. "An autopsy was conducted, and Mrs. Rosemont was found to have a heavy dose of sleeping pills in her system when she died. She told me she never took anything to help her sleep because she got regular exercise and was in such good shape."

"Oh, that does sound like Eleanor," Doctor Simpson laughed, "but I still can't, and won't, discuss her medical history with you." She remained friendly, but made it extremely clear she wasn't going to compromise her position.

Regan persisted. "The police found a half-empty prescription for Xanax in her medicine cabinet. That's one of the reasons they think her death was an accident. They theorize she took her pills but didn't go right to bed. Instead, they think she decided to climb the little stepstool she had to get things out of her high kitchen cupboards, got dizzy because of the medication, and fell, hitting her head on the tile counter with enough force to kill her."

A fleeting, slight frown wrinkled Dr. Simpson's forehead at the mention of Xanax. Regan caught the momentary change in the doctor's expression and played her final card. "The prescription for Xanax had your name on it, just like her other prescriptions," Regan said, assuming knowledge she didn't have.

"The authorities should always contact the prescribing physician whenever they suspect a medication contributed to the death of an individual. I was never contacted by the police." For the first time, Dr. Simpson's smile was gone. "I don't know whether that was sloppy work on their part, or whether you are lying to me again."

Regan didn't answer the doctor directly, instead she moved on quickly. "Doctor, I understand you must preserve Mrs. Rosemont's privacy. I'm not asking you to discuss her medical history, or to tell me what medications she was taking, or even anything about the state of her health. I think she was murdered. I think someone gave her sleeping pills to sedate her and then killed her. I think they made her death look like an accident." Regan was surprised at how emotional she had become.

"I keep remembering her on the floor in her kitchen." The pitch of her voice rose, "I'm suspecting a friend of mine of doing this horrible thing, and it may be only my imagination. It's just that I so clearly remember Eleanor emphatically telling me she didn't take sleeping pills.

"Maybe she did. Maybe none of what I'm afraid happened to her is real. Please, you don't have to tell me what medicine she *was* taking. Can't you just tell me," Regan spaced out the last five words of her sentence and emphasized each of them, "if she wasn't taking Xanax?"

Doctor Simpson stared at her for what felt like a full minute. She said nothing, she didn't move. Was this the way the interview would end? Finally, still without a word, the doctor turned away from Regan and tapped on the computer keyboard on her desk.

"If the authorities had checked with me, I would have told them I never prescribed Xanax or any other sleeping medication for Eleanor Rosemont. And, just so you know, Xanax is contra-indicated for patients of Mrs. Rosemont's age. No competent physician would prescribe Xanax for her."

22

Regan would have willingly broken her own rule about not driving and talking on her cell phone, even while she maneuvered up the twisty road toward home, but the granite underlayment and hilly surround interfered with most cell phone transmissions in Bonny Doon. She had to wait until she got home to tell Tom about her interview with Dr. Simpson.

"What do you think? Should I call Dave now?" Regan concluded with a question for Tom. She had barely paused to breathe as she recounted what she had discovered; she was still on the adrenalin high that began in the doctor's office.

"Dr. Simpson said they would need to subpoena her and her records before she would testify in court, but she will confirm she didn't prescribe Xanax for Mrs. Rosemont when the police call her.

"I sure do pity the officer who has to make that call, though. The doctor was very upset that the police hadn't questioned her about Mrs. Rosemont's use of a prescription medication when they thought it had caused her death.

She's going to have a lot to say about — and I'm quoting here — 'lazy, sloppy police work' when she gets that call."

Tom poured more after-dinner coffee into Regan's cup. She signaled 'enough' before it was half full.

"I hope they won't make Dave do it," Regan said through a small but very mischievous grin.

"I'm amazed at the change in you. You have become quite the caped avenger lately," he said, as he refilled his own cup. "You seem to be savoring the prospect of bringing down Kaivan, and even relishing poor Dave taking a shot in the ear. I know how much you like Dave, and it wasn't that long ago that you were Kaivan's defender. I thought these guys were your friends."

"The phone call probably won't fall to Dave, but if it does, he can handle pretty much anything. And Dr. Simpson is right, the police should have closed that loop. If they had her name from the pill bottle, how hard would it have been for one of them to pick up a phone? And if the Xanax prescription wasn't from Dr. Simpson, who was obviously Mrs. Rosemont's regular physician, they really should have made a call to the doctor who prescribed it, to find out why the change in her routine. One call could have changed so much." There was melancholy in her voice as she said it.

"Kaivan is quite another story," Regan sighed. Her rush was finally dissipating and she was suddenly overcome with fatigue and sadness. She added milk and sugar to her coffee and continued to stir it distractedly long after it was thoroughly blended. "This must be what it feels like to be a jilted wife whose friends tell her that her husband is having an affair, but who refuses to see what's going on.

"I really do…really did," she reluctantly put Kaivan's friendship in the past, "like him, even admired him. But if he killed Mrs. Rosemont in the way I think he did, he had to do a lot of thinking and planning before he acted. It's not like he committed a crime of passion in a moment of extreme stress. That kind of deliberate calculation and the actual carrying out of murder against such a defenseless old woman…" she shook her head. "There's no way to make excuses for him.

"He's been a friend, someone I've talked to and felt comfortable with. I can't reconcile Kaivan, as I think of him, with someone brutal enough to have killed Mrs. Rosemont. How could I have been so wrong about him? I feel betrayed and foolish, and so angry with myself — and with him. I must never have really known him at all."

"You know, we still don't have a motive for why he killed her," Tom said. "At least, I don't. How about you?"

"Umm", Regan hesitated, shaking her head slightly, "I guess because she knew about Mr. Ansari's son, and he didn't want her telling anyone about him."

"I don't buy that. Why would he care if she did, especially now that his uncle is dead?"

"I don't know, maybe to protect his uncle's reputation? Maybe to maintain his standing in the family? Something like that."

"You realize you've turned Kaivan from a calculating murderer into a regular Victorian gentleman in less than a minute? Shielding a reputation might be a reason for murder, if the person with something to hide was in a position of power or faced a tangible loss if his guilty secret came out; but that situation doesn't fit Cyrus Ansari, does it?"

Regan had to admit it didn't, and silently shook her head no.

"I could see killing a blackmailer, too, but you don't think that was what was going on here, do you?"

"Oh, no. I do believe Mrs. Rosemont and Cyrus Ansari were dear friends, just like she said. She wouldn't have been using his son to blackmail him."

Regan sighed, "I thought if I got confirmation about Mrs. Rosemont not having a prescription for Xanax, I'd be ready to tell Dave my theory and ask him if it was time to bring in the police. I'm sure Mrs. Rosemont was murdered, and I still believe Kaivan killed her, but I'm not any closer to understanding why than I was before, and honestly, I don't want him to be a murderer. I still keep hoping I've missed something that would clear him.

"I don't know what to do. Accusations have a way of making headlines, but retractions wind up in a tiny single column in Section B. You remember what happened when the O'Learys were arrested for growing pot on a remote part of the two acre property they had just bought?"

Tom nodded.

"The arrest was a front-page story in the *Sentinel*, but the 'Oops, they only owned the property for two weeks, and the plants were months old' appeared below the fold on page twelve."

"It's that old cliché about unringing a bell," Tom said.

"That's it exactly. I think it would be unconscionable to

publicly accuse Kaivan of something he didn't do. Maybe I better hold off on that call to Dave, at least until after the weekend, and try harder to come up with a motive. If Kaivan did kill Mrs. Rosemont, he must have done it for a very specific reason. It's not like he's a serial killer getting ready to murder again. Society will be safe for a while if I don't say anything right away."

It was late and she yawned.

"You look awfully tired to me," Tom said.

"Try exhausted. It's been a very emotionally charged day. I'm going to sleep on all this. Maybe I can figure it out in the morning, when I'm rested and sharp."

"Speaking of tomorrow, do you have anything besides sleuthing scheduled, any open houses or showings?"

"No, I'm free to be a full-time sleuth."

"Can I ask a favor then?"

"Have you scheduled yourself to be in two places at once again?"

"Not at all. You're the one who does that, not me. I have an open house ad running in the newspaper for the Sunlit Lane house, and I've put an ad for it online, so there has to be an open house; but my old friend Jim Petersen called just before you got in tonight. He's going to be in town tomorrow and Monday, and thinks he wants to buy a beach house. I'd like to show him what's available."

"After a nice round of golf?"

"Hey, there are some great listings in Rio Del Mar and Seascape. We'll be right in the neighborhood if we play at the Seascape course. I was able to get us a nine-forty-five tee time — which I can cancel, of course, if you're busy,"

23

Regan managed to stay asleep until three in the morning. After that, periodic checks of her bedside clock told her, tired as she was, her agitated mind was refusing her any more rest.

At first she lay very still, staring out the bedroom windows at the surrounding redwood trees. Their branches danced lightly to the melody of a night breeze.

She replayed every conversation she had with Mrs. Rosemont, looking for some phrase, some clue she overlooked before, hoping to find a motive for murder hidden there. Then she thrashed.

It was getting windier outside. The branches were becoming more agitated; a storm was coming. But even amid the increasing wind gusts, the branches still moved less than she tossed.

Finally, she accepted this would be another night when sleep mostly eluded her. She gave up, got up, and headed for the kitchen.

Harry was adjusting to life in the country pretty well. He hadn't had any run-ins with coyotes or other wild critters, but he seemed to need the security of sleeping in their bedroom at night.

Their cat, Cinco, a small, mostly black female, who looked like she had been rescued from a head-first fall into a bucket of milk that left her with residual white stains on her chest, front paws, and chin, wasn't thrilled about sharing her special space. She slept in bed with them, occasionally *on* one of them, but usually discreetly, only making quick movements when a brazen raccoon peered in one of their windows.

With the indoor addition of Harry, Cinco had taken to defending her territory by running around the edges of the bed whenever Harry moved. But sometimes she felt the need to get from one side to the other more quickly than going around the perimeter allowed, and one or both of them got trampled awake.

Harry finally realized he better keep a low profile if he was going to be allowed to sleep in the same bedroom as his three housemates. He accepted a small corner of the room, far away from their bed, as his area, and was careful not to move around much at night to keep from setting off Cinco, but he was still watchful.

When Regan got up, he followed her to the kitchen, meowing softly.

"When all else fails, Harry, make tea," she told him. She gave the kettle a light shake. There was enough water in it for her sole cup of tea. She put the kettle on the stove without emptying it and getting fresh water. Mrs. Rosemont would never do that.

The moon was close to full, resplendent in reflected

sunlight, and shone brightly through the windows of the kitchen. She had no need to turn on the lights; there was enough illumination for her to see what she was doing.

There was even enough moonlight to read the black numbers against the white background of the kitchen wall clock. 4:30.

Moments later, she caught the kettle just before it began to sound. Mrs. Rosemont wouldn't have approved.

She plunked a teabag into the cup which she perpetually kept on the counter and reused after a quick rinse-out. She added Equal instead of sugar, and no milk. Mrs. Rosemont wouldn't have approved of any of that, either. She bounced the teabag up and down in the not-quite-boiling water about a dozen times, and pronounced her beverage ready enough. She smiled to herself. Mrs. Rosemont would have been absolutely distraught at such lackadaisical tea preparation.

"Come on, Harry. Let's go find a good thinking spot in the living room. You can sit on my lap, if you like. It'll be nice sitting in the dark and then watching the sunrise begin, if we're still up when it does."

They settled on the sofa, facing where the sun would embark on a new day's journey, Regan sipping her tea and petting the cat, and Harry purring contentedly on her lap.

She had been so certain she understood Kaivan, especially when it came to what mattered to him, and what he was and wasn't capable of doing, that she had ignored all she knew about empathizing and thinking like the person she was trying to understand. Instead of neutrally observing his behavior, she had tried to make his actions fit

245

her idea of how he would behave. That had been her downfall.

If she was going to come up with why he killed Mrs. Rosemont, she had to figure out Kaivan's motivation, and she couldn't have any preconceived notions.

Regan decided to try thinking about him like she would a couple involved in an acrimonious divorce. Although most duos had a mutual goal they wanted to achieve and responded to apparent positives in a contract, angrily divorcing couples might not do that at all. Sometimes each of the splitting spouses was more interested in damaging his or her soon-to-be-ex than in getting the best deal they could for themselves. That never made any sense to her. It didn't matter. It was still her job to play to whatever moved her buyer's interests forward.

It might mean she couldn't offer encouragement when one of them said they liked some of the terms of the offer, usually a good technique. Instead she would have to remain carefully neutral so it wouldn't seem she was taking sides.

Since she always tried to establish rapport as she worked, it was counterintuitive not to engage someone who was giving her positive feedback. But she had learned it was sometimes absolutely necessary to put aside what made her comfortable and what seemed reasonable, in order to understand what motivated someone else. It was often the only way to get the result she wanted.

Regan believed people were consistent in their behavior and didn't act randomly or without thought. People always had reasons for doing what they did. Determining their reasons and using them to her client's advantage was an art, a dance, one that she did very well. She should be able to do that with Kaivan, too.

It was a given that Mrs. Rosemont represented a threat to him. There could be no other reason why he felt he needed to end her life. What did Mrs. Rosemont know that could threaten him? What did Mrs. Rosemont know that no one else knew? What did Mrs. Rosemont know? Wasn't that the title of an Agatha Christie murder mystery? No, that was *What Mrs. Magillicuddy Saw.* Regan shook her head, hoping to remove some of the giddiness her exhaustion encouraged.

"We're getting a little loopy here, Harry. We've got to focus," she said to the cat.

"Meo-oew."

"Yes, you're quite right," Regan smiled.

The answer she was looking for must involve Mr. Ansari's son in some way. What else could it be? What did Mrs. Rosemont know about him?

Well, first, that he existed.

If Kaivan thought she was the only person besides him with that knowledge, might that have been enough to get her killed? That would have to mean that the mere knowledge of his cousin's existence could cause serious problems for him.

Initially, when Tom and Dave thought Kaivan was involved in his uncle's death, they hit on a money motive immediately. She dismissed it because she didn't think he needed money or was that enamored of it. Her investigation of his properties convinced her she was right. And since she wouldn't have been motivated by money, she felt comfortable assuming the man she knew and liked, wouldn't have been either.

Suppose that wasn't true. She might be breaking one of her cardinal rules about paying attention to what mattered to others. Could it have been her own sense of morality, rather than Kaivan's, that led her to dismiss the money in Mr. Ansari's estate as a motive for murder?

Kaivan was about to inherit all his uncle's assets. When escrow closed on Wednesday, the proceeds from the sale of the house would be added to his inheritance. With the stepped-up-basis tax rules and the way trusts work, he was going to benefit financially from the sale even more than his uncle would have.

She stopped petting Harry mid-stroke; he stopped purring to register his displeasure.

But Mr. Ansari's trust might have a clause in it about legal or unnamed issue. She remembered seeing language like that in her parent's trust. They pointed it out to her and found it very amusing. She was the only child produced during a long and faithful marriage, but her parents said their attorney asked each of them if they had any children outside of wedlock. They both were about to be offended, they said, but the attorney explained it was a standard question, one that he routinely asked all of his clients, and not to be surprised when they saw a clause designed to address unnamed issue in their final trust document.

If Mr. Ansari's trust had a clause in it like that, and Eleanor told the estate about his son, would that threaten Kaivan's inheritance? Suppose one of the papers Mrs. Rosemont found in Mr. Ansari's things modified his will and added his son to it, possibly even disinheriting Kaivan? If Kaivan thought his inheritance was going to a boy who duped his uncle into believing he was his son, would that have outraged him?

But, with no Mrs. Rosemont, Kaivan could destroy the paperwork and the existence of his cousin would never come up.

Regan needed to know if unnamed-issue clauses were regularly used, and if Mr. Ansari's trust had one.

No doubt, Arlene had a copy of the entire trust in her escrow files. Never a patient person, Regan was almost ready to call her right now, before five on a Sunday morning, and ask her to go to her office and find out.

She knew she didn't have Arlene's home phone number in her files, but Regan wondered if she might be listed in the phone book. She hastily disrupted Harry's resting place and went to her office to look.

Since there wasn't much moonlight in the office, she needed to close the office door so she could turn on a light without disturbing Tom, who was asleep in their bedroom down the hall. She almost caught Harry's midsection as he squeezed in just before she fully closed the door.

"Reow," he bellowed in complaint, and hissed at her for good measure.

"Shh, Harry," Regan whispered, "I'm sorry." He forgave her instantly and jumped back on her lap as soon as she sat down at her desk. He barely complained when she disturbed his position to reach down to get the phone book out of a bottom desk drawer.

Unfortunately, Arlene's last name was Smith. There

wasn't a listing for Arlene Smith, A. Smith, or any of the other ways she could think it might appear in the phone book, so it was either an unlisted number or it was under her husband's name.

The only thing that saved Arlene's sleep was Regan's faulty memory. There were a lot of Smiths in the book, and although she was sure Arlene had mentioned her husband, Regan couldn't remember his first name. That meant she would have to wait until Monday and catch her at work before she'd know anything using the Arlene route.

Then she remembered Owen Houserling's name appeared as the attorney who had prepared Mr. Ansari's trust. She recognized his name when she saw it on the preliminary title report when the Beltran's escrow started all those months ago.

Regan had smiled to herself when she recognized his name. She knew him from when they served on the Shakespeare/Santa Cruz board during the company's earlier years.

Their time on the board was before the company had become a wildly successful organization. Back then, board members were tapped to do all sorts of unpleasant but necessary grunt work at fund-raising events, in addition to their more staid networking with local well-to-do and enlightened supporters of the arts. She remembered him as an uncomplaining wine-case-mover and table-setter-upper who was willing to do hard physical work until he was sweaty.

He was also one of the two board members who saw the pornographic likelihood in a black and white proof of the season's commemorative poster when it was submitted for approval. For some reason, he and the oldest board member, a retired psychologist in her eighties, were the only two board members with enough imagination to see what the poster would become when it was printed in full color.

The rest of the board snickered as he warned them about the poster's pornographic possibilities; but their ridicule turned to scandalized shock when the printing had been paid for and the posters, known in perpetuity to all in the company as the "flying fuck posters", arrived and had to be immediately shelved.

Company members quickly helped the posters disappear. She chuckled at the memory, and wondered if some of them still had their pilfered posters. She certainly still had hers.

Regan guessed Owen Houserling wouldn't be the kind of attorney to leave his home phone number unlisted. Besides, his specialty was trusts and estate planning. He could risk it, she smiled to herself, confident he wouldn't have to deal with too many middle-of-the-night emergency questions.

"If only he knew the danger he's in at this very moment," she told Harry.

A quick flip through the phone book proved her guess correct.

She could start by calling him and asking if he recalled whether or not Mr. Ansari's trust or will had a provision for unnamed issue. It was a long shot that he'd remember exact details off-hand, since it had been several years since he created the trust, but it was something she could do, if not immediately, at least before Monday.

Maybe, like her parent's attorney, Owen would tell her he always put language like that in the trusts he set up.

If there was such a clause, it might truly be time to get Dave involved. He would be interested if she went back to his still-favorite premise that money was always a good motive for murder. She might be able to tie everything together well enough, at that point, to suggest Kaivan as Mrs. Rosemont's murderer. She could explain he had to keep Mrs. Rosemont quiet in order to protect his inheritance.

He had opportunity, means, and now a potential motive. Oh yes, Dave would be interested, especially after she told him that Mrs. Rosemont was the only person other than Kaivan who knew Mr. Ansari had a son. And then there was Dr. Simpson's evidence about Xanax. She wanted to tell him about that, too.

Now that she had a possible, plausible motive and a plan of action, she was suddenly very sleepy. "Let's go back to bed and take a catnap, Harry, since we have to wait for daylight and a respectable hour before we make that phone call, anyway."

24

Regan missed the sunrise. It was nine-thirty when she woke again, ready to tell Tom her latest idea. His side of the bed was empty.

"Tom?" she called. Her next stop was their office. "Tom, you in here?" she said as she poked her head through the doorway. The third time she called his name and got no response, she realized it was Sunday morning — he'd want to check their open house ads. He had probably gone up to their newspaper box and would be back with the Sunday *Sentinel* momentarily.

Regan made a U-turn and headed for the kitchen and coffee. It wasn't until she discovered the note Tom had left by the coffee pot, that she remembered Jim Petersen was in town, and they had golfing plans.

"Rough night?" his note asked. "You looked so peaceful this morning, I decided to let you sleep. I'll call you after the open house. Maybe you can meet Jim and me for dinner at Café Rio."

Another quick look at the clock reminded her he had probably teed off by now. He hated to be disturbed during a round of golf; he didn't even like to have his cell phone with him when he played. He had likely left it with his street shoes in his car. If he did have it with him, it would be turned off. Regan disappointedly realized she would have to wait until much later to run her current thoughts by him.

Rain was expected later in the day, and it was blustery outside, but their house was still in bright sunshine. She looked out over Monterey Bay in the direction of the Seascape Golf Club. From her vantage point she could see it was already foggy, maybe even drizzling, near the coast where Tom was playing golf. She couldn't understand the attraction of the game, especially on a day like today, but Tom was hardly alone in his devotion to the links.

Even though it was too late to reach Tom, it was still early for a Sunday morning phone call, but she couldn't wait any longer to call Owen. His phone rang several times before he answered; when he did, he insisted she wasn't disturbing him.

Regan had decided her conversation with Owen wasn't an appropriate venue to try out her theories on uninitiated ears. She'd stick to a casual script and imply nothing other than that she was a conscientious real estate agent, just doing her job. After just a few pleasantries, she got to her preplanned questioning.

"I don't know if you remember Cyrus Ansari or the specifics of the work you did for him, but you put his trust together, and I had a couple of questions for you about it. He drowned in the ocean sometime in early February. There were stories about his death in the newspaper."

"Uh-huh, I did notice the story in the *Sentinel*…sad event…he was a pleasant fellow."

"His nephew, Kaivan Nasseri, is a real estate agent and had Mr. Ansari's house listed for sale. I was representing the buyers. My clients were about to close escrow when Mr. Ansari went missing. He hadn't signed the grant deed before his death, so the sale couldn't proceed to recording. His nephew has been very accommodating; he's even let my clients move into the house, and told them he'd be able to conclude the sale soon, since everything in Mr. Ansari's estate was in order. You get credit for that, I believe," Regan complimented Owen.

"Kaivan was right about being able to move the estate settlement along quickly; we're closing this coming week. Sorry to ask on a Sunday, but I realized my client's loan will fund tomorrow morning. I've seen some title issues pop up when an important document falls into that never-never land between being submitted for recording and finally appearing in the public record.

"I guess the title companies only rely on the posted information. It can be time consuming and difficult to get them to defend against a claim, should a dispute come up, so I'm trying to protect my clients."

So far everything she said was more or less true, even though it wasn't the reason for her call.

"Mr. Ansari's nephew is his beneficiary. However, it has just come to light that Mr. Ansari has a son still living in Iran, a son he'd been estranged from until very recently. I thought it might be a good idea to ask if you remember including any language in Mr. Ansari's will or trust that provided for him, or if there had been any recent changes to the documents to include him. I want to be able to alert the escrow officer, you know, give her a heads-up that she needs to do a last-minute extra search to catch any potential problems."

"No, I'm certain there weren't any provisions for children, named or unnamed, or any changes made to his trust or his will. I reviewed them recently, too, because Mr. Ansari made an appointment with me — let's see, seems like it was in late January, early February, and I was refreshing my memory as part of preparing for it."

"He came to see you about his estate?" Regan's interest piqued.

"He made an appointment to discuss his estate, but he didn't keep it. I remember being annoyed because he didn't cancel. He just didn't show up. Then I saw the *Sentinel* story and realized he must have had his accident before our appointment date, so of course, that was why he didn't keep it."

Time to embellish the truth a bit.

"I believe the police don't think his death was an accident. They think Mr. Ansari committed suicide. He had a brain tumor and was dying. They theorize he ended his life before he became debilitated. There was also a suicide note found after the *Sentinel* article ran."

"Now, that's rather curious. You'd think he would have kept his appointment with me, either to verify his affairs were in order, or to make any changes he wanted in his will, before he ended his life."

Yes indeed, she thought, yes indeed.

"But you needn't be concerned on behalf of your clients. There were no modifications made. Mr. Ansari's will and trust stand."

That was enough for her. She thanked Owen for his help and hurriedly said goodbye. It was definitely time to call Dave. She couldn't wait for Monday, or even for Tom to finish his soggy golf game, so she could bring him up to date with what she had uncovered. Regan hit the speed dial button for Dave on her phone.

Dave answered on the second ring, so full of his usual energy that she didn't get a chance to mention her conversations with either Dr. Simpson or Owen Houserling before he started talking.

"OK, so you're calling to rub it in, aren't you? You were right and I was wrong," he said in a singsong gibe at her.

"What are you talking about?" she asked.

"Don't you watch the eleven o'clock news? You should stay informed, Regan."

"You mean last night? No, I missed it. I was…"

"Your pal Kaivan was the lead story," Dave interrupted. "There he was, all dressed up, handing one of those giant checks to the fundraising committee for that little girl with the brain tumor."

"What little girl are you talking about?"

"The little girl in the newspaper last week. She's a cute little thing. She needs treatment to save her life, but her family doesn't have medical insurance. So, yesterday and today, a bunch of friends and neighbors have been doing a fundraiser for her."

"What does that have to do with Kaivan?"

"Well, he's a hero. He turned up with this big check, kind of like a Reader's Digest award check, made out to the little girl. The check was for over $700,000. Can you believe it? He said it was in honor of his uncle who died of a brain tumor. I figure that's got to be all the money he inherited from the old man. He said he wanted to remember his uncle and do some good at the same time.

"You were right. He's a great guy. I'm going to go shake his hand and apologize, just from me, for thinking he did something to his uncle to get the old guy's money. You should have seen it. Maybe they'll rerun it. See if you can catch it."

"Dave, I wasn't calling to rub it in or tell you what a great guy Kaivan is. I was calling...because I think he killed Mrs. Rosemont. I have some evidence..."

"Who?" Dave interrupted again. "Was she the L.O.L. who lived next door to the uncle?"

"Yes. I think Kaivan killed her."

"Why would you think that? She fell and hit her head, didn't she?"

"I don't think so. I think she was killed, and her murder was made to look like an accident."

"Let me get this straight. You think she was murdered, even though the coroner ruled her death accidental?"

"That's right."

"And you think Kaivan did it?"

"Yes."

"Work with me here. Why would you think that?"

"Because the coroner found Xanax in her system. You

told me that yourself. But she didn't take sleeping pills. I can prove it. Just ask her doctor."

"You think your pal, Kaivan, killed her because she didn't take sleeping pills?"

"I think he gave her sleeping pills so he could kill her, because she knew Mr. Ansari had a son, and Kaivan thought she'd tell someone, and he might not get his inheritance." She ran on without pausing for air, relieved to finally get her theory out.

"OK then," Dave drew the words out endlessly. "So he killed her to keep the inheritance that he gave away last night? Is that about right?"

"Not when you put it like that," she said weakly.

"Just how many conspiracy-theory websites do you visit on an average day? Where do you come up with this stuff?"

He was laughing as he said it. They were good friends, but an unversed bystander might not see it that way. They sparred and teased one another mercilessly and often sounded like they had no respect for one another, which was far from true.

"Oh wait, I get it! Today is April first. Are you trying to set me up to be April-fooled?" he asked, making a verb out of the tricks people play on one another on that date.

Regan decided there was no talking to him right now.

"I'll see if I can catch the great humanitarian at noon. They usually rerun their lead stories from the night before, then," she said. "But you have to sit down with me in a serious way in the next couple of days. Do you promise you'll make time?"

"Sure. Tuesday. How about lunch at Riva's Fish House on the wharf? I always enjoy a good fish…" he waited for the count of three, "…story," he added, amid peals of laughter.

She pressed the OFF button on her phone, missing the solid old cradle phones you could slam for effect.

Regan got ready for the open house she had promised to do for Tom, wishing the whole time that they had purchased at least a few signs that accepted waterproof magic marker, instead of chalk, for writing addresses. Waterproof was the operative word. The wind was picking up and the sky was getting darker. It would start raining any minute.

That meant many unpleasant things were going to happen to her later today. She'd get wet by the time she put out directional signs to the open house. The house on Sunlit Lane was in a quiet spot, not remote, but off the main thoroughfare, with enough branching roads that she'd need to set up at least six directional signs if anyone was going to find it. She wouldn't just be wet, she'd be soaked, she imagined, already feeling sorry for herself.

And she'd be cold, at least to start. The house had an efficient heater, but the owners had moved out already, and Tom couldn't get them to leave the furnace on at a reasonable temperature, even on its timer. They argued it wasted energy. Tom tried, with only marginal success, to tell them first impressions were critical. If a potential buyer had to shiver when they came to see the house, they wouldn't think of it as a warm, inviting home.

The owners finally agreed to set the thermostat to 60 degrees. So, whenever she showed it, the house was leave-your-coat-on-cold for half an hour after she reset the thermostat to 68 degrees.

She'd probably be lonely, too. Even after putting out all the directional signs, there might not be many people at the open house. The chalked-on addresses would wash off within minutes and become nothing but runny smudges of color. Some people would follow the arrows that were pre-printed on the signs in bright red paint, but most wouldn't. If they didn't see the address they wanted on the first sign, they wouldn't realize they had found the right real estate signs to start their house hunt.

The market had slowed, too. A year ago there would have been at least a dozen groups through, even in a country location like Bonny Doon; but now, realtors were complaining they were lucky to get half that many buyers through an open house, even in town. How many would bother to brave the rain to see a country property?

No need to print more flyers; there were plenty at the house, even if ten groups came by. But she did print out a fresh sign-in sheet to capture the names and phone numbers of any hardy attendees who made it.

Tom and Regan kept sealed bags of premixed homemade cookie dough in the freezer, ready for days like today. She took out a packet and all the equipment she would need to bake cookies. There wasn't anything more welcoming than the aroma of fresh-baked chocolate chip cookies, especially on a rainy day. If people made the effort to find her open house, they would be rewarded.

Regan kept an eye on the clock as she loaded her car. She didn't want to miss the local news at noon. Everything was in the car, and she was dressed and ready to go just before the broadcast started. Regan sat down in front of the TV and clicked it on, channel hopping rapidly until she found the right station.

Kaivan's donation didn't lead the news, but it was in the top three featured stories. Coverage started with a tired looking woman with her young daughter seated next to her. The child was leaning over with her head resting in her mother's lap. The mother was telling the broadcaster that her little girl had a brain tumor that her doctors said was operable. In fact, with the right medical care, they gave her a ninety-five percent chance of survival and full recovery.

But she was a widow, the woman said, barely getting by since her husband, a civilian contractor, had been killed in a roadside bomb blast in Iraq. The young mother was without medical insurance, and the cost of treatment for her daughter was far beyond her means.

Cut to a group of people identified as family and friends. Some were waving signs announcing a car wash in one direction, a rummage sale in another. Others waved tickets they were offering for a drawing to win a 1976 green Mercedes SL, an old car that the group was trying to say was a classic. One member of the group explained the biggest part of the fundraiser was expected to be dinner Saturday, and lunch Sunday, at Mama Mia's, a popular local restaurant, that promised to donate all the profit from the meals served.

Then, in what clearly had to be either a prearranged arrival or a reenactment for the cameras, Kaivan appeared. He was dressed in one of his most fashionable double-breasted Armani suits, and he carried a large piece of blank white cardboard under his arm. As soon as he was fully in place next to the group spokesperson, he swung the cardboard over and upright in front of the cameras. There were accompanying gasps from the gathered volunteers, and even their interviewer, because the cardboard was now a check made out to the tumor-afflicted tot in an amount that read $723,633.

The reporter thrust the microphone in front of Kaivan who, looking suitably humble and sincere, listened to the woman's question: "Sir, we are all stunned at your amazing generosity. Can you tell us why you are doing this?"

The camera zoomed in on Kaivan in such an intimate setup that it seemed he was talking directly to her. Regan leaned toward the screen, involuntarily drawn by his charm, unaware of her movement.

"I'm doing this in honor of my uncle, Cyrus Ansari, who also suffered from a brain tumor. This check represents his life's work. I'm supposed to inherit this money from him, but I don't think it should rightfully come to me. Those with whom he shared his life, know it was taken prematurely, before he could fulfill his final dream."

Regan inhaled sharply, her gasp as unexpected and as sudden as her understanding.

"This donation is my way of making up for that. I hope

seeing this little girl live will help ease my pain for the way his life had to end. I loved my uncle very much. I think some would agree that helping an innocent orphaned child is a proper way to remember him. I know it would have made him happy. I know his closest friends would approve of what I'm doing here."

Regan understood why Dave reacted like he did. Kaivan's carefully chosen words came across as almost saintly, unless you knew about a lot of circumstantial evidence tying him to Mrs. Rosemont's death.

Regan didn't just see a generous life-saving donation. She saw the motive for murder that had eluded her for so long. She saw Kaivan confessing to killing his uncle and trying to ease his guilt for what he had done.

"One sees things." Mrs. Rosemont had said it so offhandedly. The significance of that simple phrase had escaped her until now.

Kaivan wasn't trying to keep Eleanor from telling anyone about his uncle's son. Mr. Ansari had told no one other than Eleanor and Kaivan about his past. Kaivan could have denied his uncle ever told him a child existed. Unless she had made copies of Mrs. Ansari's documents, Mrs. Rosemont couldn't have challenged him effectively once she turned the original papers over to him. Family members would have confirmed Kaivan's denial, since none of them knew about the secret love affair.

And even if the heir was discovered and Kaivan lost his inheritance, that obviously didn't matter to him.

The stakes were much higher for Kaivan. He killed her to stop her from telling anyone what she had seen him do.

265

Mrs. Rosemont said she had seen Kaivan storm out of his uncle's house after they argued, and she had seen Regan leaving after she visited Stephanie and Ed in Mr. Ansari's house. She had a clear view of the comings and goings in front of 1215 Royale Street. She must have witnessed another more deadly encounter as well.

More pieces fell into place. Kaivan must have suspected Mrs. Rosemont knew he had killed his uncle, but wasn't sure at first. A second murder would come with additional risk, and would have taken some planning. He would have wanted to be certain of the need, before he committed such a heinous crime.

He returned Harry, thinking he could pretend to miss him. Visiting Harry would have been the perfect ruse to observe Mrs. Rosemont. Kaivan must have thought he could take his time, subtly probe, and watch her responses to see if she really was aware of what he had done.

The newscast had moved to another story. Regan clicked the TV off, but remained staring at the blank screen.

What would Kaivan's reaction have been when Mrs. Rosemont told him she knew he killed his uncle. She would have, of course. She had been a strong, direct woman. She wouldn't mince words with Kaivan. It made Regan smile, a small poignant smile, to think of Mrs. Rosemont telling Kaivan, in her very matter of fact way, exactly what he needed to do to redress his crime.

If Mrs. Rosemont wanted simple justice for her friend's murder, she could have gone to the police with her knowledge. But she hadn't. Obviously she wasn't looking for ordinary punishment for Kaivan. She wanted another outcome.

She must have understood the risk she was taking, telling him what she had seen. She'd been willing to accept that risk to get her dearest friend's final wish fulfilled. But then she had a history of that kind of bravery. Mrs. Rosemont had been a WASP during World War II. A high percentage of women fliers gave their lives for their country during the war, and had never been rewarded or even recognized for their sacrifice. Mrs. Rosemont had been one of those remarkable women.

Was fulfilling her friend's dying wish all that mattered to her? Or, knowing how much Cyrus Ansari loved his nephew, was it also important that Kaivan have a chance to redeem himself — to atone?

If Kaivan had let her live, would Mrs. Rosemont ever have told the authorities what she saw? Regan thought not. "It was a private matter." That was what Mrs. Rosemont told her. The uncertainty Kaivan would have endured, wondering if — when — she might break her silence, would have been his punishment.

Whatever she told him, whatever bargain she may have tried to strike, whatever opportunity she may have tried to give him, hadn't mattered. He must have seen Mrs. Rosemont's knowledge as a living sword of Damocles hanging over him. He must have considered her an unbearable menace, and decided to kill her rather than live with daily uncertainty about her silence.

Regan frowned. Eleanor had said something else. What was it exactly? Unlike the visual memories that flooded

Regan's mind, whole, Mrs. Rosemont's words came back to her in pieces. "It was a private matter he told me, as I'm telling you."

But, finally, all the words did come back.

"It was a private matter he told me, as I'm telling you. He said I would know the correct time it might become more than that, *as will you.*" That was what Mrs. Rosemont said.

You hedged your bet, didn't you, Eleanor? You told me nothing — and everything. You made me your instrument, your very own *open this if something happens to me* vessel, Regan reflected.

"He said I would know the correct time it might become more than that…more than a private matter…as will you," she repeated to herself.

Eleanor Rosemont might have been willing to let Kaivan absolve himself of his uncle's murder, but if it came to that, she never intended to let him get away with her own. If he harmed her, Mrs. Rosemont wanted someone to know what had happened; then she no doubt wanted justice, the traditional police-administered kind.

"How clever you were, Eleanor. If Kaivan hadn't killed you, I would never have recognized what I knew — what you told me," she said to the blank TV screen.

In her mind she saw Mrs. Rosemont, but not the terrible image of her that had been a torment to her for so many weeks. Eleanor Rosemont was alive, her carrot curls dancing as she shook her head. "Yes, dear. It was all carefully planned."

Regan closed her eyes for a second, filled with emotion,

equally in awe of Eleanor Rosemont's bravery and her subtle ingenuity.

The only piece missing now was why Kaivan killed his uncle. Maybe Tom was right about it happening accidentally. If not, she might come up with the reason if she thought about it some more, but there would be time enough to figure that part out later. What mattered was that she had the motive for Mrs. Rosemont's murder.

Regan tried Tom's cell just in case she was mistaken and he hadn't left it in his car while he was on the golf course. It flipped into his outgoing message, confirming what she expected.

Once she left her Bonny Doon landline, she wouldn't be able to use her cell phone. Even if he returned her call, she would have to wait until she was back home to tell him all this. In the meantime, she left an enticing message for him.

"Kaivan killed his uncle as well as Mrs. Rosemont. She saw him do it, and that's why he killed her. I've got it all figured out," she said.

She was ready to give it another try with Dave. She called him again. This time she got his answering machine. She was about to leave a similar message for him, but decided not to. Knowing how she was with answering machines, she'd flub it.

No, it was better to wait until she had him face to face to present all her evidence in an orderly and convincing manner. That way she could watch his body language. If he leaned back in his chair and crossed his arms, as he would if he wasn't accepting her explanation, she could always throw his lunch at him. That would get his attention, she mused. But she didn't expect that she'd have to make a scene at Riva's Fish House.

26

It was already twelve-forty-five. She'd be a little late for the one o'clock scheduled start of the open house by the time she stopped at each turning to put up a sign, but it probably wouldn't matter very much. It was raining steadily now and getting windier. A decent storm was heading their way to finish the rainy season. March had made it out like a lamb, but April was going to begin with a lion's roar.

A six-foot high solid wooden fence surrounded the three-acre Sunlit Lane property. It provided a great deal of privacy, but its true purpose was to discourage deer from bounding over into the interior gardens. Deer could clear a seven-foot fence, but wouldn't attempt an easy six-foot jump if they couldn't see what was on the other side.

There were two gates into the property; both were closed against the deer. The first one led to a parking area and the attractive walkway to the front porch and entry door. The second gate had a driveway to more outdoor parking and the detached garage.

She wanted anyone coming to the open house to get the

271

full impact of the prettily landscaped entry and the craftsman style lighting that lined the walkway, which, given today's gloom, would definitely need to be turned on. She decided to use the second gate and park by the garage so that her car wouldn't be visible from the house and wouldn't detract from a buyer's first impression.

She stopped at the first gate to open it and put out the last directional sign, the one which said WELCOME, COME IN, before going to the second entrance.

Regan parked her car and made a hurried dash to the covered porch which ran along the entire front of the house. She had used her umbrella at each of her stops with more skill than she expected, and consequently was only soggy, not soaked through, by the time she opened the front door.

The first indoor stop she made was at the thermostat in the hall. "You're going to seventy today," she told the furnace, as she moved the dial and overrode the stingy setting the owners required. Her next stop was the kitchen, where she put down all the cookie paraphernalia she had in her arms and set the oven for 350 degrees. Then she circled back to the entry to begin turning on lights.

The house was spacious and open. Where the ceilings weren't vaulted, they were luxuriously high. The house's openness and volume let the individual rooms share light from the home's many windows, and made it reasonably bright even on such a stormy, gray day. But she knew it took about thirty seconds for a visitor's eyes to adjust to the reduction of light they experienced when they came inside even the brightest interior. That was more than the time it took a buyer to register an impression of a home which they were seeing for the first time, so lights always went on at open houses, even when the sun was out.

Dismal as the day was, with her touches, this house was going to be cheerful, warm, and inviting, especially once she got the cookies baking.

Regan didn't need to work to project enthusiasm for this home; she loved it. It was genuinely pretty and had wonderfully inlaid hardwood floors and custom-detailed solid wooden doors. Its strongest feature was a spectacular sunroom off the kitchen, although on a day like today, there wasn't much she could do to make that room as inviting and special as it was when the sun was shining.

She went upstairs, flipping on light switches as she came to them.

Most of the living space was on the lower level. The upstairs was devoted to a well-appointed private master suite, reached by a wide balcony which ran from the stairs on one side, all the way to the other end of the house.

Looking up from the living room, the open balcony enhanced the home's feeling of spaciousness. From the balcony, the owner could survey the living room, entry, and part of the dining room, before descending the wide stairs.

The house had a Swiss Family Robinson feel about it. From the balcony vantage point, it was possible to look out several windows at the same time, thereby blurring the separation of indoors from outdoors, and giving the upstairs a tree house atmosphere.

Once inside the master suite, she turned on several lamps to give a buyer a sense of how comfortable the space would be for reading in bed or in the cozy built-in nook created by the angles of the roofline. Then she went back downstairs to the kitchen and started baking.

The first group coming to see the house arrived just as she pulled a batch of warm cookies from the oven.

"Your timing is perfect," Regan said. "Would you like one of these?"

"I don't know if we should eat your cookies," the husband said, as he did just that. "We aren't real buyers. We're just neighbors from down the road."

His wife licked her fingers where warm chocolate from her cookie stuck to them. "Ever since we moved in, we've been curious to see inside the fence and have a look at the house, so when we saw your signs, we decided to come in. Is that all right?"

"You're out in the rain and keeping me company," Regan laughed. "That's good enough for me. How long have you lived in your house?"

The couple explained they had owned their home at the end of Sunlit Lane for about four years. During that time, they had taken the property from something they bought primarily because the zoning allowed them to have horses, to their dream estate. They definitely weren't considering selling, having just completed a major addition to the house and a new barn for their horses.

They finished their cookies, satisfied their curiosity, and left.

At about two o'clock, a family came in who said their realtor had shown them the house the week before. They were back for a second time, to see what the house looked like on a miserable day.

They said the house passed their rainy day test. They were very interested in it, and were considering making an offer, so they had many questions for her.

They sat in the living room, on furniture the sellers had left behind for some modest staging, while she answered their queries. By the time they left, almost an hour later, their children were arguing over which bedroom each would have, and the parents were wondering if they would need a bigger table than the one they already owned to adequately fill the home's generous dining room.

Regan asked if they liked the one the sellers left behind, and their enthusiastic response prompted her to ask if they would like her to find out if it was for sale. Who knew, she encouraged, with the right offer, the sellers might even throw it in for free as a housewarming gift.

When she closed the front door behind them, she was smiling and anticipating that an offer would be arriving the next day.

The last part of the open house was as she expected. No one else came. She was eager for it to be over so she could go home and call Tom. She glanced at her watch every few minutes, willing the hands to move faster.

Experience had taught her she really should stay until the end of an advertised open house; prospective buyers would inevitably straggle in, pointing to their watches, as soon as she turned off the lights and got ready to leave. But with the rain and the excellent likelihood of an offer, she decided to start closing up about fifteen minutes before the advertised four o'clock end of the open house.

She packed up the cookie gear and began the process of closing up the house, starting with returning the thermostat to 60 degrees. She was upstairs turning off the master suite lights, when she heard the front door open and slam closed against the storm outside.

Why does this always happen, she asked herself, frustrated that she would have to stay now, not just until four o'clock, but probably longer. She turned the lights back on, sighed, and prepared to be friendly to the last-minute arrival.

From the balcony she could see a lone man dressed in jeans and a plain green sweatshirt. He had on a dark baseball cap. He had walked through the foyer and was heading into the living room, his back to her.

"Hi, come on in," she called in welcome as she started down the stairs.

She stopped short on the landing, where the stairs turned to face the living room, and held the railing very tightly.

"Have much of a turnout today?" a smiling Kaivan looked up and asked.

Her adrenaline surged. Her first inclination was to turn and run back up the stairs, but she didn't think there was a lock on the bedroom door. Besides, even if there was, what would that accomplish? She'd be trapped on the second floor. It might take him some time to break through the sturdily constructed door, but eventually he'd do it.

She could call for help, but even the closest neighbors probably wouldn't hear her. They were too far away and would have their doors and windows tightly closed on a day like today. Her cell phone was in her purse which was tucked in a laundry room cupboard, safely out of sight of visitors and on the ground floor with Kaivan. Even if she had it in her pocket though, she knew it wouldn't work here.

"It's time for your open house to be over. I picked up all your signs on my way in, so no one else will be coming by. Aren't I a helpful guy?"

He still smiled. She still didn't move.

"Regan, you're not being very polite. At least you could say, 'Thank you'."

"Yes, you're right. Thanks." She produced a too-bright smile. "I was just starting to close up before the owner's got back. They always want a full report on how the open house went." She struggled for composure. "I thought you were a looky-loo coming in at the last minute, so I turned the lights back on." She forced a small laugh. "I better go up and turn them out again. The owners are very conscious of energy usage; I don't want them to think I'm wasting energy when they get here."

"I don't think that's necessary," he said casually. "Remember, I'm a realtor, too. I looked this listing up on the Multiple Listing Service. It says 'vacant, on lockbox, go direct'. I don't think your clients will be coming home anytime soon, do you?"

He wasn't smiling anymore, and she didn't have an answer.

"This was a test," he said. "I badly wanted you to pass it, Regan, but I'm afraid you haven't. You don't seem very happy to see me, and that's really too bad. You see, you should always be happy to see a friend. I'd be happy to see a friend, especially if he picked up all my signs on a rainy day for me. But you're not. Now why is that, I have to ask myself?"

As he talked, he casually pulled up his sweatshirt and reached into the waistband of his jeans. He pulled out a large gun and clicked off the safety.

"Why don't you come down here? We'll talk for a while and see if we can figure it out, you know, friend to friend."

Regan walked down the stairs very slowly. Her knees were shaking and they didn't want to bend.

Kaivan used the gun to motion her to the sunroom at the back of the house and indicated she should sit on the large sofa opposite the door to the back garden. She weighed how long it would take for her to unlock that door and what Kaivan would do if she bolted for it. Better to sit down, she decided. If she tried that escape route, she would have a bullet in her back before she could get the door open.

She needed to calm down. And she needed to come up with a plan to escape. There was no use pretending she didn't know he had killed. The minute the gun came out, that possibility ended. Her best chance was to keep him talking while she figured out what to do.

He sat down at the opposite end of the sofa, facing her, with his back to the kitchen, still steadily aiming the gun at her.

"I wouldn't have figured you for a gun owner," she started.

He laughed, genuinely amused at her statement. "You know me pretty well, don't you? This is Mrs. Rosemont's gun, or rather her husband's. She told me it was a souvenir

Luger which was taken from a dead German soldier near the end of the war. Just in case you were wondering, it does work, and I do know how to use it."

"I did think I knew you, Kaivan. You know the police suspected you killed your uncle for his money. Tom thought so, too. But I was certain they were mistaken. I thought you couldn't possibly have done that. What happened? Was it an accident?"

"No, it was quite deliberate," he said calmly. "It was the hardest thing I've ever had to do. But you were right about me, I would never hurt him, or anyone, for their money."

"Then why did you do it?"

"I'm sure Mrs. Rosemont told you."

"Please, Kaivan, I need you to tell me why." *Buy time* she told herself. Her heart was still beating wildly. She forced herself to take deep, even breaths. *Calm down. Think. Look for a way out.*

"OK. I guess I owe you an explanation for this," he said, waving the gun slightly. "I loved my uncle. He was like a second father to me, a wonderful second father. I didn't want to hurt him, but I had no choice. After the recurrence of his brain cancer, we knew he was dying and we were trying to prepare for that day. He was ready, he said. He accepted what was to come.

"Then he got a letter from a woman he had loved before he left Iran, telling him she had his son almost twenty years ago. She told him she never intended to tell the young man or Uncle Cyrus about one another, but now she was very ill and frightened for her...for their son."

Regan's gaze was on Kaivan, but she was barely

listening to him; her mind struggled, trying to find a way to escape.

"He and his older brother had converted to a radical fundamentalist form of Islam. His brother had become a jihadist, a terrorist, who had blown himself up in an Iraqi marketplace, killing a dozen local people and two American soldiers. She was afraid my uncle's son would follow in his brother's footsteps.

"She wanted Uncle Cyrus to bring him to America and reform him — save his soul — before he was brainwashed into doing the same thing.

"My uncle was a good and decent man. He couldn't accept the way the world is now. And he was so happy to have a child. He said surely his son couldn't be part of the pain around us today. The kid was nearly twenty, but not to my uncle. To him it was like having a newborn. He was filled with hope and the promise of a kind of immortality through his son."

Kaivan exhaled loudly; it was a sigh filled with irritation. "Then another letter came, this time from my uncle's son, my cousin." He spit the last words out with disgust. "He said his mother had died, but before she did, he had promised her he would renounce his newfound faith, or politics, or whatever you call it, and return to Christianity. He wrote that all he wanted to do now was meet his father and make America his new home.

"My uncle believed everything his son told him…because he needed to. Uncle Cyrus couldn't understand the danger the kid represented." Kaivan looked squarely into her eyes, "But I could," he said slowly.

"I called some relatives in Iran who knew him, and asked them what they thought of our new family member. You should have heard them. They said he scared them all. He was crazy, they said, committed to jihad and bragging about how his path to heaven would be paved with American skulls.

"Well, I didn't just take their word for it. It took a while, but I managed to get a phone call through to the kid. I told him I was my uncle. He was very smooth at first. He said he was full of remorse about how he had treated his mother, and he was so eager to meet me and come to America.

"But do you know what he did when I told him who I really was?" Kaivan grew increasingly agitated. "He called me an American Satan, the enemy of Islam, and yelled 'Allah Akbar' over and over, like those sadistic masked men you see on the Internet videos, all screaming before they behead some terrified hostage.

"I told him I was going to expose him for what he was to my uncle, that he'd never get into this country. He just laughed at me. He said his father was an American fool who loved him too much to listen to me.

"Regan, I begged my uncle not to bring his son here, but my cousin was right, there was no reasoning with him. Uncle Cyrus hadn't heard what I had. He said he had plane tickets...a visa. He was determined to bring his son home."

Kaivan shook his head, "His health began to deteriorate a couple of weeks before his scheduled trip, and he begged me again to help him travel. I thought I might be able to deceive my uncle, delay him from going to Iran until he

281

became too ill to go. I thought I could prevent his son from getting to Santa Cruz that way, but Uncle Cyrus said he was going to change his will, too. He made an appointment to do it.

"If my uncle left all his money to that fanatic...well ...they say only five hundred thousand dollars was spent to bring down the Twin Towers at the World Trade Center."

He looked at her, much as he had on TV, with indisputable sincerity. "I couldn't let him do it. So much was at stake. I just couldn't take the chance. I love my country too much to sit by and do nothing when it's threatened, when it's about to be attacked.

"Finally, I lied to my uncle and told him I would go with him and help him. We had a nice celebratory dinner at his house. He was so happy," Kaivan sighed. "I've never seen him happier." Kaivan paused for a second, remembering his world before he took his first fateful action.

He continued his story in an oddly detached manner. "I laced his food with his sleeping pills. He barely understood what was happening when I helped him to my car. Then he fell asleep. Deeply asleep. I've heard drowning isn't a hard way to die...I drove him up the coast...for privacy...I wanted a chance to say goodbye. I...I, well, you know the rest. I saved my country and saved him an agonizing end to his life."

"What danger was Mrs. Rosemont? You killed her, too, didn't you?" Regan asked softly.

"I had to. I waited until it was late and very dark outside before I took Uncle Cyrus to my car, but she still must have seen me do that. I think she may have thought he was ill, maybe even thought initially that I was taking him to the hospital, but when his body was found, she figured out I was responsible.

"That Mrs. Rosemont was something," he said emphatically, no longer distant. "Phew!" he said with a shake of his head. "She started by calling me and asking me to bring Harry back to her. I was only too happy to give her that stupid cat. He was there at my uncle's house and saw everything I did. He kept looking at me with those gold eyes, accusing me. You can't explain to a cat.

"When I took Harry to her, she invited me in for tea, sat me down and told me that where Uncle Cyrus' body was found had significance. She said she knew where I lived. Toilet Bowl is pretty much right across Lighthouse field from my house. She said my uncle's death was coming home to me.

"That's when she told me she knew what I had done. There was no anger, no recrimination, although I know how much she cared for Uncle Cyrus. She said my uncle would forgive me for his death, but that I first had to atone for the pain I caused him by denying him the chance to meet his son.

"She gave me the same task Gandhi gave the Hindu man who asked how to atone for killing his neighbor because he was a Muslim. She said Gandhi told the man he had to adopt the child he had orphaned and raise him in his own home, not as a Hindu, but as a Muslim.

"Crazy old woman. She'd seen so much in her life, so many different cultures, but she, in some ways, was as naïve as my uncle. Neither one of them understood how dangerous my cousin was.

"She said if I refused to do what I should, there would be consequences. It was too risky to let her live. I couldn't let her tell anyone about my uncle's son or about what I had done.

"I lied to her, too." Kaivan worked the bottom of his chin as if momentarily stroking a nonexistent goatee. "I told her I needed time to consider what she wanted me to do. Instead I planned how to make her death look like an accident.

"I worked it out right away. I should have eliminated her quickly, but I was weak. I'm not a violent man; it's not in my nature to kill," he said, almost pleading with her to understand.

His emotional confession left him momentarily overwhelmed. He lowered the gun to his lap. His eyes were downcast as he rubbed them with his left hand.

Regan decided now was the best chance she would ever have to get away. She lunged off the seat, trying to get past him, trying to get out of the sunroom into the kitchen. But he was on his feet before she cleared his end of the sofa. He grabbed her arm and swung her around, throwing her back down to the seat. He stood over her, aiming the gun down at her.

"I waited too long and she had a chance to tell you everything. I can't make that mistake again. I'm sorry," he almost screamed. "I've got to stop this from spreading. I'm sorry I have to do it this way. I was able to put both of them to sleep first. Neither of them was afraid. Neither one felt any pain. I'll try to make this as clean as I can, I'm so very sorry." His words came out somewhere between a sob and the rage he would need to kill her.

"Take off your jewelry," he commanded. "This has to look like a robbery."

"Please, Kaivan, I don't want to die. I understand. Really." Regan began crying, "I promise I won't tell anyone."

"Now!" he shrieked.

All 6-feet 3-inches of Tom appeared at the entrance to the kitchen. He leaned against the doorjamb, casually, his body at an angle, one leg bent at the knee and crossed in front of the other, and his arms crossed on his chest.

"You want to explain how you're different from your cousin?" he asked in a conversational tone. His sudden appearance startled Kaivan who swung the gun in Tom's direction as he backed away from Regan a step.

Tom had at least five inches and forty pounds on Kaivan. She thought he was going to try to attack him and grab the gun. She knew size and strength would never be enough to overcome a bullet, and was terrified she would have to see him die before Kaivan killed her, too.

But Tom didn't move — and Kaivan didn't pull the trigger. For several seconds it appeared that an unarmed Tom had forced a standoff of sorts.

"Get over there with your wife," Kaivan finally barked harshly, when he realized he was still in a position of power.

Tom straightened up and walked toward Regan. His movements were molasses slow. His eyes, locked to hers, never broke contact. His eyes were always very blue, but now they seemed more intensely colored than ever, and he squinted just a bit. Regan recognized the look. He was as angry as she had ever seen him.

It seemed like it took several minutes for him to reach her.

"Sit down!" Kaivan yelled. "Do it."

Tom sat on the forward edge of the sofa. Instinctively, Regan tried to put her arms around him in a protective gesture, and to make sure he wouldn't try any sudden leaps at Kaivan, but he pushed her arms aside, angling his body to protect her from the gun firing line as much as he could. She put her hand on his back. His shirt was warm, wet and clinging, not from rain, but from perspiration.

He leaned forward with deliberate slowness, forearms on his knees, his wrists crossed. Again his demeanor was seemingly relaxed and conversational.

"I heard everything you said, so you'll have to kill me, too," he lectured. "How many will that be? Four? Four innocent people? Or maybe it will be five. I was on my way here when I saw you stopping to pick up the last sign. I didn't recognize you at first. You had a truck, not your BMW, and you usually don't dress like you did today. I didn't put everything together until you were already in the house. Since I couldn't get Regan away from you, I called for help."

Kaivan only needed a second to think. "No, you didn't," he said mockingly. "Cell phones don't work here. You're bluffing." But he was calmer now, mirroring Tom's tone.

"I didn't use my cell phone. We sold the Healys their

house across the road just last year. I ran to their house and used their phone to call for help. Sean was there and heard everything I said. You'll have to kill him, too. He'll make five.

"His wife, Sherrie, came home just as I was running back over here. He's probably told her what's going on by now. Six. Maybe you should kill their baby, too. He's only a few months old, but you don't want to leave any loose ends. Seven."

"Stop it!" Kaivan demanded.

"You were about to tell me why you're not just like your cousin," Tom said.

Regan couldn't believe how hard Tom was pushing. He was taking a huge calculated risk that Kaivan wouldn't pull the trigger just to make him be quiet. If he guessed wrong, they would both be dead and Kaivan might well go across the street and execute everyone in the Healy's house, just like Tom suggested. If Kaivan had any idea how long the police response time was in Bonny Doon, Regan thought, he would know he could do all that without even having to hurry.

Kaivan was breathing as fast as Regan was, but he didn't shoot them.

"I'm not anything like him," Kaivan stammered. "Everything I've done has been to save lives. I've had to sacrifice people I care about for the greater good. Do you have any idea what that's like?"

"I'm sure it's been difficult for you, but this is war, isn't it? We're all just collateral damage. That's probably what your cousin's brother thought when he was getting ready to blow himself up in that marketplace. Sometimes innocent lives have to be sacrificed for the cause," Tom shrugged his shoulders. "That's the way war is. I bet your cousin would agree, wouldn't he?"

Tom had left the front door open when he slipped into the house, not wanting to risk the noise that closing it might have made. The storm had passed. The wind and rain had subsided. It was quiet outside again. Regan could hear crunching and then soft thumps and sharp clanks as a car pulled into the pea gravel driveway so rapidly that its tires sent tiny stones flying into the fence on one side and into the metal water storage tank on the other side. Two doors slammed almost simultaneously. Regan thought she could hear a siren in the distance.

"Eight. Nine," Tom said, inclining his head in the direction of the slamming car doors. "It's too late Kaivan. You can't stop people from knowing about your uncle and Mrs. Rosemont, anymore.

"But you already did what you needed to do. You stopped your cousin from getting to America. You got rid of your uncle's money so your cousin couldn't claim it. You did save lives. I could be wrong about you, Kaivan. Maybe you're not like your cousin. Make me wrong. Put the gun down and stop this. You don't want to hurt more innocent people."

There was no longer any doubt about a siren. A piercingly shrill one, still two or three minutes away, Regan guessed, was definitely moving in the direction of Sunlit Lane. More cars began arriving. There were now several voices outside.

"I don't see any smoke," one of the voices announced.

"I don't see any either. I'm gonna check around back."

Without a word, Kaivan abruptly poked the gun back in his waistband and covered it with his sweatshirt. He unlocked the sunroom door and rushed outside, heading away from the voices and toward the garage where he had parked his truck next to Regan's car.

Tom was ready to follow him, but Regan held his arm. "Don't leave me alone," she pleaded, as uncontrollable tears began. "You called the fire fighters?" She was half laughing, half crying.

"I asked Sean to call the police after I left and then go down to the start of Sunlit to direct them in, but when I got 9·1·1, I told them this house was on fire and to sound the fire call. The police aren't here yet, but the Bonny Doon Volunteer Firefighters are here in force," he grinned triumphantly.

He found a crumpled tissue in his pants pocket and began wiping her tears.

The police arrived about twenty minutes after the firefighters, and took statements from Tom and Regan. Kaivan's truck, borrowed it turned out, had four-wheel drive, and there was a trail left near the end of Sunlit Lane where he had crashed it through some low fencing, crushed a leafy hedge, and grooved the landscaping of a very disgruntled neighbor on his way over private property back to Empire Grade Road.

From there, the police couldn't tell for sure whether Kaivan had turned left or right. Left would have taken him to several roads off Empire Grade Road, all of which would have eventually led out of the county. If he turned right, he would have headed back toward Santa Cruz.

It was possible he drove right by at least three police cars rushing to Sunlit Lane with their sirens screaming. If he had, he probably pulled to the side of the road to let them pass unhindered, acting like a good driver in careful compliance with motor vehicle laws.

If the police passed him, they didn't notice him as they hurried to Sunlit Lane.

27

Dave didn't wait for lunch on Tuesday to see Regan. Even though she had already told him all the details of their ordeal, he came by their house the next day around lunchtime with takeout Chinese food and bottles of Sapporo beer.

Tom made note of the beer. "You brought a lot of those, I hope?" he asked, holding out his hand and pretending it was shaking.

"I did. I figured Regan would need some, too," Dave answered, putting the take-out bags on the dining room table. "Your sodas and tea probably aren't doing the job right now, are they?" Dave asked Regan, who was bringing in plates and chopsticks.

The men sat down at the table and started unloading white paper containers and opening tall beer bottles.

"No, she's handling this surprisingly well," Tom said. "She just gets teary at unexpected moments, like every time she looks at Harry, or sometimes when she looks at me."

"That's because you're my hero," Regan said, putting her arms around Tom's neck and kissing the top of his head.

She joined them at the table. "I thought he was brilliant the way he handled Kaivan," she said to Dave, "although for a while there, I did think he'd lost his mind, pointing out to Kaivan that he called for help from the Healy's house and then telling him they lived right across the street."

"But that was just until I told you about sending Sean down the road to wait for the police, right?" Tom asked.

"Yes, my brilliant, *sane* hero," she murmured.

Tom turned toward Dave with a proud smile on his face. "Of course, Sherrie and the baby weren't there, either. I made up the part about them coming home. Sean said Sherrie was in Indiana with the baby, visiting her parents, but I needed to boost my innocent victim numbers," he laughed.

"That was the right thing to do in a hostage situation," Dave jumped in as the authority. "The idea is to make the hostages real people. It's harder to kill one real person than a group of abstract people."

"But we weren't hostages," Regan said. "We were intended victims."

"Same thing. Premeditation killers usually downgrade their Vics to objects or obstacles by the time they kill them, or convince themselves they have the right to take their lives." Dave turned to Tom, "You knew that, right? That's why you talked to the guy the way you did, isn't it?" Dave asked approvingly.

"No, I didn't know that," Tom said. "Regan, the behavioral science major, has explained to me all the things

I did right, but I'm a computer guy turned real estate broker. I was just winging it. The only plan I had was to stall as long as possible and wait for the cavalry to arrive.

"Well, maybe that's not quite true," he chuckled. "The whole time I was by the kitchen door, I was trying to spot something I could use to brain him. That was my real plan. I just couldn't find anything big enough and portable enough to work.

"But while I was looking for a weapon, I was listening to him. I got to hear his whole justification for what he had done and was going to do to Regan. He was apologizing — there's no other way to describe it — and trying to rationalize murder. I hope you won't take this the wrong way, sweetheart," he said to her, "but if I were him, I would have just taken care of business and shot you right away."

Regan clasped her heart in feigned shock.

"Instead he let Regan ask him questions, and then tried to explain why he had no other choice but to start killing people. He seemed to be talking himself into what he was going to do.

"When he got to the part about not being a killer by nature, I believed him."

Dave asked Regan, "That's what you said about him, wasn't it, until your now famous flip-flop?"

"That's what I thought at the start of this whole misadventure, but as I collected more information, I realized I was wrong about Kaivan. I didn't flip-flop. It's not flip-flopping when you change what you think in light of new information," she said rather righteously.

293

"You know, I don't think you were wrong about Kaivan, at least not completely," Tom said, pointing a chopstick at Regan. "He would have lived his whole life being a decent sort, like most people, if his cousin hadn't turned up. He didn't want to kill you any more than he wanted to kill his uncle or Mrs. Rosemont. He just couldn't come up with a way not to.

"I suspect he really believed the only way he had to stop his cousin was to kill his uncle." Tom scooped some Gan Pung chicken onto his plate. "And his uncle was already under a death sentence, so he could rationalize what he thought he had to do fairly easily. He probably worked that murder over in his mind until it was even noble in some sort of way.

"Mrs. Rosemont's murder must have been much harder for him to justify because he was killing her primarily to protect himself, although he may have convinced himself, at least in part, that he was doing it to be sure he kept his cousin from inheriting Mr. Ansari's money."

"What about Regan?" Dave asked. "Her murder would have been totally self-serving."

Tom interrupted his analysis to take a sip of Sapporo. "I don't think it was, to him. He was already trying to say he had to kill her to stop her from putting anyone else at risk. It's bizarre logic, given that he was the reason for their danger, but he might have convinced himself her murder was justified, too, given enough time to massage his guilt.

"I gave him a way to stop killing by pointing out more murders weren't going to protect him or accomplish anything else. He took it," Tom shrugged.

"You know what I keep thinking about?" Regan asked. "I keep thinking about what Kaivan said about his cousin — how dangerous he thought the young man was, and about how he was trying to protect his country.

"I remember Kaivan never referred to himself as Iranian-American. As soon as he could, he became an American citizen.

"Dave Samuels, the broker of the Century 21 office where we worked, used to set aside the weekly office meeting on each Election Day to review all the initiatives on the ballot. Kaivan wasn't a citizen when Dave started holding Election Day debates, so he couldn't vote, but he always studied all the initiatives and could lead an intelligent discussion on the ramifications of a yes or no vote on each one. No one else could do that, not even Dave, who loved politics and relished being seen as the resident expert on anything and everything.

"I remember the Election Day when Kaivan arrived in a new Armani suit with an 'I VOTED' sticker on his lapel. He stood so straight and was thrilled as he announced to the office that he had become a citizen, and had voted that morning for the first time. He told us it was one of the greatest privileges of his life, and said how proud he was to be an American.

"We all squirmed and felt a little embarrassed. Every one of us probably remembered at least one time since we were of voting age when we had been too busy, forgetful, or just disinclined to go out in the rain to vote. I bet he shamed every one of us into fulfilling our civic duty that day.

"You may be the one who really understands him, my clever hero," Regan flashed Tom an adoring look. "I think you're right. He may have genuinely believed he was protecting his beloved country and felt that justified murdering his uncle. He may also have worked out some flimsy rationalization that excused his killing Mrs. Rosemont, and I guess if you hadn't arrived when you did, me too," she said to Tom.

"But I wonder why he didn't just kill his cousin. That's what I would have done," Regan said.

Tom and Dave both stopped eating and stared at her.

"What?" she shrugged, taking a sip of Tom's beer. She made a sour face. "I don't know how you can like that stuff," she said, going back to her soda.

"Wouldn't that have been a cleaner thing to do? He could have gone to Iran, eliminated his cousin, flown home and gone on with his life. Maybe he could have even skipped going to Iran. Maybe he could have taken out a contract on his cousin. Do you think they have some sort of mob in Iran? I bet they have hit men for hire there, if you know where to look for them. He might have been able to do it long distance, without even leaving home."

Regan put forth her ideas so brightly, Tom and Dave weren't sure if she was kidding or being serious.

"Now, he's killed his uncle, whom I don't doubt he loved…Mrs. Rosemont…almost us. His life is totally messed up…and I bet he feels overwhelmed by what he did, now that he's had some time to think about what Tom laid on him in that well-timed guilt trip…you know, about him being just like his cousin."

"I won't tell anyone on the force how your wife thinks, I promise," Dave laughed.

"Well," Tom said, shaking his head as if mystified, "I've always thought everyone's capable of murder, given the right circumstances."

"Even female realtors?" Dave asked.

"Oh, *especially* female realtors," Tom replied.

Epilogue

They all made the front page of the *Santa Cruz Sentinel* on Monday. For the next couple of days, the local media coverage of what had happened gave new meaning to the phrase "media circus" as far as they were concerned. Regan and Tom's phones wouldn't stop ringing. They received over four hundred emails and so many faxes they turned off their fax machine.

Everyone wanted comments from them, but they declined all interviews, and didn't answer any questions. They did see two of their neighbors on TV who were being interviewed about them. One said they were quiet people who seemed to like their privacy; the other said they had loud parties at their house most weekends.

Some of Kaivan's neighbors were interviewed, too. They said he was a quiet person who valued his privacy, except when he had wild parties.

The tape of Kaivan handing over the check was played again and again.

Kaivan had signed everything he needed to sign the week before, so escrow closed on Stephanie and Ed's house on Wednesday, as scheduled. The proceeds went to the fundraising committee he had selected, and they passed it on for the little girl's brain surgery. She was doing well a month later.

Kaivan's parents wrote Regan and Tom a formal letter of apology for their son. Regan tried to go see them, but was told Kaivan's mother was too distraught to see anyone.

Dave kept them informed about the search for Kaivan. At first, witnesses saw him often. Sometimes he had grown a mustache or a beard or both. He had bleached his hair. He was seen at a soccer game in the company of a woman and two children. Finally, after several weeks, there weren't any new imagined sightings of him, although Dave said there was still an APB out for his arrest.

About three months later a letter arrived, postmarked Iran. Regan made Tom open it. Inside was a single Polaroid photo of Kaivan with his arm around the shoulder of a young man who looked a lot like him. Someone had printed on the back of the photo in English. It read "Kaivan and his cousin, Teheran, Iran."

"What do you think," Regan asked Tom, "Gandhi?"

"Or assassin," he replied.

About the author

Nancy Lynn Jarvis has been a Santa Cruz, California, Realtor® for almost twenty years. She owns a real estate company with her husband, Craig.

After earning a BA in behavioral science from San Jose State University, she worked in the advertising department of the *San Jose Mercury News.* A move to Santa Cruz meant a new job as a librarian and later a stint as the business manager of Shakespeare/Santa Cruz.

Nancy's work history reflects her philosophy: people should try something radically different every few years. Writing is her newest adventure.

She invites you to take a peek into the real estate world through the stories that form the backdrop of her Regan McHenry mysteries. Details and ideas come from Nancy's own experiences.

If you're one of her clients or colleagues, read carefully — you may find characters in her books who seem familiar. You may know the people who inspired them — who knows, maybe you inspired a character.